Sated

Truth Devour

Published in 2014
by Truth Devour

Interior layout and design
by Publicious Pty Ltd
www.publicious.com.au

Book cover design by:
Brightpixel Design
www.brightpixeldesign.com.au

Catalogue-in-Publication details available
from the National Library of Australia

ISBN: 978-0-9922999-4-1

Also available in ebook
ebook ISBN: 978-0-9922999-5-8

It was when I looked into you're eyes that I could truly see the reflection of me. Two hearts synchronised to the same beat. Two halves of the one soul, never forgotten, never lost, destined to find their way home. I have said my vows and intend to keep my promise. You are the love of my lifetimes. Amor Vincit Omnia

~ Yours ~ Forever ~ Faithfully ~ Always ~ Truth Devour ~

Believe

We held each other in an embrace which represented familiarity and a mutual desire never to let go. Neither of us cared about our surroundings. Bodhi and I paid no heed to the people who were now staring in curiosity. I had waited my whole life for this precise moment and for the longest time never believed it would arrive. In my mind's eye, I could see the little girl who was so familiar to me clapping her hands, dancing around us, and then she stepped closer to join in our embrace. Seeing this only made me squeeze him tighter.

I whispered in his ear, "One of us has to make the first move to break."

With no hesitation he replied, "It will never be me," and then repositioned his embrace to lock me in. "Now that I've finally found you, I'm never going to let you go."

I closed my eyes and inhaled deeply, drinking in his words. There was an unspoken strength and confidence in him; he showed no doubt about what he wanted. It was intoxicating.

I finally had to make the first move. "I have to pee," I said as I started to release my grip and shift back.

He didn't lighten his grasp. Instead he stepped in to reclaim me and held on tighter as he replied, "I'm coming with you."

I laughed; it was such a cute response. "As much as I love the concept, I think it might be a little advanced for our first meet. I'll take a rain check on the offer. Remind me again post our third greet."

He took a deep breath, squeezed one more time, hard enough to force my breath from my lungs, and then released me. "Hurry back. We have a lifetime of catching up to do."

"Yes, we do."

I headed to the ladies' room. I could feel him watching and I liked it.

When I returned, he had organised a table and was confidently watching me as I approached. His eyes held steadfast to mine. I sat down and reached across to hold his hands. It was the greatest gesture I could provide him. I never held hands with people, as I always felt its unspoken promise and intimacy. All I wanted to do right now was hold his hands.

"How did you know it was me?" I asked.

"When Eddie came back on stage I saw your name. I couldn't see through the crowd to be sure it was you but somehow I just knew it was. I was trying to read the phone number he had written on his arm so I could program it into my phone when he asked for a phone to dial your number. It was perfect. I gave him my phone, he called you and I kept the number."

"What are the chances you would be at this bar, watching this band and I walk in? You have no idea how much I cringed when Eddy made such a scene. I wanted to crawl under a rock. The only reason I gave him my number was to make it all stop. Actually that's only partially true. I also had made a promise to say 'yes' rather than default to the safety of my usual 'no'. I've been haunted by universal messages telling me to say yes more."

He released a sigh of relief and squeezed my hands. "Well, whatever the reason I'm glad you did."

"Were you there because you like the band?" I asked, trying to inadvertently ask if he was with someone.

"I manage bands for a living so the chances of me being there were pretty good. I organised for their mini tour around the US. They're starting to develop a solid following here. You, on the other hand, are harder to find than a needle in a haystack."

"You've been looking for me then?" I secretly wanted the answer to be 'yes'.

"I've never stopped," he said, squeezing my hands.

My heart melted at hearing these words. I looked at him and knew what he was saying was true. "We danced at the masked ball. Why didn't you tell me then?" I questioned.

"I wanted to but my girlfriend interrupted me as I was about to introduce myself. If you remember, you quickly exited when she came on the scene. I tried to look for you but you were nowhere to be found. I contacted your office and left countless messages but I assumed they never passed them on because I didn't hear from you."

I slowly reclaimed my hands. "We should order a coffee. Would you like one?"

He looked at my hands now placed on the table in front of me then gently smiled as he retrieved them. This time he interlocked our fingers to prevent escape. "I don't have a girlfriend. I'm single." He stared deep into my eyes, addressing my unasked question.

"Okay," I whispered, feeling unexpectedly relieved.

His head tilted slightly and his lips pursed as he said, "I'm sorry about your parents. I wish I had been there to support you."

"You know? How?" I asked.

"When I was eighteen I went back to Haiti to backpack. I was drawn to spending time there. After my first week I realised I was unconsciously searching for you. I stumbled upon Marlee's village. She recognised me and invited me to stay with her and her family for a few days. She told me everything. Marlee also told me I wouldn't be able to find you until you were ready to be found," he said.

I nodded my head and smiled. "So I should really have posed the question 'what the fuck took you so long' to myself?"

He laughed. "Precisely."

I looked down at the table and felt sad for the amount of time that had elapsed. It had been akin to a life sentence of aching and desire unfulfilled. The sound of his voice, the confidence in the way he communicated his thoughts and the touch of his hand made me feel I had finally arrived home. There was an instantaneous comfort in being in his presence, which made me awakened to the depth of my yearning.

Bodhi used his thumbs to stroke across my hand. "Talia."

I looked up and smiled at him.

"You have to speak out loud for me to hear your thoughts."

"Sorry, I was just thinking how this feels like the comfort of home. I've never really felt settled anywhere. I've been comfortable, familiar, but never truly settled. Here we are meeting in a coffee house for the first time in thirty-four years and I feel like I've arrived home." Tears started to form once again in my eyes.

"Don't make me come over there and hug you. I promise this time I won't let go." He reached across to collect a single rolling tear. He placed it in his mouth and laughed. "Salty."

The words instantly transported me to when we were six in my bedroom in Haiti. He had kissed a tear then and said the exact same words. It felt as though we were picking up right from where we had left off.

"You're doing it again, Talia. I seemed to have lost you to your thoughts."

"Sorry, I've been silent for so long I don't realise I'm not speaking out loud."

"Well, you'd better get used to it. I'm here and I have no plans to be anywhere else. I want to get to know every aspect of you. No stone unturned, no secrets."

I smiled. "I'd like that."

I took a deep breath and exhaled, listening to his words, feeling grateful to hear them. It was surreal to be instantly drawn to a depth unparalleled by any other and yet he was a stranger before me. I felt as though he had the key to unlocking the connection to my soul. I had never felt like this before and we had only just begun. Is this what all the philosophers, painters and poets were trying to capture when describing love?

Bodhi laughed. "You weren't kidding when you said you were silent. You're doing it again." He shook my hands as if to wake me from a dream.

I laughed and reclaimed my hands to cover my face. "I'm sorry. I seriously don't realise I'm doing it. I'm bad at this."

"We'll just have to break the habit. I'll buy a cattle prod online tomorrow. That should help to drive the change."

I moved my hands down so my eyes were visible. "What if I like it?"

"Hmm, dirty birdy. I see how it is."

"What?" I tried to feign innocence while smirking.

"You use your sultry sexual allure to distract and command a situation." He demonstrated by biting his bottom lip and returning my smirk.

"Ha, maybe. Sometimes," I said, admiring his insight. It was refreshing and a little disconcerting. I may have met my match, or worse, he may be able to run rings around me. I could see I wasn't going to get away with much in his presence.

"Do you need to go back to work?" he asked, once again drawing me out from behind my thoughts.

"No."

"I have a meeting I need to go to. When I'm finished I'd like to spend some more time together. Do you have any plans tonight?"

"No," I said, amused at my succinct responses.

"You do now. Send me a text on where I can pick you up. I'm thinking we can start with dinner. I want to take you out on our first date."

I smiled as I felt the flushes of a shy little girl surface. He knew he was making me blush and didn't hide that he was enjoying it.

"Okay," I said.

He stood up and leant in to whisper in my ear. "Hiding behind short responses won't help you." Then he kissed me on the cheek and left.

I sat there smiling like a giddy schoolgirl experiencing her first crush.

Discovery

I went back to the Solution Manifestation office to gather my things so I could head home and prepare for my date. I had been working on replies to some letters from men who had misguidedly declared their undying love for me and needed to be let down gently, so I printed off the letters I had already written and passed them across to Michael to address and post. Now more than ever I wanted these people to know never to lose faith in what they desired.

When I arrived home I jumped into the shower. While I was washing my hair I wondered how I should wear it. Then I started to consider my wardrobe. What do I wear to a first date? Can I get away with jeans or is that too casual? I didn't want to wear a dress only to feel as though I was making too much of an effort. Oh my, I was starting to sound like a girl. Fretting about what to wear, indeed. This needed to stop before it started.

I decided to leave my hair wet. I put some product through it so my natural wave of surfer curls stayed in a nice shape. Carefully I applied some liquid eyeliner, added mascara and finished off with lip gloss. There were two items I always carried in my bag: lip gloss and my perfume, Rive Gauche, by Yves Saint Laurent. It was the only perfume I ever wore.

The attire for the evening was more of a challenge. I didn't know where he was going to take me so I felt a little lost. I looked at my phone and wondered whether I should text to check. I cringed, knowing I was feeling slightly anxious about making the right impression. I had never experienced this before.

I opted to take a safe route, so I put on a few outfits and then messaged my friend and employee Ash in Australia to ask her which one I should wear. She thought it was priceless to witness me being indecisive. She instantly knew it involved a man and more so that I was obviously keen to make the right impression. She picked the black jeans and turquoise top with a plunging neckline. It was feminine and not too revealing. I agreed with her. It was probably the best combination out of the selection I had sent her. I threw on some open-toe sandals and I was ready.

As I walked across to the lounge room a text came through from Bodhi. *"When will you be available?"*

I responded with my address and confirmed I was ready when he was. As I pressed the 'send' button on the phone, butterflies fluttered in my stomach. I laughed, acknowledging I had placed an enormous amount of importance on my reconnection with him. This was either going to be the most amazing love affair of my life or the saddest.

I pottered around the apartment while I waited. Time seemed to have slowed. I banned myself from looking at the clock on the wall, as it seemed not to move as fast as it ought to. I had never experienced this aspect of my nature before. I wanted to sit outside myself to observe and taunt me for my behaviour. I was equal parts amused and surprised. If this was what I was like after such a brief interlude, what the hell was I going to turn into when we became intimate?

A text came through. Bodhi was downstairs. I wondered why he didn't attempt to come up. I grabbed my purse and keys, switched off the lights and headed out the door. He was in the foyer, dressed in jeans, a white shirt only partially buttoned and a blue suit jacket. He looked me up and down as I approached. I shook my head and laughed.

"Subtle," I said.

He laughed and leant in, giving me a kiss on the cheek. His hand found mine. I could feel an immediate surge of electricity catapult up my arm to my stomach, where the butterflies once again stirred.

"Let's go," he said.

We walked out the door and proceeded on foot down the street hand-in-hand. It was a nice balmy evening for a stroll. It felt natural to hold his hand. It was as though mine and his made a matching pair. I loved how his grip was so secure, an unspoken sign of not wanting to let go. It felt comforting.

"You might be pleased to know I found a two-for-one sale on cattle prods online this afternoon."

I laughed. "I thought you were going shopping tomorrow. I'm thinking you're a little too eager to deliver punishment." I squinted at him.

"Well, after your performance today I was motivated to get right on it."

"Geez, I wasn't that bad, was I?"

He laughed loudly. "Yes. Yes, you were."

I took a breath and exhaled, smiling. "Give a girl a break. I'm an inward thinker."

"I get it, but I need you to be present. I've waited a long time to find you. I started to think I had made you up. If I hadn't accidently found Marlee and had our love plait I might have convinced myself you were an ideal or a ghost."

I looked at him. He was referring to the nanny who had cared for me at the time of my parents' untimely death in Haiti and the plait she had made for us before we parted. "I know exactly what you mean."

"Why were you looking for me all these years?" I asked.

"I knew the moment I laid eyes on you when you were standing in the classroom in Haiti that I loved you. It might sound crazy, but I knew I wanted to be with you always."

"We were six. You were sure when we were six?"

"Yes. I was sure that you were the only one I wanted to play with. You were the only one I wanted to share with. I didn't understand it fully back then, but when I had to leave to go back to the States with my parents I knew. I cried for weeks, I refused to eat, I begged my parents to take me back. My mum tried to reach your parents through the school; however, they advised you had left too and there were no forwarding details."

"You tried to find me back then?" I said, amazed.

"Yes. I didn't even know your surname so I couldn't look you up if I wanted to."

I stopped walking, turned to face him and reached across, touching his cheek as we gazed into one another's eyes. I stepped close to his torso and felt his nurturing arms wrap around me like a warm blanket. I clasped my hand around his and breathed.

"I'm sorry I didn't believe you existed," I said.

10

Bodhi squeezed me tighter. "It's okay. I had enough belief for both of us."

Everything he said was so perfect. He was so sure of himself, knew what he wanted and was holding steadfast to ensuring I knew too. He stood before me without fear. I had never experienced anything like it. I was already falling for him and we hadn't even known each other for a day.

"Okay, we have to get to the restaurant or we'll miss our reservation." He peeled me off him and re-engaged my hand.

"Which one have you booked?" I asked.

"You'll see in a minute."

When we turned the corner there was a little restaurant in the middle of urban sprawl. It had a green neon light displaying the word Trattoria. A little green-and-white awning created an undercover space on the outside to protect the tables and chairs. As we drew closer I heard music playing and an operatic male voice resonated through the glass. It sent shivers up my spine.

"This place looks amazing," I said as we headed inside.

"Just wait. It'll be mind-blowing soon," he said with an excited expression.

"Billy!" called out a man, who waved his arms as he walked towards us.

"Hi, Sergio. This is Talia," Bodhi said.

"Hi," I said, slightly taken aback as Sergio stepped in to kiss me on both my cheeks.

"Bella, bella, you are beautiful. Billy, you keep this one or I take her," said Sergio, now waving his finger at Billy.

Billy pulled me into his arms. "She's not going anywhere, Sergio."

He looked at us both as he clasped his hands together and waved them in joy. *"Amore,"* he said, before turning to guide us to our seat.

We were taken to a private courtyard where a table was set beneath a pergola with an overgrown grape vine snaking through it. Delicate fairy lights were entwined through the twisted trunk of the vine. The effect was enchanting. Hidden speakers released pleasant instrument music, which was carried softly through the air. The tablecloth was a red-and-white check, and a single red rose in small vase and some small tea-light candles in the centre of the table created the perfect finishing touches.

Bodhi pulled out my chair for me to sit. "Madam."

"Thank you, kind sir," I said, now seated.

When he was seated he poured the red wine from the decanter into our glasses. He raised his glass, indicating for me to do the same. I raised mine and stared into his eyes.

"To never giving up hope," he said.

"To the reunion of our souls," I replied.

The wine was delicious, the atmosphere captivating and Bodhi beyond amazing.

"I pre-ordered our meals so we wouldn't be interrupted. I want you all to myself tonight," he said, smiling.

"Just tonight?" I asked, being cheeky and playing on his words.

"What do you think of the place?" he asked, ignoring my dig.

"It's such a lovely restaurant and the atmosphere is so …"

"Romantic?"

I nodded shyly. "Yes, romantic."

"Do you mind that I ordered for you?" he asked, his head tipped to one side.

"No, but I hope you don't mind if I don't eat it. I'm very selective about my food."

"I know you're a vegetarian. Everything I selected is vegan and the pasta is made fresh each day so it's out of this world in flavour."

"How did you know my food habits?"

"You were in the paper and magazines. They had little profile breakdowns and I noted you weren't a carnivore," he said with a smile.

I shook my head. He was referring to the debacle when a reporter, Mila Jones, had written an article on me and against my wishes and to my great annoyance revealed the vast extent of my wealth. "What a nightmare. I spent my whole life keeping under the radar and 'bam' I get thrust into the spotlight under a false allegation. Then some bizarre fascination developed and the media followed me around. They tried to label, classify and rate me. People are so strange. I really dislike the lack of respect they have for others' privacy."

"Are they still harassing you?"

"No, since I've been back I haven't noticed anyone lurking behind bushes. I'm hoping it's a sign that the interest has waned."

An attractive girl delivered our entrées. She placed mine down and then Bodhi's. As he looked at her to say thanks, she blushed. When she scurried away I laughed and took another sip of my wine.

"What's so amusing?" asked Bodhi.

"The waitress went red when you looked at her to say thanks. It was cute to watch. I found it amusing."

He smiled at me and then looked at my entrée. "It's homemade olive tapenade with roasted eggplant infused with garlic and rosemary on linguine. Try it."

I picked up my spoon and fork to collect a sample. I placed it in my mouth. The aromas were fantastic and the flavours simple and clean. He was right: this was delicious.

"It's really nice. The fresh pasta makes a world of difference."

"I told you," he said with an expression of satisfaction.

As we finished eating the entrée a good-looking rotund man walked up to us. He looked like a classical Italian Papa Giuseppe. His energy was wonderful. I was trying to finish my mouthful in order to greet him when the music changed and he took a deep breath, lifted his arms and released sounds of an enormity I had never heard before. I couldn't take my eyes off him and Bodhi couldn't take his eyes off me.

I listened, completely immersed in the song. The words were Italian but that didn't stop me from feeling moved by what he was singing. The height and depth of his range was impressive. What a pair of lungs this man possessed. He sang three songs for us and then finally took a bow. I rose from my seat and gave him a big cuddle. I couldn't get my arms around him but he squeezed me like I was a toothpick.

"Your voice is sublime. Thank you so much for sharing it," I said.

"Billy asks; Billy gets," said the man.

I looked at Bodhi, who was sitting back in his chair sipping his wine, enjoying my reaction to his surprise. The man reached down and gently kissed my hand, bowed once more, waved at Billy and left.

"He was wonderful, thank you," I said, not knowing what else to say. It was all becoming a little overwhelming. A week before I had been giving up hope of ever finding love, stating I didn't believe in fairy tales, and then in a blink of an eye this had happened.

"I manage him and he loves a good love story, so he wanted to be part of our first date."

"I'm speechless. This is all so overly perfect I don't know what to say," I said.

He leaned across and kissed me on the cheek. "Just enjoy."

The waitress came out with our mains. I was still full from the entrée. They were not overly large portions but I rarely ate pasta so it was very filling. Some garlic bread and a fresh garden salad were placed in the centre alongside our mains, *pappardelle con funghi*. Once again the flavour was exquisite. The chef really knew how to keep the flavours light so they were distinct but not overpowering.

"This restaurant is a real find. I can't believe I didn't know about it," I said.

"I'm glad you like it." He continued to watch me.

"You know someone should have taught you it's rude to stare," I said in jest.

"I've waited a long time for this night. Surely you wouldn't begrudge me my desire to drink in the view."

I shyly looked at my food and whispered, "I guess not."

The dessert and coffee came soon after. I was too full to consider eating another bite but the presentation of the little traditional Italian cakes was wonderful.

"Aren't you going to try some?"

"No thanks. I'm so full from the meal. I'm not used to eating pasta and having entrée and mains. I tend to eat a lot of salads, so this was delicious but way too much for me," I said, patting my stomach.

"More for me then."

"Go for it." I pushed the cakes towards him. "Tell me, Bodhi, do you have any other siblings or is it just you?"

A serene expression came over his face. "I have a younger sister. We're pretty close. She knows all about you."

I laughed. "I'm sure it's a distorted perspective. We'll have to get to know each other all over again before you can really decide how you feel."

"No, I know how I feel. I knew when I was little, I knew when I danced with you at the masked ball and I knew when I saw you at the coffee shop. It's more how you feel that's going to be the deciding factor here."

I admired his certainty. I wished I could be the same. I really liked him. I could feel a love for him, but he was right: I was not certain. I was flying blind.

Bodhi gently kicked me under the table. "You're doing it again."

I nodded. "I know, but these thoughts I need to keep to myself for now, if it's okay. I need to process some things on my own."

"Take all the time you need."

At the end of the meal Bodhi once again resumed holding my hand as he walked me home.

"Do you want to come upstairs?" I asked.

"No, I'm not coming up until I know you're sure." He kissed me on the cheek. "Good night, Talia."

I didn't try to change his mind. I understood his position but it didn't make my desire for him to come upstairs dissipate. "Thanks for an amazing day and evening."

"You're welcome."

I turned and headed inside while he watched. I could feel there was a level of sadness, perhaps anguish, he seemed to internalise. I needed to understand where his emotions stemmed from. It was almost as though he was relieved to have found me but annoyed that I didn't appear ready to receive him. It could have been my imagination overreacting too. This whole space was new to me.

Upstairs once more alone in my apartment I decided to have a hot bath and go to sleep. As the warmth of my bed enveloped me I drifted off to sleep with a sense of sadness. I wished he had kissed me on the lips. Bodhi could be the love of my life, yet I didn't know how to connect with the intensity of feelings being offered. I had underestimated the impact of keeping myself closed off emotionally for so long. I felt like a pebble being swept into the promise of his ocean of love.

The next day I didn't feel motivated to get out bed so I didn't arrive at the office until after 10 am. When my assistant, Michael, who had been with me since the start of Solution Manifestation, noticed I had finally made an appearance, he rushed into my office.

"Morning, Talia," he said, clearly busting to tell me something.

"Morning, Michael, spill it."

"You had a gentleman caller this morning. He arrived in the office and was hoping to take you out for breakfast. He said his name was Billy. Oh, my god, he's hot."

I ignored his comment about Billy's looks and searched in my bag for my phone. "What time did he come in? I don't have any missed calls."

"He was here at 8 am and stayed for thirty minutes. I kept him company," said Michael, swaying from side to side.

"How lovely of you. Did he leave any other message?"

"No, he said it was nice to meet me and then left."

"Okay, thanks. I'll give him a call."

As Michael walked out the room I wondered whether I should call Bodhi or leave it for later. I had some thoughts floating through my mind that I needed to process so I decided not to call. I spent the better part of the day immersed in my work so I didn't have to think about anything. I wasn't sure overthinking was the answer. Sometimes the best results are born from distraction.

"Are you up for some lunch?" asked Blake, trying to swing from my door jamb. He was my rock, the one who, along with Michael, I could rely on to keep Solution Manifestation thriving in my absence.

"I'm not hungry but I could use a break," I said as I grabbed my coat and bag.

"Would you prefer a walk in the park?"

"Yeah, that sounds like a better idea," I said.

"So, tell me about Billy." He interlocked his arm with mine as we headed out the door.

I looked at him and shook my head. "I know him as Bodhi. He and I met when we were kids in Haiti. It was a short burst of time, four maybe five months, from what I can recall, but we were thick as thieves. He was always by my side. Just before his parents were headed home to the States, my nanny Marlee executed a voodoo ritual and plaited our hair together. He kept one portion and I was allocated the other. I had forgotten about him but he never forgot me. He says he's been looking for me for years."

"Wow, I had no idea your history together was so deeply entrenched," said Blake, squeezing my arm.

"Yeah, our foundations are set back in childhood but the duration was marginal. The part I'm struggling with is the contrast between him remembering, even searching for me, yet I didn't really carry the same passion for him throughout my life."

"Does it matter? How do you feel about him now?" asked Blake.

"I'm drawn to him like a moth to a flame. I find comfort in his arms. I love the way he seems so sure of himself. He has an air of confidence which almost crosses into arrogance."

"The office girls, and Michael, of course, were all swooning at the sight of him. Apparently he's noteworthy."

"Michael carried on this morning. The funny part is I never really noticed too much about Bodhi's appearance. I've had more than my share of beautiful looking men. It was the way he looked into my eyes and the connection I felt when we touched that was intoxicating. That's what awakened my senses."

"He sounds like quite a find."

"I think he might be the one. I just need to figure out what it means to me." I headed towards a park bench to sit.

"Perhaps you need to do less thinking and more feeling. You seem to have been closed off from the world for so long. I'm assuming you're probably struggling to find a way to connect and yet you want to."

"When did you become the smart one?" I said with a light laugh.

"You could see my psychologist, if you like. She's great."

I held my hand up to Blake so he would stop. "No,

thanks; I'm good. This is something *I* need to work out. A journey of self."

"How do you plan to take your journey of self?"

"I don't have all the answers. I'm not even sure of the questions. I just trust they will come."

"Well, if there's anything I can do to assist, please let me know. I would love nothing more than to see you truly happy."

"Thanks, Blake."

My phone vibrated in my bag. I reached in, checked the display and saw it was Bodhi.

I looked at Blake. "I'm going to take this."

"No problem. I'II see you back at the office."

I nodded to him and then spoke into the phone. "Hello."

"Hey, you. I swung past your office this morning hoping to take you out for breakfast but you were a no-show."

"Hey, Bodhi. Yes, Michael told me you rocked up. I decided to sleep in. I don't think I walked in the door until 10 maybe 10:30 am."

"Must be nice for some," he said with a little laugh.

"I'm just a token gesture there these days. The place runs itself really. It's a credit to the team."

"You sound flat. Are you okay?" he asked, concerned.

"Yep, just trying to process some stuff."

"About?"

"You, me, the idea of us," I said, knowing he wouldn't leave it at that.

"Let's catch up so we can talk."

"I'm thinking I might need to work through this on my own. Just to get some clarity on my thoughts before we speak," I said in attempt to buy myself some time.

"No, you've had a lifetime of talking to yourself. If it involves us then we should work through it together. I promise I won't push you to be ready before you are, but I do insist that you don't hide. Make the effort to be present."

I paused for moment before confirming, "Okay."

"Good, I was expecting a fight. I'll come to you. Where are you?"

"I'm at the park. It's half a block from the office. The one with a big lake. I don't know its name."

"It's okay. I'll head in that direction and look it up. See you soon."

"Bye."

I sat there watching the native water birds floating past, foraging for food. Life would be simpler if I were bird. I didn't know where to start with Bodhi or even how to talk to him about what was going through my mind. I had this profound desire to be with him, but I didn't know how to push past the emotional barrier I had unintentionally created throughout my lifetime.

Arms glided around my shoulders and his face leant into mine from behind as he gave me a gentle kiss on the cheek.

"Hello," he whispered.

"Hi." I attempted a half-smile.

He walked around the bench so he was standing in front of me. He held out his hands to gesture I stand. I gave him mine, entered into his arms for a beautiful embrace and released a big sigh.

"There you go," he whispered as he heard me exhale.

"I'm not good at this, Bodhi." A tear welled up in the corner of my right eye.

"Sure you are. You're good at everything you put your

mind to. We just have to find a way to switch your brain off and your emotions on."

"Sounds simple." I was already exhausted before we had begun.

"Come with me." He gestured I follow his lead, holding my hand while I lagged slightly behind.

At the base of a magnificent oak tree, he looked up and then turned to me with an eyebrow raised. "Are you game?"

I looked up at the branch that he had pinpointed and then traced a pathway with my eyes as to how I might get up there. "Sure."

"Okay, you first. I'll follow you up."

I tucked my bag into my jeans so both hands were free. Climbing the oak was easier than I had expected because all the rotted knotholes provided a sure footing. Once I was safely up I straddled the branch and waited for Bodhi to join me. He shuffled in behind me so he was leaning on the trunk and I was leaning on his chest with his arms around my waist, our feet dangling.

"Are you comfortable?" he whispered.

"Yes, it's nice up here with this light breeze."

He squeezed his arms around me. "I like it when you smile."

"Me too."

"Talk to me, Talia. What's going on?"

"I'm not sure what to say or where to start. Honestly, I haven't had much of a chance to consolidate my thoughts so they won't be coherent," I said.

"Just talk through whatever is on your mind and we can string it together from there. It's okay if it doesn't make sense right now."

I released a big sigh and allowed my body to relax

into his chest. I stared up through the tree canopy to focus on the shifting clouds roaming in the mottled blue skies. The last time I had had to work on pushing beyond my instinctual refrain was with my cousin Brad in London all those years before. Somehow this was infinitely harder. I had more invested in the outcome of this exploration.

I could feel Bodhi's warm breath near my ear. "Aloud, please," he whispered as he gently bit the bottom of my lobe to reinforce the request.

I semi-smiled and looked down at my clasped hands. "I honestly have no idea where to start."

"Do you want me to help you?"

"Yes, no, maybe?"

He laughed and nuzzled his head into the back of my neck. "Are you attracted to me?"

"Yes. Yes, I am."

"Is it more than a friendship attraction or don't you know yet?"

"It's more. I'm just not sure how to process how I'm feeling," I said as I closed my eyes.

"What are you feeling?"

I took a deep breath and exhaled. "You're really familiar to me. My body reacts to your touch in a way I haven't experienced with anyone else. I'm not sure whether we had an amazing bond as kids that managed to last through the ages or whether Marlee cast a love spell which enchants us to this day. There's something very different in the way I feel about you in comparison to the rest of the world and I'm struggling to process it. I find myself daydreaming about curling up in your arms and sleeping like a baby. I want to tell you everything and anything about my life experiences but I can't understand why." I paused to calm my breath and opened my eyes to reacquaint myself with the skies once more.

"Don't stop; keep going. I'm listening." He pushed into the nape of my neck with his head.

"What is it you see in me that's so attractive?" I asked.

"Don't turn this on me. I'll tell you everything, but it's important you go first and work through this. I know it seems hard, but it will become easier the more you try. Back to you."

I shook my head. "I had forgotten you existed," I whispered. "All those years you remembered me and I let you go. I have an amazing memory, yet the significance of you I released."

"I didn't lose my parents and wasn't swept away to a foreign country to be raised by strangers. It's completely understandable. You were six and your whole world changed. I had both my parents, was returned to a life I was familiar with and I held enough memories for both of us." He squeezed his arms tighter around me as I heard him take a deep breath. "I'm so sorry I wasn't there for you." His voice was broken and genuinely sad.

"Me too." A tear fell from my eye.

"Hey, you guys, you're not supposed to be up there." A voice layered with a thick Scottish accent called out from below.

I peered over the edge of the branch and saw a portly man with a moustache looking up at us and shaking his finger in disapproval.

"Okay, we'll come down," I said, tapping on Bodhi's arms for him to release me.

"I'm not ready," he whispered.

"Excuse me, sir, can you get us a ladder, please? I

don't want to fall on my way down. It might be safer," I called down.

"Okay, I'll head across to the park's maintenance shop. I'll be back in ten. Don't do anything silly." He scurried away.

"Thank you," said Bodhi.

I ran my hands along the length of his forearms exposed around my midriff and settled my hands on top of his. Gently I encouraged him to release his grip, and then opened his arms to rest them on his legs. I shuffled forward and made an easy turn so I was facing him. Bodhi's hands were now on the branch and he was leaning slightly forward, looking down. I paused when I realised the splashes on the trunk were his silent tears. I shifted closer and lifted his face to have him look at me.

His eyes were slightly bloodshot and moist. His gaze held steadfast to mine. I felt a connection of our souls. I placed my hands on either side of his face and leant in so my forehead was now on his. Closing my eyes, I synchronised our breath.

"I feel you," I whispered.

Bodhi's hands lifted from the branch and gravitated towards mine. He gently removed them from his face and kissed the inside of both palms before placing them in front of me. I opened my eyes to be greeted by him staring intensely at me. His right hand glided across my neck and held in position as he drew me closer. He shifted his head slightly to the side and hovered his lips over mine while I felt him draw breath. The lingering of his intent sent electric pulses through my body. I shuddered as the tingles increased like tiny bubbles rising to the water's surface. In this moment he succumbed and connected our lips. I could taste the salt from his tears as he increased and released the pressure on our mouths. It was the most perfect unrehearsed dance of synchronicity. He yielded when I intensified and I did the same for him. I was overwhelmed with emotion and could feel my connection to him amplify.

As he slowly pulled away he used his thumb to trace the outline of my lips and swept the tear falling down my cheek.

He smiled as he said, "I'm in love with you, Talia Jacobs."

I stared at his mouth in silence.

Bodhi lowered his head to get my attention. "It's okay. When you're ready and not a second before. I don't want to be robbed of the moment I've been dreaming about my whole life."

I nodded. "Okay," I said as I internally sent my truth to the universe: *I'm falling in love with you, Bodhi.*

Mable and Walter

I hardly slept that night. My thoughts were consumed with flashbacks of my past experiences interwoven with an intensity of foreign emotions enveloping my core whenever I focused on the idea of Bodhi. I silently admitted to myself I was fighting my desires. How was it possible to know so little about a person and love them with such depth? None of it made sense. I recognised the timeless tales of romantic stories suggesting the concept of love at first sight, but this ran far deeper than the superficiality of his looks. I felt implicitly connected to his soul.

When I woke in the morning I was drowsy and drained of energy. I wanted nothing more than to conclude the inevitable. I was in love with Bodhi. Bodhi who? I was in love with him and I didn't even know his surname. I smiled and shook my head as I slowly gathered my things to shower. I didn't feel like going to the office. Today I planned to wander the streets and allow myself the luxury to indulge in thoughts.

My first stop was a random coffee shop. No morning should ever be started without a good brew. I planned to order it to go but noticed a magazine on the bench, which had the title "How to know when you have fallen for him?" I collected my coffee, inconspicuously grabbed the magazine and headed towards a vacant table with seating for two. I was really conscious of my surroundings. I didn't want anyone to notice my choice of magazine, let alone the article I was reading. Under normal circumstances I wouldn't have cared but today I was present to my vulnerability.

I flipped to page 86. "Have you fallen?" was the title of the article. I sat there and read the core content and then pulled out a pen from my bag to do the quiz.

Does he give you butterflies when he looks at you?

Do you think about him all the time?

Do you consider whether he will like what you are wearing?

The list of questions seemed endless. I trawled through it, tallying up the figure at the end to see my results were "Congratulations! You are deeply in love". I slammed the magazine shut and sipped my coffee while looking out the shop window. I'm not sure why I was so irritated by the quiz confirming what I already knew. Perhaps it was because I was resorting to guidance from a quiz in the first instance. I put my face into my hands and thought, *What am I doing? Jesus, what next? Am I going to seek council in horoscopes?*

"Can I sit with you, dear?"

I peered through my fingers to see a sweet old lady in a classic straw hat with a fresh but withered daisy poking from the brim.

"Sure, please take a seat." I gestured to the vacant chair.

She smiled and sat opposite me. "I'm Mable."

"Hi, Mable. I'm Talia. Pleased to meet you."

"Oh, and you, my dear." She glanced across at the magazine.

"I just grabbed it to pass the time while I drank my coffee. Would you like to read it?" I offered.

"No, I would rather chat, if that's okay."

"Sure, Mable, what would you like to talk about? Any topic, your choice," I said, trying to present as jovial.

"How about love?" she said, once again looking at the cover of the magazine.

"Love? Okay, why not? It seems to be a regular theme among people. Talk to me about love, Mable."

Her eyes followed my coffee cup as I picked it up to take a sip.

"Before we start, if it's alright with you, I'd like to buy you a cup of coffee or tea. Which would you prefer?" I asked.

Instantly her face lit up as she straightened her posture and clasped her hands together. "A cup a tea would be just lovely."

"Okay, I'll be back in a moment." I headed to the counter to place the order.

"Let me guess: a cup of tea?" said the barista, who had watched me come towards him.

"Indeed. I assume she's a regular, then?"

"A regular moocher. She seems to find the right people to sit with and she manages to get them to buy a cup of tea for her every time without fail. She's been here at least once a week for as long as I've worked in the joint."

I could see he seemed to hold her in quiet contempt. He glared at her as he proceeded to prepare the teapot.

I stepped across to block his view. "If it makes her day for me to buy her a cup of tea, then it's my choice and my pleasure. She's not swindling anyone. Not today."

He refocused on the task at hand. I could feel his annoyance at my desire to protect her. I wasn't sure why it was such a big deal to him. She was harmless and possibly lonely. This weekly outing could be her only lifeline to connect with others. It was brave of her to approach random strangers to talk to. I admired her gumption.

I paid for the tea and arranged for an assortment of small muffins to be heated and delivered to the table. As I headed back I was ultra careful not to tip the teapot or the miniature vat of milk. I was not a waitress's arsehole. If there was something to spill, break or burn, I was the person for the job. It took all my concentration to deliver her order intact.

Mable reached up with a charming smile to take the tray from my hands and place it on the table in front of her. "Thank you so much, my dear. This is lovely of you."

"You're welcome. There are some mini muffins on their way. They're just being heated."

"Ohhhhh," she said, impressed with the unexpected extras.

"So, you were going to educate me on the concept of love," I said as I settled back into position.

"I can only tell you about my experience of love." She took a sip of her freshly poured tea.

"I'm all ears. Go ahead, Mable."

"I was married for forty-two years to Walter Moss. He's passed now just on five years and I miss him every moment of a day."

She shifted her hands so they were now clasped together once more. I pursed my lips and smiled at her to acknowledge the depth of the emotions she was sharing with me.

There was a glint in her eye as she leant forward. "He knew before I did, you know. Walter was clever like that. He was so certain of his love for me he said he had enough to carry us both through life."

I could feel myself getting a little choked up. This was not going to be easy for me to listen to without associating it to Bodhi.

"We met at a social charity dance. He was the man of the hour, doing the work as an MC." She paused to sip her tea while she seemingly studied me.

The barista came across and placed the muffins on the table and quickly walked away before either of us could say thanks.

"Oh, my. This is lovely, my dear. Thank you." She reached across to touch my hand.

"You're welcome. They're all yours. Enjoy."

"Aren't you going to have some?" she asked.

"No, I'm not a real fan of dough-based products. Honestly, I bought them for you. If I wanted something I would have it."

Her face lit up as she drew the platter of muffins closer to her. "I think I might start with the chocolate chip one first." She wiggled her fingers.

I enjoyed seeing her delight and happily watched as she took her first delicate bite.

"It's delicious," she said.

"I'm glad."

"Now, where was I?" She tapped a single finger against her mouth. Her face lit up once more. "Oh, yes. We met at a charity dance for the local church group. The ladies were swooning over Walter. He was quite the charmer, you know." She paused to take another bite of her muffin.

"How old were you?" I asked.

"I was twenty-seven years young," she said as she giggled at her own words. "Walter was five years older than me. He was always so upright in his posture. When our eyes locked his didn't leave mine. I was shy. I quickly looked away, all flushed with emotion. I wanted to look to see if he was still watching but was too frightened. Scared that he might be and terrified that he wasn't."

I nodded and smiled. "Go on, this is fascinating." I knew exactly the feelings she described.

"I continue to stare at the floor when a pair of shoes appeared in front of me. I slowly raised my head to be greeted by Walter's warm smile. He introduced himself and asked me to dance. Oh, my. How we swanned around the dance floor. Our movements were aligned. We just seemed to glide. I kept looking at the ladies, who were staring at me. Walter made me focus on him and told me that there was no one else in the room, just him and I."

"Sounds like a fairy tale meeting, Mable," I said, swept away by the romance of her tale.

"He was my prince and I was his queen."

"Wouldn't that make him your king?" I asked.

"No, Walter always insisted on being the prince and me his forever queen."

"I'm sorry I never got to meet Walter. He sounds like an amazing man." I was genuine in my statement. It was so rare to witness true love. I would have enjoyed the privilege of seeing these two together.

"He would have loved you, my dear. I'm certain of it." She patted my hand.

"Thank you. I'm going to order another coffee. Can I get you anything?"

"Goodness no. I'll wait." She reached for a raspberry muffin.

I went across and placed my order and then headed to the ladies. When I came back out my coffee had already been delivered to the table. I waved my thanks to the barista. He acknowledged my gesture and then glanced back at the old lady. I shook my head in amazement. She was harmless. What was it about her that warranted his contempt?

Once seated at my table, I smiled at Mable. "You have my full attention."

"After the dance, we were inseparable. Every spare moment we had we shared together. Walter kissed me on our third meeting. He told me he loved me by the fourth and by the sixth time we caught up he proposed. On one knee, sonnets a-ready, he proposed and even had a ring." She held out her right hand to show me her wedding band.

I gently supported her fingers while I inspected the ring. "Wow, he really knew he wanted you."

"Yes, and he wasn't afraid to let it be known. I was the one for him," she said, beaming.

"Did you have any children?" I asked, before considering how personal the question was.

"No, sadly we weren't blessed with any children. We wanted them but the stork never came to our door."

"I'm sorry, Mable. I didn't think before I asked the question. I apologise if it was too personal."

"Don't be silly, dear. I've had my time to come to terms with this and made my peace. There's nothing worry about. I'm too old to harbour guilt. We did the best we could with what we knew then. Besides, Walter would always remind me I was more than enough for him."

I smiled. "Mable, I'm afraid we might have to stop

talking about Walter or I might find myself falling in love with him too."

"Everybody did, dear," she whispered as she gently patted the top of my hand.

I took a sip of my coffee and looked out the window at the people scurrying past. Somewhere between arriving and talking to Mable the weather had become feral. The wind was howling and rain pelted down. Rubbish from some of the overflowing bins received a second lease on life as pieces of wrappers and other lightweight garbage randomly whirled in the air.

She touched my hand again to draw my attention. Her head was tilted and she wore a gentle smile. "Do you have someone special?"

I looked into Mable's sweetly aged eyes. "Yes, I think I've met the one."

"Is he like my Walter?"

"There seems to be some commonality between them. They know what they want; they aren't emotionally afraid to make it clear. There is a sense of certainty to their conviction, a confidence or knowing."

"Yes, it makes you want to doubt your own feelings, doesn't it?" she said, patting my hand once more.

"I guess he's so open and it accentuates how closed off I seem to be in comparison. I know what I'm feeling; I just seem to have lost the bridge between feeling and conveying. Does that make any sense?" I asked.

"I didn't tell Walter I loved him until three weeks after he proposed."

"Really? So when did you say 'yes' to his marriage proposal?" I craved to understand the finer details.

"While he was down on one knee he reassured me he knew I was in love with him too and I could take the rest of my life to discover it. He asked me to trust him and say yes. I was overwhelmed, as you can imagine, but knew I had to say yes." She paused for a moment to reflect and then she looked at me, shrugged her shoulders. "I said yes."

"Then you got married and lived happily ever after for forty-two years. That's outstanding and a rare story indeed."

"It wasn't all smooth sailing. When Walter was around I was certain and felt secure. In his absence I would allow doubt to creep into my mind. I would get caught up in 'what if' scenarios that made my feel very confused."

"What did you do to correct it?"

"I ran away." She folded her hands in front of her, smiling.

I leaned forward. "Nooooo, really? You walked away from Walter?"

"Yes. I got scared and convinced myself he had some magic hold over me, so I ran away. I caught a train across country to break his spell. It might not seem like a big distance now, but in our day that was a world away for me. I had never been anywhere outside of my home town, so it was very scary."

"What happened next?" I asked, eager to know.

"I stayed a few nights to allow myself to think. I may have physically taken myself to another place but I realised I took him with me. Everything reminded me of him – everything. I had no escape from how I felt. On the third day I recognised I was just scared. I had never fallen in love before and felt completely vulnerable."

I sat back again. "What did you do?"

"I knew I had to go home and tell him how I felt. On

the train ride back I decided to give in to love, to trust him and to trust how I felt about him. To give it my best chance so we could see if he was to be my forever."

I raised an eyebrow and bit my bottom lip. She was brave in her realisation and decision. "I have to say, Mable, I'm impressed. You pushed past your own fear to ensure you didn't deny yourself the opportunity to explore love."

"When I saw the look on Walter's face as I approached him any remaining uncertainty melted away. He was completely in love with me and I felt replete with love for him."

"So all was forgiven?"

"Well, let's just say by the end of the week we were married. Walter insisted. He didn't want to take any chances." She covered her mouth as she giggled.

"I understand. Walter was wise to secure the flight risk." I released a hearty laugh.

I looked outside the window once more. The weather had settled. The ground provided the only evidence that there had been a downpour. The skies had cleared and the sun was beaming on the ground, causing steam to rise.

"So you see, sometimes we just need to believe without seeing." Mable drew my attention back to the topic at hand. "If you feel love for him, allow it to happen. You have nothing to lose, my dear."

"Your words are wise."

"But?" she said, expecting me to provide some futile resistance.

"No 'but' exists. I agree with you. I just need to bridge the gap between what I feel and how I convey it. I've spent a lifetime keeping my thoughts to myself. Now I'm in a position where I need to share them and I'm struggling to find a way that feels natural to me."

"Fake it until you make it," she whispered.

"What does that mean precisely?"

"Walter used to say, if you're sad and you cannot find your smile, smile anyway. Even if you feel it's a lie, before you realise it starts to become your truth. Fake it until you feel it."

"I'll take that on board. Thank you," I said, smiling.

"Dear, it's been such a pleasure to sit with you."

"I enjoyed it too. Do you think you could meet me here again at the same time next week?"

Her face lit up as her hands cupped her mouth. "Oh, I'd love to. Yes, please."

"Great. What I'd really like to see, if it's not too much trouble, are some pictures of you and Walter. Is that okay?"

"It would be my pleasure. I'm so glad we met, Talia."

"I do believe the pleasure has been all mine, Mable. I'm grateful to you for sharing your most treasured of experiences with me. I'll carry them for my lifetime. Thank you." I stood up and gave her a cuddle.

As I looked down at her face she adjusted her hat and said, "I used to be taller."

I laughed, and as I headed to the door I turned and called, "Same time next week, remember?"

She smiled to acknowledge my words and then I glanced across at the barista to give him a salute. I knew he would be pissed that I was now encouraging Mable to come back.

The sun may have been shining but the air was crisp. I quickened my pace to warm my body with a bounce in my step. It was as though I had obtained a new level of freedom. Perhaps I was going to give myself permission just to be in the moment. This was a once-in-a-lifetime opportunity for me and I knew I loved him.

A figure hovered near the entrance to my apartment building. When I got closer, I saw it was Bodhi. He had his hands tucked in his pockets and was pacing up and down. I skipped up the stairs and waved to catch his attention.

"Hey, I wasn't expecting you," I said with a big smile.

He looked at me with relief and wrapped his arms around me. "Why didn't you answer my messages?"

"I left my phone at home. I went out this morning to grab a coffee and sort of got side-tracked. I wasn't expecting any calls so it never really crossed my mind."

"It's three in the afternoon. I called your office, tried your mobile. I thought you'd skipped the country."

I would have laughed but I could see he was pale as a ghost, genuinely concerned. I squeezed him tight and swayed him from side to side. "I'm seriously sorry. I had no idea. I had no idea you would be looking for me or be worried, for that matter."

"It's okay. I just became a little vulnerable after telling you how I felt yesterday. I thought I could handle not knowing but I didn't sleep a wink last night. I just can't stand the idea of losing you after spending my whole life trying to find you."

"Shhhh, I know. I couldn't sleep either. I went for a walk this morning to clear my head. I was hoping to get some answers, but instead I was overwhelmed with feelings that I should have shared with you yesterday."

Bodhi pulled back from the embrace to look at me.

I took a deep breath, touched the side of his face and said, "I'm in love with you."

"You're not just saying that? You mean it?"

"I've never felt this way about anyone and doubt I ever will again. I felt connected to you when we met at the coffee shop. That night at dinner I was completely drawn to you and yesterday when we kissed I knew I loved you. Yeah, I mean it."

Bodhi picked me up and swung me around in circles. The intensity caught me by surprise and knocked the wind out of me. I tapped him to put me down while releasing a squeal of laughter.

"I have to catch my breath and I'm a little dizzy," I said as I bent over to open my airways.

"I'm so happy, Talia. Seriously, you have no idea the relief and joy I'm feeling right now."

I stood upright while laughing. "I think I'm getting an inkling."

Bodhi regained his composure, took a deep breath and then stepped into my personal space. He ran his hands down my arms towards my hands and intertwined his fingers with mine. He kissed me with forceful passion as he gripped my hands tighter. I responded in kind and felt myself melting into the intensity of the moment. Kissing him was electrifying.

"Get a room."

Distracted by the comment I released our lip lock and looked to see my neighbour, Mr Hodgkins, staring at us as he left the foyer.

"Let's go up to mine." I turned to head inside towards the elevator, still holding Bodhi's hands.

Bodhi pulled back slightly. "Ah, I'm going to take a rain check. I've been here for hours and I really need to get back to the office to get some paperwork finalised. Can I call you later?"

"Okay," I said, looking into his eyes.

"Great. Keep your mobile close." He widened his eyes as a warning and gestured with his hands, threatening to tickle me.

"I will. I'll chat to you later then," I said, trying not to show my disappointment.

Bodhi stepped in and gave me a quick kiss on the lips, paused to look at me and then headed down the street, smiling.

I went upstairs, had a shower to warm myself up, and then settled on the couch with a cup of tea. There was something bothering me about Bodhi not wanting to come up to my apartment. This was the second time he had avoided it.

I scrolled through my phone and saw I had nine messages from Bodhi and a text from Michael letting me know Bodhi was looking for me. Geez, we were only on the cusp of a relationship and I already felt pressure to inform him about my whereabouts. It was something I would need to get used to. This was a big shift from a lifetime of answering to no one.

I spent the rest of the afternoon responding to some emails and randomly harassing Ash via text. The time zone difference meant it was heading towards the end of her day but I didn't care and she never seemed to mind. I had grown accustomed to sending her cryptic messages, laughing at her attempts to retaliate and hang shit on me. She was such a laidback, funny creature. Her current focus was trying to pry information out of me regarding my "mystery man". I wasn't ready to talk about Bodhi but I enjoyed taunting Ash. The less she knew the more fixated she became in her desire to know. It was perfect.

Bodhi sent me a text indicating something had come up and he was going to have to work late. I looked at the message and rolled my eyes. I had somehow transitioned into 'that person', the one who waits beside the phone for a call. Yikes, this was not sitting well with me at all. I re-read the text again and wondered why he would choose to not engage with me verbally. I knew I should respond so he was aware I had received his text, but I just didn't want to. I switched my phone to silent and headed off to bed to read.

The next morning the door buzzer drew me out of a fantastic slumber. I stumbled out of bed to check the security monitor.

"Hey, Bodhi, I'll buzz you up. I'm on the ninth floor, apartment 307."

"No, that's okay. Let me take you out for breakfast. Can you meet me downstairs?"

I paused for a moment, watching him through the monitor. "I'm still in my PJs and I'm not really hungry so I'll pass on the offer. Thanks."

"Let's go for a morning walk then. I'll wait here for you to get dressed."

"Bodhi, seriously. Come upstairs or go away." I knew I ran the risk of him walking off, but I was really annoyed by his lack of desire to come into the apartment.

"Buzz me up. I'll be there in a minute," he said, sounding annoyed.

I pressed the button to unlock the entrance and left my door ajar so he could let himself in while I went into the bathroom to take a quick shower and get ready.

"Hello?"

"Have a seat in the lounge. I'm just getting dressed," I yelled from my en suite.

I took my time getting dressed because I needed

space for my own annoyance to subside. When I finally emerged he was sitting on the couch flipping through some of my coffee table books.

"Hey," I said as I approached.

He stood up to greet me. "Hey." He kissed me lightly on the lips. "You took all that time for jeans and a T-shirt?" he said, trying to lighten the mood.

"I was annoyed with you so I decided to take my time. I needed to calm down."

"Did it work?" His bottom lip pouted.

I looked at his lip and then into his eyes. "Why is it like pulling teeth to get you to come up to my apartment? It kind of made me feel like a leper."

He placed his hands in his front pockets and stiffened his posture. "You've got it wrong. I was avoiding coming up here because I didn't want to be tempted or have things escalate before we got a chance to really know each other. I want our first time to be special." He looked at the floor as he swayed back and forth on his tiptoes.

"Why didn't you just tell me that?"

"I guess I didn't want you to try and persuade me. Seriously, Talia, I'd like nothing more than to throw you on the bed and have my way with you right now. It's really hard for me to be here at the moment without feeling the draw of temptation." He tilted his head and gave me a pleading look. "Can we go now, please?"

I collected my bag and headed out the door.

Bodhi followed.

In the elevator I turned so I was positioned in front of him. I didn't provide any time to resist my intentions. I leant in and kissed him hard. As I pulled back I took his bottom lip with me and smiled. The elevator doors opened.

I whispered, "We should have stayed upstairs." I flashed a cheeky smile, feeling very triumphant, then walked out the doors into the front foyer.

I put my hand out for Bodhi to hold. He grabbed my hand, kissed it and then held it tight with his eyes focused forward. As we walked out the door I kept glancing at him. His expression was pensive. I couldn't wipe the smile from my face. I felt better knowing his hesitation wasn't based on a lack of attraction.

"Don't," he said, squeezing my hand.

"What?" I said in a high-pitched playful tone.

"Not funny, Talia. This is why I didn't want you to know. You're doing this flirty cutsie thing." He paused for a second, took a breath. "Stop."

I swung our arms back and forth as we walked, still not able to remove the smile from my face. I did my level best not to glance across at him. I could feel the tension building and it only made me want to be cheekier.

Just as we passed the main street Bodhi pulled me down a cobblestone side lane and forcefully pushed me up against the brick wall. He swiftly placed my arms together behind my back and pressed into my body with his to secure them into position.

I bit my bottom lip. "What do you ever plan to do with me?"

He glared into my eyes as his hands firmly ran from the sides of my hips, up my torso, brushing the outline of my breasts and onto my neck, where they cupped it like a collar. One thumb then shifted up the length of my neck towards my lips, where he worked to separate them. Using his thumb, he drew my bottom lip down and ran his digit across the surface from side to side before leaning in and grabbing my lip with his teeth and gently pulling. His hand glided to the back of my head, where he pulled me firmly into his, deepening into a kiss that threatened more.

He used a single finger to run down the side of my neck across the length of my collarbone and down towards my breast. He traced the outline of it and then used his palm to run along the surface until he could feel my nipple rise to greet his touch. I groaned as he pulled at it, then he released it to use his whole hand to squeeze. As he shifted his torso both his hands gravitated to the back of my buttocks, where he held me firm while he persistently ground slow and hard up against me with his engorged manhood, all the while kissing me with fervour.

I opened my eyes as I felt him pull away. He held out his hand to me. I was still dizzy from the experience. On autopilot, I passed him my hand, speechless. He intertwined our fingers and led me back onto the main street.

"Let's find somewhere to eat. I'm starved," he said.

Still reeling from the experience, "Okay," was all I could say in response.

Enable Mable

I walked into the coffee shop and saw Mable was sitting at our table awaiting my arrival. She was wearing the same hat with a different fresh flower, a small yellow gerbera.

"Morning, Mable, I'm glad you could make it," I said as I patted her on the shoulder.

Her hand reached up and patted mine in return. "I've been looking forward to this all week, dear."

"Me too, Mable. Can I get you a cup of tea?"

"That would be lovely."

I went across to the barista to place my order. Much to my surprise, he placed the tray in front of me with my long black and a pot of tea already prepared. "Am I that predictable?" I said in jest.

He laughed. "Your order may be, but you don't strike me as predictable in any sense of the word."

"Hmm, I'II choose to take that as a compliment. Can you bring out a few of those mini muffins heated too, please."

"I'm already onto it. I'II bring them out when they're ready."

I squinted my smiling eyes at him. Something had shifted in his attitude and I was curious about his demeanour. "Thanks."

"No problem." He stepped back in front of his coffee machine to continue filling his orders.

Once again I managed to deliver the tray without spilling a drop. Mable swiftly assisted in unloading the tray while I sat down.

"Did you have an eventful week?" I asked.

"I spent the whole week gathering some photos to show you. It's the busiest I've been in years," she said with delight in her voice.

"I've been busy too. I was inspired by our conversation last week, which led me on some creative pathways that actively revolve around you. No obligation or pressure. They're just ideas which we can discuss a little later, if that's okay."

The barista arrived with the muffins. "Ladies, these are compliments of the house." He bowed his head and clicked his heels as he placed the plate on the table.

"Oh, how sweet. Thank you, my dear," said Mable.

I looked at the barista, bowing my head, and smiled to acknowledge his gesture. He winked in return and headed off.

"Life is different since I met you, Talia. People seem to be so much nicer to me." She reached across to touch my hand. "I'm starting to think you may be an angel."

I shook my head. "I'm far from being an angel, but I'm glad to hear people are being nicer to you."

Mable's expression changed as she looked thoughtfully at her wrinkled hands. "It's the strangest thing getting on in years. You don't feel changed inside. Sure, you notice some physical limitations and your appearance alters, but it's the way people treat you that makes you feel old and dispensable."

"My philosophy is simple – we can only ever be harmed by what we allow to harm us. It starts and ends with you. Free will is the governor. Mable, choose to accept and understand people may default to a perception or stereotype. It doesn't mean you need to conform and buy into it," I said.

"Yes. It was easier when Walter was alive. I was stronger than I am now," she said with deep sadness in her voice.

"Mable, you're stronger than you think. I believe you are an amazing gift and it's time we considered unwrapping you so the world can share in this too."

"If I had a daughter I would have wished her to be you, dear," she said with tears in her eyes.

I was touched.

"Hello."

"G'day. You're right on time. Take a seat," I said as I looked up at Mila.

"Mable, I'd like to introduce you to Mila Jones. She's a reporter."

"Hello, Mila."

"Hi, Mable."

"What drink would you like me to organise for you?" I asked Mila.

"I've already had two cups of coffee today. I'll be bouncing off the walls if I have another."

"Okay, I guess I'll explain why I asked you here. Mable and I have been getting to know one another and I'm inspired. I want her story to be captured. I'd like you to spend some time with her listening to her experiences with the intent of creating a biography of her life. The primary focus will be her relationship with Walter her husband, who has passed. Thoughts?"

"I'm not sure what to say. Why me?" Mila asked.

"Every reporter is an aspiring writer. I'm making an assumption that you're no different."

"You're correct, but I still don't understand why you would ask me of all people to do this. After I unintentionally misrepresented you in that article, I assumed you hated me. "

"I could hire a stranger to do this, but I'd rather engage someone who I know is capable and is also driven by obligation to ensure the right amount of heart and soul is placed in this endeavour. Did I choose right?"

Mila thought about it for a second. "What's the catch?"

"None from my perspective. You can choose to be part of the journey or decline. You need to let me know which it is by the end of the week if possible. The terms and conditions are simple. You provide me with a quote on the cost of your services. You will be paid for your time and retain full credits for writing the book. I'll pick an editor and Mable and I will have final say in the changes, but I'm happy to work in consultation with you. All the sales and any spin-offs from it are fully owned by Mable to do with as she chooses."

Mable gasped. "No, dear, I couldn't."

"Sure you can, Mable. You can donate it all to charity or anything you like. Just say yes. Allow me to organise for your and Walter's story to be captured. This can be your legacy, your baby that lives forever. What do you think?"

Mable burst into tears and covered her face with her hands. I got up from my chair and stood behind her, gently placing my arms around her fragile frame. "It's the least I can do. You're truly amazing and I want the world never to forget it," I whispered.

"I'll do it," said Mila with tears in her eyes.

I looked at her and nodded.

The barista came across, providing some tissues for Mable. "I don't know why you're crying, but it's making me want to cry too," he said as he gently placed the tissues in her hand.

I was surprised when he bent down to look into Mable's eyes. "Please stop. You're too sweet to shed tears."

"It's okay. She's just a little overwhelmed by an opportunity that's been presented to her. These are tears of joy," I said.

Mable finally managed to compose herself. "I just don't know what to say."

Mila piped in, "Say yes, Mable. I'd really love the opportunity to write your story."

The barista also said, "Say yes. I don't know what it's about but say yes." He patted the corners of his eyes to prevent the formulating tears from falling.

"Okay, dear, I would love to share my and Walter's story," she said, wiping her tears.

"I'd like you to consider the title *Once in a Lifetime, Mable's Story* for the book. We can reassess it again later but for now use it." I gestured to Mila to write it down.

The barista went back to serve some customers and I reseated myself.

"I'm busting to see a photo of you and Walter. Gimme, gimme," I said as I wiggled my fingers in a manic wave of excitement.

Mable carefully opened a thick leather-bound album and started to pass across some of the images that were loosely sitting between the pages. Mila shuffled her chair closer to mine so she could see at the same time.

I studied the faded black-and-white image of a young Mable and her Walter. He was standing tall and proud, just as she had described, with his arm around her. She was looking up at him with admiration. You could feel the potency of what they shared ooze from the image.

I looked at Mila. "Can you see what you need to artistically translate into words?"

"Yes, I see it," she said, not shifting her gaze from the image.

"He was a very handsome man, Mable, and you were quite the looker. You still are," I said.

"No, I was back then, but now I'm just sparkling eyes with wrinkles," she said with a laugh.

I looked at Mila. "Write that down as a quote. We can use it." I pushed my coffee cup away and then stood.

"Okay, ladies, I have to head into the office. I haven't been there for almost a week so I should try to make an appearance. Feel free to stay. I'll organise a tab so you can both meet here regularly. The beverages, lunch, anything you need, just order it and place it on the tab. If you need a private place, call my office and I'll have Michael arrange a room for you. Whatever you need can be arranged; just let me know."

"Okay, what do you need from me?" asked Mila.

"I'd like you to quote for the cost of your services. List any terms and conditions you feel are important for me to consider. I'd like to have an outline of the time you feel you will need for the initial draft (say three chapters), second (over halfway complete) and final manuscript. If you have any questions or additional ideas add them to the considerations. Please email me by the end of the week. In the meantime I'll have my lawyers draft a high-level outline of the engagement. When we are agreed on the terms and conditions we can sign and start."

"Oh, my. It all sounds very complex," said Mable.

"It's standard business practice, Mable. Don't worry about it. You just need to keep focused on remembering the story. Mila and I will do the rest."

"I'll get started on it straight away," said Mila, typing into her Blackberry.

"Good. There's one more thing. When you've finished catching up here, can you bring Mable by my office, please? I have something I want to show you, Mable, that you may be able to help me with if you're interested."

"I already want to say 'yes' and I don't even know what it is. This has been my most exciting day in years." Mable shuffled across so she could stand up with her arms open.

I gave her a cuddle.

"I'll see you both later then."

I walked across to the counter to settle the bill and set up a tab. I watched the barista as he organised the paperwork.

"Can I ask your name?"

"It's Ryder," he said, stretching his hand across the counter to shake my hand.

"I'm Talia." I shook his hand.

"I know."

"You know my name? How?" I looked at him a little closer to see whether I should recognise him.

"After you left last week a couple of the patrons told me you were Talia Jacobs, the secret millionaire," he whispered.

"Ah, right. Last week you held Mable in contempt.

This week you were considerate, and even displayed compassion. Is this all because you found out something about me that you deemed favourable?"

"No," he said, looking a little defensive.

I watched as he shifted to fold his arms. "Your body language indicates a different story. Can you tell me why you were so annoyed at her in the first place? I'd like to understand."

"Every week she comes in, looks around and tries to find someone to sit with. She's annoying the customers and always mooching for a free cup of tea. It was pissing me off. Just because she's old doesn't mean she should make nuisance of herself," he snipped, pursing his lips.

"Ryder, have you ever walked into a room full of strangers and tried to make a connection?"

"Sure, I've had to do it once or twice," he said.

"Was it easy or did you have some angst about doing it?"

"It was awkward. I wouldn't say it's the nicest feeling in the world."

"How many times did you witness Mable get rejected by your customers in here?"

"A lot."

"Did you ever try to console her or offer her a free cup of tea?" I asked.

"No, she got enough free tea from everyone else."

"Look over my shoulder at her." I waited until I was sure his eyes were locked onto her. "Imagine the amount of loneliness that drives her to venture out week after week in an attempt to connect with the world. The only person she knew and loved died and left her in uncharted waters. Instead of hiding, this vulnerable woman chose to continue to attempt to engage with the world. Look at who you choose to hold in contempt."

I could see he heard my words and felt the message as I watched his body melt into shame. "I understand," he muttered.

I passed across some money. "That's for today and the rest can be allocated to kick off the tab. I'll come in weekly and fix up any outstanding balance owing. Just so we are clear, I want you to give them anything they ask for and bill me. No questions asked. Understood?"

He stared at the pile of money on the counter, only responding with, "Yes."

"Okay, have a nice day." I turned to walk out the door.

"Talia, for what it's worth, I'm sorry," he said.

I continued to walk towards the exit. Turning my head slightly in his direction, I responded, "Right gesture, wrong person, Ryder."

Outside the shop I tapped on the window to give the ladies a final smile and wave goodbye.

Mila indicated she wanted me to stop. I shrugged and nodded. She said something to Mable and then left the table to join me.

"What's up?"

Mila looked into my eyes. "I just wanted to say thank you."

"No problem. I know you'll do a good job."

"Actually, I was referring to what you did to prevent me from getting fired from the paper. I didn't deserve your kindness and in spite of my horrid behaviour you stepped in and protected me. I just don't understand why?"

"How do you know about that? It was meant to be confidential," I said, returning her gaze.

"The liability contract and covering letter were

accidentally or perhaps on purpose sent to me to be archived. I read what you wrote around the terms and conditions. It stipulated the company needed to own its responsibilities and improve their work practices and were not allowed to utilise me as a scapegoat. You put a clause in commercials stating the agreement would be null and void if I was fired for reasons related to the article." She dropped her gaze. "I treated you poorly and in return you saved me."

"No one's perfect. We all make mistakes and all deserve the benefit of the doubt. Yes, I was really annoyed with you for thrusting me into the public eye, but I knew even though you were misinformed and had clouded judgement your intent was to expose corruption. You just went about it the wrong way. It was as much the paper's fault for blindly printing articles before facts are validated. If they had enforced the discipline it never would have been printed. The root cause of what happened was directly linked to companies' process and policies or lack thereof. I only did what I believed was correct, in spite of how I felt about you at the time."

She clasped her hands together. "You hated me, didn't you?"

"Hate is a strong word. You came in guns a-blazing with an attitude and tone that wasn't endearing. I didn't hate you; I hated what you had done. Anyway, let's not rehash the past and I'd prefer we never spoke of it again. Can you manage that?"

"I'll try," she said.

"Do better than try. The chapter is closed. We are about to embark on a great journey. It's time to reset and start anew."

"Okay."

"Good, I'm off. Don't forget to bring Mable to my office this afternoon. I also want to reintroduce you to the team." I intentionally turned so I couldn't see the expression on her face as I mentioned the reintroduction. I gave Mable one last wave through the window and proceeded down the street towards the office building.

When I arrived most of the staff were at lunch. Michael was on the phone, as was Blake. I waved and went to my office. The first thing to catch my eye was an amazing bunch of flowers. The message on the card was "Patience". I laughed. It was Bodhi trying to bait me. Ever since my stunt in the elevator he had been randomly attacking me with short bursts of delicious sexual interludes and then, quick as a whip, he withdrew as though nothing had happened. I don't know how he had the ability to stop. I was in a frenzy, wanting to succumb to the delights every time. He was truly driving me insane but I refused to admit it, knowing full well that he already knew. That cheeky monkey was going to get some serious payback. I planned to strike when I had the right opportunity. All's fair in love and sexual tension, I say.

I pulled my phone out of my bag to send a text of thanks. Brad had sent me a message, saying: *"Do I hear correct? My Talia is in love? I expect full details when you're ready. Which is now."* The next text from him only had the word: *"Waiting ... "* It had been sent thirty minutes before.

My first response went to Bodhi: *"Thanks for the flowers. They are lovely."*

Ash was next: *"Don't think I don't know it was you who baited Brad. Nice try. I'll tell him everything and make him promise not to tell you anything. Backfired!!!! Stay tuned. You will be punished. ☺"*

My final message was to Brad: *"There may be some foundation to the rumours. It's too early to tell. I'll keep you posted when I know more. Who knows? I might even bring him home to meet you guys. ☺ Make sure you don't tell Ash anything … I know she put you up to this and therefore she must be punished. (LOL) Pass on hugs and kisses to Suzanna, the kids and the rest of the gang."*

I walked out into the main workspace to speak with Michael and Blake. They were just finishing up on their calls so I waited.

"G'day, guys, I wanted to let you know Mila Jones will be coming around soonish with a lady called Mable."

"Mila," snapped Michael with a scowl on his face.

"See that look, it's not allowed. Be nice to her when she arrives. I've hired her to write Mable's autobiography, so she will very shortly be within my employ. I therefore expect the whole team will embrace our new team member. Got it?"

Blake laughed. "I have no idea what you're up to, but I don't hold any grudges towards Mila. Thanks to her incompetence Solution Manifestation gained notoriety. She might have been one of the best accidents to happen to us."

I nodded my agreement and looked at Michael. "Ask any question you want now or forever hold your peace. What she did was not personal. It was a mistake and we are all entitled to make them. I need you to be on board because the rest of the team will look to you. Leading by example is a responsibility not to be taken lightly. Thoughts?"

Michael folded his arms; he was clearly struggling with the idea. "I just don't know why you would trust her. She was horrible to you."

"Yep, she was a righteous cunt at the time. She also believed she was exposing corruption. Mila wasn't doing it for personal gain or interest. The paper and she got it wrong, she's paid the price so I want to put the past to bed. There is no point in holding grudges. It serves no one to be bitter." I waited for Michael's response.

"Do you trust her?"

"No, I trust me. That's all I need. It'll be fine, I promise. Let's face it, if there is an issue you know I'll handle it. Are we good?"

"Yeah, I guess so."

"Excellent. Mable, on the other hand, is somewhat of a treasure. I want you to ensure the gang make her feel like this is her home and you are all her children. It's important me, okay?"

"We can do that," said Michael with a smile.

"Awesome. On your way back from lunch can you please organise some snacks for the staff and call them into the conference room to let them know what's going on?"

"Will do."

"Thanks, Michael. Blake, are we good?"

"Everything is perfect at the minute," he said.

"Alrighty, I'll let you get back to it. Thanks, guys."

I went into my office and started searching for information around self-publishing. The idea of submitting the manuscript to a known publishing house didn't appeal to me. I liked the freedom retained with doing it all ourselves. I spent the rest of the afternoon educating myself on the pros and cons.

"Talia, Mila and Mable have arrived," said Michael, who was standing at my door.

"Did you inform the crew? Are they on board?"

"Yessss," he hissed.

"Did you put on your best welcome face for Mila?"

He rolled his eyes. "Yessssssssssss."

"How seriously cute is Mable?"

Michael's face lit up. "Oh, my god. She reminds me of my nanna. She's so cute."

I laughed. "Good. Go get them and bring them in."

I heard Michael directing them to my office. Before they reached the door, Mable was already talking. "You have a lovely office, dear."

"Thanks, both of you have a seat." I looked at Mila, who was showing signs of feeling a little awkward. The last time she had been in my office it was on very different terms.

"Are you okay, Mila?" I asked.

"Yes, fine thanks," she responded.

"How did you both go today? Are there any questions or concerns?"

"No, Mable stepped me through her photo album while I took some preliminary notes."

"Sounds like a good start," I said with a reassuring smile.

Mable shifted in her chair to lean forward. "The boy who makes the coffee came and apologised to me. He said he was really sorry if he had appeared rude in the past and told me I was welcome to come in for a free cup of tea while he's on shift anytime I like."

I smiled. "This day just keeps getting better and better for you, doesn't it, Mable? Well done. I'm glad."

"Whatever you said to him must have left quite an impression." She nodded her head approvingly.

I stood up. "Follow me, ladies." I walked out of the room and led them to the back storage area, where I picked up a pile of letters, sifted through a couple of layers and then passed one to Mable. "Have a read of this letter."

Mable put her glasses on and carefully read the letter. When she was finished she looked at me. "This poor soul needs a little direction."

"My thoughts exactly. Mable, this room is full of people just like him who need a moment from a stranger. I believe a kind word, a wise thought, a simple consideration, could make all the difference perhaps giving them something in return for their extension of thoughts misdirected at me. I'd like to offer you the job of being the person who reads the letters and hand-writes a response. It doesn't need to be an essay. Most times simple is the best. Are you interested?"

"I've never had a job before. This would be wonderful. I'd love to," she said, gushing with excitement.

"Awesome. You can keep your own hours. I'll have Michael allocate a desk so you can be here with the team. There's no race. Feel free to respond to as many or as little as you like in a day. Just do as much as you feel you're able to. No pressure, okay?"

"Oh, we must respond to them all. None of these should go unanswered. They all deserve some return. Wouldn't you agree?"

"Sure, but the pile gets higher every day so let's just aim to do our best. I'm keen for all these lonely hearts to get the gift of Mable and Walter's wisdom."

Mable stepped in to give me a huge embrace. "You are an angel," she whispered.

I graciously returned her embrace as I smiled. Mable was such a lovely soul. I felt blessed to have met her.

I took them both out to the main section of the office again. "Michael, Mable will be joining the team, effective from tomorrow. She's going to be responsible for responding to all the lonely heart letters on my behalf. Can you organise a desk, security pass and get some office supplies for her? Quality parchment paper, matching envelopes and a super nice writing pen."

Michael gave Mable a hug. "Welcome on board. It's going to be wonderful to work with you. Let me give you a quick tour of the place." He offered his arm to her and off they toddled.

"Guess that just leaves you and me," I said to Mila.

"What you're doing for this woman is just amazing. I'm speechless," she said, stepping into my personal space.

I shifted slightly back. "Let's make something crystal clear. Anything you learn about me is strictly off the record. Not the paper, your best friend, no one gets to know anything when it comes to me. I'm clandestine by nature. Please respect that. Do we have an understanding?"

Her lips pursed. "Absolutely. I just wanted to say I'm in awe."

"Hmm, hopefully that'll pass," I said, making light of it. "Do you need me to organise desk space for you too?"

"No, Mable and I will meet at the coffee shop so we're not distracted."

"No problem. If you change your mind, let me know. I'm going to get back to work. Try and get me your terms and conditions before Friday, if you can."

"Okay, I'll see you and thanks again," she said chirpily.

"You're welcome, Mila. Enjoy the rest of your day." I headed back into my office. My mobile was buzzing. "Hello."

"Are you intentionally ignoring my messages?"

"Brad? It's a bit late at night for you to be calling, isn't it?"

There was a pause on the phone and then a shift in tone. "Is this a joke? Who's Brad?" asked Bodhi.

"Oops! Hey, Bodhi, sorry the number was blocked. Your voice sounds similar to his. How are you?" I said as I laughed.

"Me, I'm still wondering who Brad is."

"Brad's my cousin. We grew up together and are really close. He sent me a text earlier today so I guess he was on my mind. You do sound alike, at least on the phone."

"Phew, you gave me heart palpitations, woman."

"I never pegged you as the jealous type," I said, feeling surprised.

"Do you recall the singer who got your number so easily?"

I felt annoyed at his tone and the suggestion of 'easy' hit a nerve. "Yes."

"After the gig when he was passed out, I smudged your number on his arm. The next day he called me to see if I still had it in my phone. I told him it had been wiped. I didn't want him calling you. Talia, when it comes to you I am insanely jealous."

Calmly I responded, "Okay, I'm kind of stuck on your choice of the word easily."

"Well, you didn't seem to put up much resistance. Come on, Talia, don't take it the wrong way. I didn't mean anything by it."

"The thing is, Bodhi, I'm not sure there is a right way to take the word 'easy' in this context."

"Look, perhaps it was a poor choice of words. Forget I said it."

"See, even the word perhaps tells me you intended

to use the word easy and because I'm challenging you to define it further you're modifying the dialogue because your desire to appease and move on is greater than your need to stick to your initial statement and provide context."

"Wow, what's up with the psych babble? You're really not going let this go, are you?" he said, starting to get annoyed.

I thought about his words for a moment before responding, "It makes me wonder whether your desire to withhold sexual union has anything to do with a perception that I'm easy. You tease me mercilessly and then go cold. Why?"

He didn't respond.

I paused, waiting for a response that never came. "The silence is deafening, Bodhi. I'll chat to you later. Bye." I hung up the phone, switched it off and threw it into my bag. It was just shy of being two and a bit weeks into us being together and already there was trouble in paradise.

Alignment

Time didn't stand still but internally I wished it would. Three days had passed since Bodhi and I had spoken on the phone. It was starting to get harder to breathe. I know my withdrawal into silence wasn't assisting the situation but I was completely out of my comfort zone and this was my default position. I knew I needed to harness my emotional bravery and reach out to him.

I switched on my phone and listened to the flurry of beeps come through to notify I had messages. There were some from Brad, and Ash, responding to my taunts, and a few from Bodhi. I went straight to his to see what the collateral damage was.

"I'm really annoyed that you hung up on me. Call me."

"I've tried to call and your phone is switched off. Seriously, Talia, come on. Call me."

"Two days, really?"

"Roses are red, violets are blue, some of what you said does hold true, but all that matters is I'm in love with YOU. Call me, please. We can make this right."

I stared at the last text and saw it had been sent that

morning. I would have called him but I had no voice. I was emotionally drained in a way I couldn't recall ever feeling about another man, not even Brad. I definitely had more invested in Bodhi than I'd had in any other man. I really loved him and felt myself being pulled apart.

I messaged back:

"Roses are red, and violets are blue. I really need for us to always speak the truth because I know how deeply I have fallen for you. Come over when you are ready so we can talk."

I pressed the 'send' button and stood up to get myself organised. I hadn't taken more than three steps when the phone beeped.

"Thank god, I thought I had lost you!!! I'm coming over right now."

I still felt numb and knew it was my way of protecting myself from the pain that surged around the core of my being. I didn't want to feel anything, yet I knew I had to. I jumped into the shower and brushed my teeth for the first time since I had arrived home three days before. In movies they depict people curled up in a ball, wearing the same clothes for weeks, dropping their hygiene standards. I used to be the viewer who would look at this and think, Ugh, as if? Now I was living the dream. Perspective can be a bitch.

No sooner had I slipped on a fresh pair of jeans and a plain T-shirt than the buzzer sounded. I let Bodhi up and opened the door while I went back to the bathroom to do a quick towel-dry of my hair. I heard the door being closed. As I threw the towel on the hook Bodhi walked into the bathroom. His eyes were bloodshot and swollen from crying. It made my stomach sink to see him like this.

I walked into his arms and burst into tears. "I'm sorry, Bodhi, I'm just not good at this." I squeezed him tight and buried my head into his shoulder.

"I wasn't exactly helping the situation. I was scared of losing you so I started to get caught up and insecure. I wanted you to want me so bad that you could never leave me. I'm sorry if I hurt you," he said as he kissed the side of my head and heaved to gulp in some air.

The release of my emotions was awful. They came as an unannounced flood of tears, and all I could do was hold him tight while I allowed it to be released. I didn't want to keep it in or feel like this for a second longer than I had to. Bodhi was also caught in the intensity of the moment but his concern for my wellbeing overruled his ability to lose himself. He rocked me gently, holding me tight as I howled.

Finally I exceeded my tear ducts' ability to produce any more tears. I didn't feel better for the release, just exhausted. Bodhi didn't move. He continued to rock me gently and hold on tight. I wasn't looking forward to seeing what my eyes looked like. My head was clouded and there was a looming ache that I knew would grow if I didn't address it.

I gently pulled back. I couldn't look him in the eyes; I wasn't ready. "Let's go to the lounge. I need to rehydrate and we should look at getting some takeaway. I haven't eaten in three days and I'm starting to feel it."

As I turned to walk out the door Bodhi readjusted his arms so they were wrapped around me. He placed his head on top of mine and followed closely behind. When we got to the lounge I released his hands and turned to look at him as I pushed his torso to sit on the couch. I then lay across him with my legs bent so I was neatly snuggled in his arms. I found myself holding my thumbnail between my teeth.

"What do you feel like eating?" I asked.

Bodhi squeezed his arms around me. "I don't care. You pick; anything will be fine."

I shifted slightly so my face could nuzzle into the crook of his neck, put my arms around him and whispered, "I love you so fucking much it scares the shit out me."

He lifted my torso into his arms, used his lips to shift the hair from my ear and whispered with a heavy breath, "Never stop telling me you love me. Never. I love you like crazy, Talia Jacobs."

"Thank you," I whispered.

He gave me another big squeeze and then released me. "Come on, we have to organise some food to be delivered so you can eat."

I nodded and shuffled across so he was free to move. My headache was starting to make its presence known so I went into the bathroom to take something for it. While I was there I stared at my reflection in the mirror. I looked awful. My colour was drained, black shadows under my eyes and red bloodshot eyeballs. Yep, I was a real catch.

Unexpectedly Bodhi came to the bathroom door. "How's Thai sound?"

I jumped. "You startled me." I raised my hand to my heart.

"Sorry, honey," he said, releasing a little laugh.

"Thai's fine. I'll have some steamed rice and veggies, no sauce."

"Okay, I'll go call them."

I left the bathroom. Nothing good was going to come

from me inspecting my appearance too closely this day. I organised the cutlery and set a nice shiraz to breathe while we waited for the food to arrive. When I walked back into the lounge Bodhi was lying on the couch looking very comfortable. I threw a blanket across him and went off to get some tea-light candles to give the room some ambience.

When I returned, I settled down on the floor near the couch with my head resting on his arm, looking into his lovely eyes. He smoothed the hair from my face, placing it behind my ear, and then used a single finger to trace the outline of my face, down my nose and across my lips. He kissed me softly and then placed his forehead against mine.

"Everything about us seems so intense," he said.

"I know."

After dinner, he resumed his position on the couch while I sat beside him on the floor, sifting through my text messages to reply to everyone who had tried to reach me during the last few days. The whole time I was texting Bodhi quietly lay there stroking my hair. It was surreal to feel such an enormous flood of amplified emotions for him. I was totally enamoured.

I placed the phone on the coffee table. "I'm exhausted." I released a big yawn.

"I'll head off so you can get some sleep."

"Not a hope in hell. You aren't going anywhere."

He propped his head up with his arm. "I don't think now is the right time for us to spend the night together."

"I disagree. Tonight we 'have' to spend the night together. I want … no, I need to sleep in your arms. I want to wake up and see you beside me in the morning."

Bodhi gently ran his thumb down the side of my face. "I can do that," he whispered.

I stood up and held my hands out to help him off the couch. As he rose he looked down at me, dropping his head to softly rub his face against mine. I closed my eyes to heighten the temporal sensation. As he turned he wrapped my hands around his taut torso and led me to my bedroom.

"Do you have a preference for side?" he asked.

"Nope, let's both sleep in the middle."

I pulled back the layers and crawled into bed fully clothed. Bodhi took off his shoes and did the same. We wrapped the blankets around us so we were snug. I had my back to him and he nestled into the curve of my body so I could feel his warmth. He placed his arm around me and held my hand. His head rested on the crook of my neck. It didn't take long for me to fall into a deep sleep. I was knackered.

I woke in the early hours of the morning, feeling groggy but satisfied with the amount of slumber I had acquired. Bodhi was curled over on the other side of the bed, fast asleep. I watched as his chest rose and fell with each breath. The concerns of the previous day were no longer present on his manly facial features. I hoped his dreams afforded him some joy.

I snuck into the bathroom and had a shower. There was something wonderful about the cleansing sensation of water. It was a symbolic washing away of all the woes, an opportunity to obtain a clean slate for a new day. I towel-dried my hair because I didn't want to wake Bodhi. I slipped on fresh bra and knickers, an oversized plain white T-shirt and then snuck back into bed.

In a daze, Bodhi turned and shifted closer, pressing hard against my body. I placed a hand on his arm, which was now lying across my chest, and gently kissed his bicep. I watched as a sleepy smile appeared. He kept his eyes shut as he raised his head to find my face and kissed me on the cheek. I slowly shuffled so I was facing him. I stroked the side of his face and then kissed him softly on the lips. At first Bodhi didn't stir. Instead I watched as he lay still in a way that falsely indicated he might be drifting off to sleep again. I waited patiently.

Without warning his arm tightened and he drew me to him. He raised his head to rub his nose against mine and then he hovered over my lips as his fingers ran through my hair at the back of my head. Shivers shot through my body in anticipation of what was to come.

"Are you ready?" he whispered.

I placed my hand under his shirt and ran an elongated stroke with a single finger from the top of his shoulder blade to the crest of his buttock. "Yes."

Our lips connected in a balanced rhythm. The intensity of his motion was amplified as he used his tongue to gently caress mine. His hands increased in pressure as he pushed my head deeper onto his mouth. I found my hand automatically gravitated towards unbuttoning his shirt. I wanted to feel his flesh against mine. We had only just begun and my body was already on fire.

I pulled away from his kiss momentarily. "Take your clothes off."

Bodhi reconnected our lips and masterfully peeled his layers off, only leaving his briefs. I instantly allowed my hand to glide across his abdomen and torso. I needed to explore every inch of his flesh. His breath altered when I brushed across his nipples. I was tempted to remain there but chose to continue my tactile adventure.

Initially I avoided going near his manhood. I traced the outline of every contour and muscle on his upper body. My annoyance started to rise when he maintained his conscious restraint not to touch me. My body ached all over with desire. I was wet with anticipation and the scent arose from my southern region, releasing the perfume of my arousal.

Gently I pulled away from his kiss and waited for his eyes to open so I could meet his gaze. As he looked deep into mine I ran my fingers across the horizon of his lower abdomen, just above his briefs. Lightly I scraped my nails against the skin on his inner thighs towards the outline of his scrotum and the sides of his penis. Bodhi instantly released a groan as he forcefully recommenced our kissing. His hand shifted from holding the back of my head to travelling under my T-shirt and straight to my breast. He slipped the strap of my bra down my arm to unveil my bosom. Lightly kneading and pulling, he focused his fondling to that region as I ran my hand with a firm grip slowly up and down his shaft.

I lifted my leg so it leant across his. Instantly Bodhi's hand moved down my abdomen towards my hip, settling on my buttock, where he squeezed hard and pulled me near. The length of his hand extended as he used his fingers to caress my swollen passion through saturated panties from behind. I pushed against his fingers and groaned. Without warning he lifted me onto his body so he was straddled. He raised his torso up to kiss me as he guided my arms in the air and swiftly removed my T-shirt. His face dropped to engulf my exposed breast in his mouth as he worked the back of my clasp to remove the bra.

I found myself naturally grinding against his swollen member. Placing his hands on my arse, he pushed my hips down while he thrust up against me. My breath was heavy and I felt dizzy from our long-awaited connect. I leant forward so his body fell back on the bed. I hovered my face over his, looking into his eyes. I could feel his breath on my skin as he exhaled. Maintaining eye contact, I grabbed his bottom lip with mine, gently tugging before I released and started kissing my way down his chest. Using my tongue, I circled around his nipples and then gently blew some air until they stood at attention. I placed one in my mouth to play while I tweaked and pulled at the other. He released a series of noises as I worked my magic, his hands scratching my back and intermittently pushing my head hard against his rigid torso.

When I did something that excited him his clawing would deepen, which encouraged my need to provide further attention. I was completely aroused by the freedom of expression. I wanted to continue to drive him wild but was unable to contain my own needs.

I rose up to kiss him with deep passion and then whispered in his ear, "I want you inside me." Then bit the bottom of his lobe.

Bodhi's used his hands to guide my body off his and onto my back. Swift as a leopard to its prey, he pounced to now be partially on top, securing me in position as he sucked on my neck, ripping at my knickers and removing his briefs before repositioning himself between my legs. I could feel his erection resting on the entrance to my swollen vagina. I tried to shift my torso to force his entry, without success. He wasn't allowing this to be driven by me.

The pressure of his body increased as Bodhi hovered his face to look into my eyes. I braced my hands on either side of his arms as he slowly entered me for the first time. I felt compelled to turn my head, but without words Bodhi communicated by stilling himself every time I lost contact with his amazing eyes. He wanted me fully engaged.

His pace was steady and deep. I shifted my hands to run up and down the length of his back while our eyes were locked. As he altered from quick thrusts to achingly slow I could feel myself getting lost in the pulsating build-up of sensation. I bent my knees and lifted my torso to reposition the pressure of his gyration. He placed my hands above my head and clasped them as sweat beaded on his brow and a pensive expression appeared.

I knew he was close.

I held my gaze steadfast to his. I opened my mouth and bit my bottom lip as his eyes started to falter. I stilled my gyrations to regain his focus and smiled as he looked upon me again. I then lowered my body and spread my legs as far apart as I could so he was able to have total immersion. I released a groan as he plunged hard and fast over and over. I felt the delights of the breeze created as his balls kept slapping against me.

I freed my hand from his grip to watch with satisfaction as his eyes half-closed when my hand ran down the side of his body, travelling across his stomach and down towards my clitoris. As I extended my fingers to touch the base of his thrusting penis the intensity rose to a new level. My sensations increased exponentially as I self-stimulated. Waves of electric pulses ran through my body. The build of its presence forced my breath to quicken. Lifting my head to kiss him, I released loud gasps as my body surrendered to orgasm. Bodhi gritted his teeth as he thrust harder for a few final strokes before pulling out, placing his penis on my abdomen, where he released his juices of satisfaction.

We both lay there panting. I stared at the ceiling while Bodhi lay on his side gazing at me. I turned my face to look at him.

"Morning," I said with a smile.

He kissed me softly, sucking on my bottom lip as he returned his head to the pillow. "Morning."

Bodhi headed home to change his clothes prior to work and I stayed back to tidy up the place before I too ventured into the office. Thoughts of the day before seemed so distant now. Yesterday I was fighting to breathe, consumed by unhappiness, and now I couldn't contain my elation.

The sound of my mobile vibrating disrupted my thoughts. I picked it up and sat on the lounge to answer. It was Brad.

"Hey, you," I said.

"What's with the silent treatment? Is everything okay?" he asked.

"I'm sorry. I did respond to you last night. Didn't you get the message?"

"Nope, I've received nothing. I figured if I couldn't get hold of you today I would have to jump on a flight to hunt you down."

I laughed. "I know you would but there's no need, honest. I did take a sabbatical from the world for three days but I'm officially returned to the land of the living. I'm good. Actually, I'm feeling more than good. How are Suzanna and the kids?"

"The family's fine. Tell me about this fella. Are you an item?"

"Yes. We haven't really spoken about it officially, but I would say we're dating."

"Wow, he must be quite a guy for you to consider dating him."

I could hear strain in Brad's voice. "Are you okay?"

"Yeah, of course. When I didn't hear back from you I felt a little lost, so I guess that's the vibe you're picking up."

"To answer your question, he is indeed amazing," I said as I reflected on the morning's event.

"When are we going to meet him?"

"It's early days. We have to work out our rhythm, but I thought I might bring him across to Oz in a month or so if he can get some time off work."

There was silence.

"Brad, are you there?"

"I'm here. I wasn't expecting you to say that. You really are into this guy, aren't you?"

"I am," I said, now feeling cautious of Brad's reaction.

"How did you meet?"

"We first laid eyes on one another when we were six years old in Haiti. Bodhi and I were in the same class together. His parents moved back to the US not long after. We bumped into each other recently through fate and good timing. I'II give you the full blow-by-blow one day, but I'm going to have to head off to the office soon, so I don't have enough time right now."

Brad's voice changed. There was an air of sadness in his tone. "Okay. Well, I'm glad you're good. I'II let you go. Make sure you keep in touch; don't forget about me."

"Brad, forgetting you is an impossibility. I always will keep in touch. Give my love to everyone and I'II chat to you soon, okay?"

"Sure." He hung up.

It was obvious Brad was feeling a little threatened by Bodhi's importance to me. I would have to tread carefully to ensure he felt secure. Bodhi's presence would never take away the connection Brad and I had. It was different. This emotional space with my intensity of love for Bodhi was momentous. I had now gained perspective with new eyes of experience on what it felt like to be truly in love.

On my way to the office I stopped off at the coffee house to see how Mable and Mila were progressing. Ryder beamed a smile and waved as he saw me walk in the door. I saluted him and headed for the ladies' table.

"How are we today?" I said with melody in my voice.

"You sound chirpy, my dear," replied Mable, who was wearing the same straw hat, adorned this time with a perfectly formed purple iris bud that was so top-heavy it drooped.

"Yes, you seem to be glowing," said Mila, looking at me with suspicion.

I seated myself and grabbed the notes Mila had in front of her. "Pen and paper, that's old-school," I said.

"Yeah, I find there's something wonderful about the texture of paper. All my rough notes are on hard copy and I transcribe them of an evening into my laptop."

"Isn't that double handling? Wouldn't it be easier to just do it straight into the lappy?" I asked.

"It would, but I find reading the notes at the end of a day allows me to cement my thoughts and feelings on what has been captured. I then translate this to my virtual notes. It helps me add depth to my work."

"I'm impressed. Well done, you." I patted her on the shoulder.

I leant in to whisper to Mable. "How is coffee boy treating you these days?"

"Oh, he's been wonderful. He's always smiling. The

other day he even ran across and opened the door for me," she said with an expression of satisfaction.

"I'm glad to hear it. How is everyone in the office treating you?"

"What a lovely family you have there. All of them are so nice and they cannot say enough wonderful things about you. I told them you were my angel and they all said you were theirs too." Mable's weathered hand extended to touch mine.

I was moved by her words. Perhaps being in love made me susceptibly mushy. "Thank you. How are you managing with responding to all the broken hearts? Do you need assistance with anything?"

"I've written a few and left them on your desk. I'd like you to read them and tell me if you're pleased for me to proceed. I am, after all, representing you. If you like them I'll continue in the same vein."

"I trust you, Mable. I wouldn't have offered you the job if I didn't believe in my heart that you had the right level of sensitivity and compassion to respond."

"Thank you, dear. All the same, I want you to check just to be sure I'm representing my angel."

I patted her hand. "Okay, I'll look at them today and enough with the reference to angels. I don't want to obtain a reputation I might not be able to sustain. Is there anything else you ladies need before I head off?"

"Would it be too much trouble to get a desk lamp? My eyes are not what they used to be and my reading glasses seem to be a little blurry."

"I'll have Michael arrange to take you to the optometrist this afternoon so we can get you a fresh prescription. The lamp will be on your desk by the time you come in. No problems at all."

Mable shifted in her chair to look at my back and proceeded to pat me down.

I smiled as I asked, "What are you doing?"

"I'm checking for wings. They must be tucked in here somewhere." She straightened up in her seat again and covered her mouth as she chuckled.

Mila laughed too.

I shook my head and smirked. "I walked right into that set-up. At least you're being creative and not using the 'A' word. It's a start," I said as I rose to my feet. "Enjoy the rest of your day, ladies. I'll see you around."

They both said their goodbyes to me and I waved at Ryder as I walked out the door. I could see by the expression on his face he was hoping I would chat with him. My inclination was to avoid any further banter for now, especially given the reason for his initial change in demeanour.   As I walked to the office I noticed I had a bounce in my step. People passing by seemed to look and smile. I guess I was glowing. I checked my phone to see if Bodhi had tried to reach me. There was one text.

"I cannot stop thinking about you. Dinner tonight? Say yes. I'll send you the details. This day is going to take forever to end. I can still taste you on my lips and smell you on my skin."

I had butterflies reading the message and felt the exact same way. I had missed him from the moment he walked out the door that morning. It was amazing to feel this way. I couldn't stop smiling like a fool.

I replied to his text with three separate messages:

"Who is this?"

"Dinner – yes assuming no better offer comes along … will let you know either way."

"I missed you before you even stepped out my door this morning. You have ruined me for all others. (True Story) xoxo"

When I arrived at Solution Manifestation, my first point of business was requesting Michael to make the arrangement to purchase a desk lamp and organise an appointment for Mable to have her eyes tested. I was keen to read the responses Mable had written to some of the solitary hearts' club. I made myself a coffee and settled into my comfy office chair.

I began by reading the letters that had been addressed to me and then read Mable's response. The first one had signalled his undying love for me. He believed I could be the one to save him from himself. Mable's response was:

Dear Wayne,

Firstly, thank you for taking the time to write to Talia to let her know your thoughts. I can feel the ache in your heart from the words you chose to use. I do believe you have good taste in whom you seek but she is not the one for you.

My dearly departed husband Walter used to say 'never mistake admiration for love'. You, my dear, hold Talia in high regard. She is worthy of your praise but reserve your love for the one you need to continue to seek. She is out there. You just need to make your heart available so your eyes can see.

Blessings and good faith,

Mable Forrester

The next letter was from a man who spoke of the resonance of twin souls and how the picture of me in the paper had stirred his heart to feel again.

Dear Tom,

Your words moved me when I read them. My dear sweet soul, please know that your heart beats in the tune of the one who seeks to identify to the same rhythm. The image of Talia may have evoked your desire to be open for love to be received. This is a blessing and you should take it as such.

My dearly departed husband Walter used to say 'you will

know when love is true as their heart will beat just for you'. Keep the faith, my dear. I feel the right person is closer than you think. True love is often easiest found when we silence our mind and close our eyes. The heart knows its way home.

Blessings and good faith,

Mable Forrester

My favourite of the letters was this fellow Maverick, who managed to make prose and humour fuse with eloquence.

Oh Lovely Maverick,

You captured my heart with your choice of words and tickled my soul with your humour. If I were fifty years younger I would be tempted to be improper and ask you out on a date. How delightful you are on paper and a gift no doubt to those who surround you. Thank you for extending your thoughts to Talia.

We all look for that special person, the one to call our own. I feel through your words you may undervalue the beauty of whom you are and the importance of the role you play within this life. There is so much talent that resides in you. The world would be better for its receipt.

My dearly departed husband Walter used to say 'pursue what you love and like a beacon of light, love will find its way'. Walter and I met at a dance. He was passionate about dancing and oh how we used to dance.

Take a risk, Maverick. Go and follow your true passions and have faith that pure love will find you on the crossroads of the journey. With all my heart I wish you the grandest of lives.

Blessings and good faith,

Mable Forrester

I sat back in my chair looking out the window, smiling. What a gift it was to have such an amazing person enter my life at this particular juncture. To think all the people who passed her by, not willing to offer her the kindness of a smile. My sweet Mable, complete with dear Walter's philosophies on the world, were set to change lives. It was satisfying to be a part of this particular journey.

There was no need to read any of the other examples she had left for me. It was clear that she was going to execute the role in the exact manner that was required. What an absolute treasure. I took one of the post-it notes from my desk and wrote the words: *Mable, outstanding responses. They are perfection. Please go ahead.*

A text came through just as I was about to place the letters back on Mable's desk. It was Bodhi.

"I can't wait until the end of the day; it's been too long already. Meet at Franklins for lunch in 10 min. Okay?"

I loved his impatience and willingness to share it with me. I had experience being desired by countless suitors. The difference here was I craved to feel his hunger for me.

I responded:

"I feel compelled to play hard to get …. I'll be there in 15. xoxo"

I made a couple of calls prior to heading out. I wanted to spend the rest of the afternoon getting some beauty treatments done. My complexion had taken a beating when I became dehydrated during my recent bout of pneumonia. I decided I would treat myself to a body scrub, seaweed wrap and rehydrating massage at a day spa near my apartment. It seemed like a nice way to spend the afternoon post lunch with Bodhi.

As I walked into Franklins I could see Bodhi was already seated. I smiled when I witnessed his face light up as I walked towards him. He got out of his seat and met me halfway, wrapping his arms around me for a welcome embrace.

"I was almost there," I said as I released a laugh.

He leant into my ear and whispered, "I couldn't wait."

I melted into his arms with his words like syrup dripping the sweetest message of promise. My body seemed to respond to his presence. Just a simple hug and a few words had me aching for more. I moved slightly to encourage him to release me. He didn't budge.

"Come on, let's sit down," I said.

He shifted his head so I could see his face. He gave me a peck on the lips and then turned to head back to the table while holding my hand. Without fuss, he pulled out my chair to seat me and then sat down himself. I looked across at him and saw he could not stop smiling.

"What?" I whispered.

"Fuck, you're beautiful,' he said, loud enough for people to hear, while he stared directly into my eyes.

I felt flush with all the attention. "Stop it. Look at the menu."

Elbows on the table, he placed his hands on his face as he leant forward and continued his focus on me. "I don't need to. I already know what I want."

I laughed. "Well, I'm going to look at the menu then. Give me a minute." I lifted the folder so it blocked his view of my face. The words seemed to be a blur. I couldn't focus. He was so deliciously distracting.

My mobile buzzed. I looked down to see a text from Bodhi.

"I miss you. PS: I already ordered for both of us. xoxo"

I burst out laughing as I dropped the menu to look at him again. "Really? How long had you been here before I arrived?"

"I was already here when I sent you the text. I was hoping you were free to join me. I'm usually at Franklins a couple of times a week so they always make sure I get seated quickly."

"Do I get to know what you ordered for me?"

"Marinated capsicum bruschetta with a rocket and pear salad. I asked them to put the dressing on the side so you could choose to use it or not. I've noticed you seem to have an aversion to sauces."

"It's not an aversion. I just like to know what I'm eating. Sometimes I feel as though restaurants over-utilise sauce. It makes me wonder what they're trying to mask with the overkill."

"Would you like a glass of mineral water or still? I ordered both for you."

I laughed. "I prefer still. I drink mineral water sometimes but mostly I like to keep things simple. You know, you might find it easier if you just waited and let me order for myself."

"Now where would the fun be in that?" he said as he poured the still water into my glass.

I looked at the three ladies on the table to our right. They kept glancing at us and then resuming their conversation. "Have you noticed how many women gawk at you?"

"I don't care." He reached across for my hand.

"Don't get me wrong; I'm not insecure. It's more a curiosity about how you manage the effect you obviously have on these women. Even the office girls and Michael all swooned when you came in for the first time. They were fishing for information about you, all so desperate to know more. It was very amusing to watch."

"Mostly I ignore it. When I was younger it had its advantages, but it also has its disadvantages. It's almost like I'm there but they can't see me. They're distracted by superficial attraction. It's empty."

I smiled. It seemed that Bodhi and I had some common experiences of people and their incessant clamouring. The waitress arrived to deliver the order. I hated to say it, but Bodhi had chosen well again. The meal looked delicious. His selection of *fettuccine pescatore* looked equally yum.

"I was wondering if you would be up for a visit to Australia some time soon."

A wicked smile appeared on Bodhi's face. "Are you suggesting that I'm worthy to meet your extended family? Sounds like you're getting serious about us."

I laughed. "Just answer the question."

"I could take a couple of weeks off at the end of the month. It's possibly the only window I have left until the end of the year. There's lots of promotional work and launches I need to be present for."

"If you send across all your passport details to Michael I'll make the travel arrangements. You just need to confirm the dates."

"Does this mean we're going steady?" he said, laughing.

"Whatever. I don't even know what that means. Let's just go with the flow. No expectations, no rules. No need for the 'talk'."

Furrows appeared on his brow. "I can't agree to that. You are significant to me. I want to be exclusive. I need to know you're as committed to me as I am to you. I don't ever want to share you with anyone." He shrugged. "It's important."

"We're exclusive," I said as I shifted my right hand to touch his forearm.

He stood up and leant across the table and passionately kissed me.

As he sat back down, I said, "I do have one request."

"Almost anything. Shoot."

"Can we not be the couple that need to know how many people we slept with, who they were? You know, all the details that exist in the past and should remain there?"

He raised an eyebrow. "Should I be worried? How many have you slept with? I think at the very least I need to know your number."

"It's not the number that counts; it's what we both bring to the party as a benefit from our previous experiences which should matter. Let's just give silent thanks to our respective interludes and leave it alone. Agreed?" I said, hoping for a quick closure on the topic.

"Partially. I do want to know about any relationship of significance. There is something I've been meaning to tell you, but I haven't felt there's been a right time."

The mention of significance brought Brad to mind. Bodhi had a point. There were some things I would need to tell him before I took him home so he had context and an appreciation for the bond Brad and I had. I would need to ensure he understood the difference between what he meant to me and how I felt about Brad. Especially now that I knew he had a propensity for becoming jealous.

Bodhi waved his hand in front of my face. "Talia, I've lost you. Thoughts need to be spoken out loud," he whispered.

"I was just thinking about what you said and reflecting on some of my key relationships. There are some things I'll need to share with you. I agree to your terms, o wise one."

He leant back in his chair and burst out laughing. "She confirms she's exclusive, which makes her officially my girlfriend. She agrees with my thoughts *and* calls me wise. Where is a recording device when you need one?"

"'She' might change her mind if 'he' keeps teasing her," I warned with a playful glare. "Tell me about this relationship you just mentioned."

"What, now?" asked Bodhi.

"Yes, now. There is no right time and the reality is now that you have mentioned it I don't want to be left wondering about it. Just tell me and I'll listen."

"Are you sure?"

"Yes, of course. Hesitating is only going to make me nervous. Just spill it, woman."

"Woman?" he said as he artfully raised an eyebrow.

"Yes, when one acts like one, one deserves to be called one," I said with a chuckle. "Stop delaying and talk. I'm all ears." I took a sip of my water, feeling very curious about what he was going to say.

His lips pursed as he dropped his head to stare at the table, a single digit used to tap his half-filled glass of water. "I was engaged to Lexie Mathers. We had been together for three years but I had known her for much longer. She's a fashion designer and the creator of Sexy Lex lingerie." He paused to take a sip from his glass.

"She knows all about you. Long before we started dating I used to talk about you so she knew my dream was to find you and spend the rest of my life with you. At one point she even tried to help me track you down. Just recently Lex started to get a little obsessive, wanting to know where I am, who I'm with. She would call the office several times a day to check I was there. It might sound a little crazy, I know. I feel stupid saying it but she was into all that psychic mumbo jumbo and kept saying she '*knew*' I was going to leave her. I had no idea what she was talking about. There was no convincing her. Lex used to be happy person. I looked forward to going home. Her obsession with me leaving created a manic insecure angry version of the person I thought I knew. Her constant accusations took their toll. I got to a point where I couldn't look at her anymore. I didn't want to go home. I became so unhappy that I decided to leave. To me it was a self-fulfilling prophecy."

"How long ago was this?"

"Two weeks before I met you." Bodhi took another sip of water.

The waitress arrived with our food. We smiled, politely said our thanks.

"So technically I'm the rebound girl," I said in jest, knowing my mouth was quicker than my consideration for its appropriateness.

Bodhi leant forward and grabbed my hand. "No, don't say that. You are the love of my life."

"I know, you're the love of mine too, Bodhi. I shouldn't have said that, I was trying to be funny."

"The thing about Lex is that she doesn't want to give up. She leaves me messages all the time. Tries to sabotage my business leads. The other night when I told you I had to work late. It was a lie. She had threatened to kill herself if I didn't go and see her. I'm at a loss. I don't know her anymore and I don't know how to help her. She seems hell bent on destroying herself and taking me with her."

"That's sounds horrid. What happened? Did she try to suicide?"

"No, she used it as a ploy to get me to come over and talk. It worked. I stayed there half the night trying to talk some sense into her but she wasn't herself. I don't even recognise her anymore. She has gone totally off the rails and I can't help but feel it's my fault. I never should have got together with her or with anyone knowing I was still searching, hoping for you."

I reached across and held his hand. "Hey, you can't blame yourself for how others behave. It's a choice and there are consequences to the choices we all make. I know it's a crappy situation but you're going to have to make peace with it somehow. Hopefully she'll come around to see it's better not to have been with a heart that yearned to be with another."

"I know. I just feel like I've ruined her. Anyway, if it's okay with you I don't want to talk about it anymore," he said in a sad voice.

I offered him a consoling smile. "We had better eat before our food goes stone cold." I didn't know what else to say.

Bodhi immediately used hand gestures to zip his mouth, lock it and throw away the key. I nodded in approval and proceeded to eat our meals, changing the conversation to general banter.

At the end of lunch we walked hand-in-hand to his office. We stood outside like two nauseating lovebirds kissing and cuddling before we parted ways so I could attend my beauty appointment. We agreed on where we were to meet for dinner that night so I was free for the rest of the afternoon to focus on pampering myself.

In the evening I decided I would wear a dress to dinner. It was a purple velvet classic plain-cut swing dress that I had found in a secondhand thrift shop a few years back. I loved the texture and the opulent saturation of colour, which changed its hue depending on the lighting. I had never worn it before.

Bodhi was waiting outside when I arrived in a taxi. Once again his face lit up when he realised I had arrived. He opened the cab door for me and offered me his hand to alight. I had a goofy smile on my face as I watched his expression change when I was standing in front of him.

"You look breathtaking," he said as he slowly inspected me from head to toe.

I chuckled. "Thanks. You wear your jeans and shirt rather well too."

"Wow, I mean wow."

"Okay, now it's getting embarrassing. Let's go." I grabbed his hand and headed for the restaurant door.

Without warning, Bodhi swung me around into his arms and kissed me. As he pulled away I reached in and kissed him back with an elongated passionate edge to it. I then slowly separated our lips, lingered for a moment, gave him a wicked smile and resumed heading into the restaurant.

Inside it didn't take long to be seated. It appeared that Bodhi was more popular than I was aware. People seemed to instantly recognise him and offer priority service. We were shown to our seats and, before I had tucked in my chair, a bottle of wine, compliments of the house, was delivered.

"What am I missing here? People seem to be aware of you and treat you differently. What's up with that?" I asked.

"In my industry you get to know a lot of famous people. I guess by default if you're around them for long enough to get your mug shoved in magazines standing next to them or are seen at A-list parties then people are going to make assumptions. Either I'm someone or I know someone that they want access to."

"Yikes, I'll leave that part all to you. I'm a clandestine creature. I like living and flying under the radar." I reached for my freshly poured glass of red.

"Tell me about it. You're the only person I know who doesn't have a social media footprint. It wasn't easy to find you and when I did I still wasn't able to track you down. It was so frustrating. There were times I started to think it was all too hard and perhaps I was chasing a pipe dream."

I smiled. "I do have a social media profile thanks to that shitty article about me. I googled myself a few months ago and cringed at half the crappy photos and other junk that was on there. I haven't tried since and I'm not sure I'm going to. It's not pleasant."

Bodhi smiled as he glanced at the menu. "Will you allow me the honour of ordering for you?"

I sat back in my chair with my red. "Sure."

The waiter came across when Bodhi gestured. "Can we please have the tomato basil soup for starters, and for the lady's main the chilli fennel risotto and I'll have the twice-cooked roast duck with fennel salad."

"Are you right for drinks? Can I get you anything else?" asked the waiter, who turned to look directly at me.

"No, I'm fine with the wine, thanks for asking."

The waiter smiled and left to place the order.

"Apparently I don't exist at this table. Did you see how he focused on you?" said Bodhi.

"Yep, I get that all the time. It's an energy thing."

"No, it's a 'well, damn; she's fine' thing," he said, making exaggerated hand gestures.

I laughed. "Whatever, Bodhi."

We had a really nice time at dinner. Something shifted for Bodhi that allowed him to be completely relaxed, happy. I think offloading his concerns about Lex made him feel more at ease. He exuded a glow and I once again saw glimpses of a wry smile that suggested he had secrets about me I was yet to learn. We exchanged banter easily and although at times my mind drifted to our shared delights partaken in the early hours of the morning, for the most part I maintained being present.

"What are the plans now?" I asked as we were walking out the door.

"You're coming to mine," he said as he flagged down a cab.

I reached across and poked his rib. "A little presumptuous, don't you think?"

He looked into my eyes and smiled.

"There's that look again. I've seen it appear all night. You have a secret. What is it?"

He opened the door of the cab and gestured for me to get in. "All in good time. Patience."

In the cab he placed his arm around me, drawing me close. I put my head on his shoulder and an arm around his waist. I would have been happy to stay right there, being driven around all night. I loved looking at all the nightlights, people walking around, and most of all feeling Bodhi's warmth against mine.

When we arrived at the building Bodhi paid the cab driver and we headed inside. Much to my surprise his place was designed in a similar style of minimalistic furniture and decorations. The colour pallet on the walls was a neutral tone and adorned with artwork, posters and photos. What I loved was the warehouse-style open-plan space with floor-to-ceiling windows.

"This place is beautiful," I said as I glanced at some of the photos.

Bodhi was in the open-plan kitchen preparing some drinks. "You seem surprised. Did you think I lived in a dump?"

"No, it didn't even cross my mind. I just didn't expect the place to be so open and big. It looks like it's three times the size of mine."

"It is. Do you like it?"

"Nope, love it. There's a nice feel to the place and the windows are amazing. I really like the view. You picked well."

He smiled as he walked over to me and passed me my glass of red. As he leaned in to kiss me he whispered, "I do pick well."

Electric pulses ran up and down my body at the receipt of his words. I wasn't sure I would ever get used to his effect on me but I also never wanted it to stop. Bodhi placed his glass on the coffee table that looked like an old twisted tree trunk shaped and polished. He then went around the apartment lighting candles before dimming the overhead lights.

He sat on the couch and patted the seat beside him. I took one last look around and then sat down.

"So, give it up. Something's changed since lunch. You seem more relaxed, dare I say comfortable. What made the difference?"

He smiled again in a way that confirmed I was onto him.

"Give it up or I'll work it out."

"Hmm," he said, retrieving his wine glass and leaning back on the couch.

"Okay, did the change happen this morning?"

He sipped his wine in silence.

"That would be a 'no'. Did it happen at lunch?"

Once again the cheeky monkey did his best to maintain his composure.

"Let's narrow it down. Did the change happen when I agreed to be exclusive?"

The muscle spasm under his eye indicated that had assisted but it was not limited to that event.

"Okay, so 'yes' but not completely. Hmm." I paused for a minute to think. It couldn't be the discussion about Lex. It had to be something else. After lunch, the next time we caught up was for dinner, so my guess is it happened between me dropping him off at work and us meeting at the restaurant.

"Did it occur at work?" I watched closely, as he was extremely guarded now, which also indicated I was getting closer. "No. Was it when you got home this afternoon?"

He sniffed and then cleared his throat with a cough.

"Gotchya. Whatever had an influence occurred here. In this room, yes?"

He nodded. "That's actually very impressive. I thought you would get stuck on lunch because of the conversations we had."

I pouted my lip and in a whiny voice I said, "Stop delaying and show me what you've been hiding. Pleeeease."

He grabbed a letter from underneath the coffee table and passed it to me. He repositioned himself on the couch so he was facing me. I glanced at him and once again saw that look. I knew this was what had made all the difference to him today. I put my wine glass down to give the letter my full attention.

Dear Billy,

I read your letter and felt overwhelmed by a flood of raw emotions. Your words seem to evoke a depth of unspoken connection to my own personal journey around the concept of love and chasing ghosts. I've received many letters from suitors over the last twelve months and in truth I haven't read any. Yours was selected by my team as one of a handful of the letters they believed I should read. Of the few I did glance over yours was the one that drove me to reflect within myself.

You see, I only recently admitted that I too want to fall in love. I want to share the remainder of my life with a person whom I have a deep connection with. I've never believed in fairy tales yet secretly I find myself wanting to. I suspect my life would feel more complete if I was blessed with the opportunity to be in a space of true love.

In your letter you mentioned this girl from your childhood. The way you describe your bond makes me want to help you find her too. I understand the level of disheartenment that comes with not knowing where to look or what you're actually searching for. Chasing ghosts, as it were.

My only message to you is never give up. Keep an open mind and heart. Ask the universe to guide you and most of all believe. She's out there waiting for you to find her. I'm sure of it. I recognise as I write this it is as much relevant to me as it is to you. Perhaps we are kindred.

I wish you all the best. Thank you for your extension and trust in sharing such intimate thoughts with a stranger. Please always remember you are not alone.

Blessings,
Talia Jacobs

"What are the chances?" I said to Bodhi.

"It came in the mail a few days ago but I only opened it today when I realised it had come from your office. I was blown away that my letter had actually managed to reach you and felt touched that you wrote back personally."

"I did. I divulged my soul's secret desire to you."

"My doubts were never about our union or whether it was right. All my concerns revolved around whether you were ready. This told me you are ready and, even better, seeking to be in love." His delicious smile beamed.

I placed the letter on the coffee table and shuffled across so I was in Bodhi's arms, placing my head on his chest to listen to his heartbeat.

"I'm in love with you, Bodhi."

He gently used his hand to guide my face so I was looking into his eyes. "I know."

Introductions

The flight across to Australia seemed to take longer than usual. I wasn't sure whether it was because I had Bodhi beside me chatting or due to me taking him home to meet the gang. I guess if I dug deep there was an underlying concern about whether he and Brad would get along. It would bother me if they didn't.

We managed to get caught in customs on the way through. The timing of this flight must have been the same as a few others. The queues were large and moving very slowly. I had made arrangements for Ash to pick me up so the poor bugger was out there waiting.

Finally through the checks, we walked out the doors of the international terminal and there, much to my surprise, were Ash and Brad waiting for us. Ash's face was suspenseful; she must have thought I would be annoyed with her for allowing Brad to tag along. I beamed to reassure her that it didn't matter. I knew Brad would have insisted and it was okay.

"Hey, guys, so sorry to keep you waiting. The queues in customs were a ball-buster. Brad, Ash, this is Bodhi."

Brad was the first to offer his hand. "G'day, Bodhi,

Talia hasn't said much about you but she's brought you home to meet the family so you must be alright."

"Thanks. Well, Talia has told me a lot about you; and you too, Ash, so I'm really glad to put the faces to the stories."

I burst out laughing as both of them looked at me, wondering what the hell I might have told him. "Relax, guys, he doesn't know everything, just the incriminating stuff."

Brad shifted across to give me a big bear hug, which I gladly embraced. When I was released from Brad's vice grip I leaped forward to punch Ash in the arm. She laughed as she rubbed it.

I smiled. "You know what that's for and I'm sure by the time my visit's over there will be more where that came from. I hope you like the shade of black and blue."

Bodhi laughed. "I'm not going to ask."

I smiled at Ash and Brad. "See, he's attractive and intelligent." I turned and winked at Bodhi.

We grabbed our bags and headed to the car for the long drive home.

We went straight to my place so Bodhi and I could settle in and get ahead of the jetlag I felt starting to wash over me. Ruth, in her true style, was organising a family gathering for that evening. I had asked her to postpone by a day to give us a chance to recover but she wouldn't have a bar of it. She was so excited she said she couldn't wait. I let it be.

The inside of my house smelt fresh and clean. I looked over my shoulder at Ash and mouthed thank you.

Bodhi walked around exploring, touching the wooden walls and looking up at the cathedral ceilings. "This place is cool. It's a real architectural find."

"Go have a look at the other rooms. I'm going to put our stuff in the bedroom and make us a cup of tea."

Bodhi didn't need any encouragement. He was off down the hall to look at the other rooms while I got organised. When he was finished he met me back in the kitchen and walked around to where I was standing. He leant against my body as I continued to make the tea.

"Do you feel like going for a walk to see the outside?"

"I do but I have some other ideas I'd like to explore first." His hands glided across my midriff and then up to cup my breasts. He squeezed them as he pressed himself against my back.

I placed my arms on the bench so I didn't fall forward.

"Whatever do you have in mind?" I asked in a syrup-like tone.

"Shhhhhh."

He wasn't intent on wasting any time with small talk. He undid the zipper on my jeans and brutally forced them midway down my legs. He lifted the back of my shirt and softly kissed the length of my spine as his hand ran under my knickers, exploring my buttocks, and then down the narrow path between my legs to my clitoris. He started stimulating me and then inserting a finger in then out just as quick to lubricate and continue his fondle. My head bowed forward and I groaned with every insertion. I could feel I was already dripping.

Bodhi then torturously removed his hand and used both to run up either side of my body under my shirt and then he knelt down to remove my shoes, take off my jeans and peel my soaked knickers from my waist. As he stood up he guided my body to turn so my back was against the bench and he was facing me. His look of desire transitioned my body from a tingle to a slow burn. I wanted him so badly.

He smiled as he leaned in with his head tilted towards my lips. Just as I could detect the heat he pulled away. He inclined his head to come at me from the opposite side to once again tease me with the prospect of a looming kiss. As he pulled away I grabbed his head with my hands and connected our lips. I couldn't stand it anymore. I wanted him. I pulled his head towards mine as I kissed him deeply.

Bodhi pried my hands off his head and placed them on the bench behind me. He then took the lead in our kissing frenzy as he started to unbutton my shirt and release my breasts from their delicate lace caging. As he shifted to kissing my neck I lifted my head so he had full access. Gently he nuzzled and then kissed my breasts, his hands firmly positioned on my waist. Without warning he lifted me onto the bench and used a hand to run up my torso. He placed it around the edge of my neck and guided me to lie back.

As I felt him kiss my abdomen and snake his way down to my southern region I felt like my skin was on fire. The moment his tongue touched the velvet of my clitoris I could feel my breathing change. Initially he persisted with slow torturous gentle strokes, transitioning to hard lashings which compelled me to wriggle as I groaned. He used his muscular arms to pin my waist down while he consumed all I had to offer. When the moment came for me to climax I squealed as I tried to wriggle from his grip. Sweat was falling from my brow as I released an almighty series of groans.

I reached across to grab his hand to pull away from my playground. "I want you inside me," I whimpered.

At these words he stood up and kissed me with his wet lips. The taste of me on him made my vagina pulsate. I reached down to undo his jeans, only to discover he had taken them off. He continued to kiss me with intensity as he adjusted my hips to be closer to the edge of the bench. I widened my legs and wrapped them around him as he entered.

I released a moan in his mouth and whispered, "Fuck me."

Bodhi's head dropped to bite at my nipples while he gyrated in a frenzy, pounding against my flesh. I could feel myself building up to the delights of another orgasm. I arched my back so my breast was fully in his mouth as I screamed, "Oh, my god. Fuck! Ohhhhh, my god."

Bodhi stood upright and arched his back so he could release deep inside me. His face at the point of ecstasy was beautiful. It was one of my favourite moments to witness. His body was heaving to catch his breath as he leaned his torso on mine to rest. I lay back and felt the tension dissipate from our bodies.

The afternoon quickly disappeared and we were all on our way to Ruth and Shane's. When we arrived the kids were nowhere to be seen. They had made arrangements for a sitter to look after them at Brad and Suzanna's so we could have an adult gathering. I was really disappointed. I had wanted to see all my little rug rats. I expected they would have grown like weeds.

Inside, everyone made their introductions, complete with not-so-subtle glances at me to indicate their approval of Bodhi. I knew he noticed but skillfully maintained his expression so they were unaware. I liked that we were able to read each other so well. It didn't take long for us to be ushered to the table. Ruth had gone all out. This time around we each had a seating card. Brad organised the drinks while Suzanna and Ruth did the typical synchronised hosting routine.

"Looks like you passed phase one," I whispered.

"I noticed. It was funny to watch. Did they really think they were being subtle?"

"Yes, they really, really did," I said as we both quietly chuckled.

When everyone was seated and the food had been served I watched as they looked intermittently at us both. They were champing at the bit to ask questions. Bodhi was the only man I had ever brought home to meet them, so their curiosity was understandable.

"Ruth, the seating cards are new," I said to break the silence.

"I've been taking a calligraphy class and just used this as an opportunity to practice." She smiled as she flicked her glance between Bodhi and me.

"Ah, good to know. I thought you might have developed some control issues."

Shane piped up. "No, they were present and well developed since before we got married."

We all laughed as Ruth pinched him under the table for his efforts.

"Okay, guys, let's have it. You're all busting to ask questions. Shoot," I said.

Surprisingly, Suzanna was first in. "How did you meet?"

"As kids we went to school together briefly while we were in Haiti. Recently we met at a coffee house. Next question."

"Are you both in love?" asked Ruth.

The question caught me by surprise which was evident by my response of semi-choking on my half chewed mouthful of food. "Wow, I was expecting the 'L' question to be much further down the pile. Yes, we are very much in love."

Bodhi nodded to them as he shifted his hand under the table to rest on my knee.

Brad tapped his fork against his plate, looked at Bodhi and asked, "How long did it take you both before you knew you were in love?"

Bodhi responded, "I knew on the first day we met as kids that I loved her. When I saw her again for the first time as adults I once again knew she was the only one for me. By the time we exchanged our first kiss I was irrevocably in love. Talia, on the other hand, took a little more convincing." He gave me a wistful glance.

"Actually, that's not true. I knew I had intense feelings for you at the coffee shop. I just wasn't willing to convey it, as I was trying to process the concept of your existence. I never believed I would find my other." I reached across and touched his face. "You are the yin to my yang."

Ruth, Sammy and Suzanna all had tears. I looked at them and pouted. I knew this was their expression of relief. I had been closed off for a lifetime. To have them witness me openly speak about love, to demonstrate the depth of how I felt for this person, moved them. I even noticed Shane and Tommy seemed to be in silent awe. Brad, on the other hand, was disengaged. His lack of eye contact indicated to me that he was struggling.

The questions continued into the night. I hoped to see the wane of their curiosity but they seemed insatiable. The jetlag and extra-curricular activities of the day were finally catching up with me. I could see that Bodhi had also hit a wall but he was too polite to say anything.

"Folks, we're going to head off. I'm afraid with a full tummy and wine in my belly the jetlag is finally winning. I think Bodhi and I will call it a night and catch up with you again in a few days."

Ruth jumped to her feet. "Of course. You must be exhausted. I've made you some food to take home so you don't have to worry about tomorrow."

She went into the kitchen to retrieve it from the fridge. Meanwhile Bodhi and I kissed and cuddled everyone.

When Ruth returned I looked at the two bags of groceries. "You have vegetarian moussaka, I made you homemade falafels and there are some wraps, hummus and salads so you can make them up yourself."

I kissed her on the cheek as she passed me the bags. "Thanks so much. You know you didn't have to."

"I know," she said as she shifted to her tippy toes and swung her hands.

I could tell she was over the moon with the idea of me being in a relationship. She felt responsible for my happiness. I guess it was her prerogative to feel an obligation to do the best by her sister's child. It was nice to see her so happy.

Everyone walked us out to the car except Brad. I made the excuse that I needed to go to the loo before the drive home, heading back inside to see what was up.

He was standing in the lounge, tracing a finger around the edge of his wine glass.

"Hey, is everything okay?"

"Yep, I thought you were going," he said, without looking at me.

"I am, but I needed to know you're okay, that we're okay."

He looked up at me with the saddest eyes. "I don't know. Are we?"

I stepped in closer to touch his arm as he stepped away. "Don't be like that, Brad. Nothing's changed for me. I still care about you."

He didn't respond.

"Clearly something's up. I'll call you tomorrow to organise some one-on-one time so we can chat. Okay?"

His gaze returned to the wine glass as he responded with a single word, "Sure."

I stood there for a moment looking at him and then quietly left the room. In truth I felt completely gutted that he was in this negative headspace. Ideally I wanted him to be happy for me. I hoped somewhere deep down he was. It was evident that we had some work to do to readjust to the new version of me.

Bodhi and I spent the next few days settling in and taking the opportunity to look at the local sites. He seemed to take a shine to Ash and her girlfriend Jenna. Whenever I was off on an errand I would return to find the three of them having a laugh. I was pleased; Bodhi seemed to fit right in.

I decided to head across to find Brad. I sent him a text to warn him I planned to hunt him down that day. It had been four days since dinner and he hadn't returned any of my texts. Before we had come to Australia I had explained my full history with Brad to Bodhi so he knew there might be some alignment to be done and I would need to do that without him. I loved that he understood the importance of this relationship to me but was very conscious of his ability to become very jealous. I needed to strike a balance between these two important men in my life.

When I arrived at Brad's house he was nowhere to be found. The car was also not there. I tried his mobile but once again he refused to answer. I sat on the porch to gather my thoughts. Where would he be? No sooner had I completed the thought than the image of his possible location appeared. I shook my head. He was such a sentimental creature. I jumped in the car and drove across to Ruth's.

As I arrived, Ruth was coming out the front door to put rubbish in the bin. She waved as I parked the car.

"Hey, Ruth."

"Talia, I wasn't expecting you. Is everything alright?"

"Actually, I was looking for Brad. He wasn't home so I thought I might swing past here and try my luck. I can see his car is here so I guess he's around somewhere." I smiled and watched Ruth's body language shift.

"He told me to tell you if you come looking for him that he's not up for chatting." Ruth diverted her gaze to the ground.

"Is he inside?"

She shook her head and pointed to the pathway.

"Thanks, Ruth, I'll go spend some time with him."

As I headed towards the path, Ruth called out, "Talia, be gentle; he's in a lot of pain. I've not seen him like this before. I'm really worried about him and Suzanna."

I smiled at her. "Trust me; everything is going to be fine. I promise." I turned and continued down the path once more.

I reached the edge of the river and crossed the bridge to the meadow. Sure enough, Brad was there, lying on the ground staring at the sky. He didn't acknowledge me as I lay down beside him. I searched in the clouds for shape formations.

When I saw one I pointed in its direction and said, "What is it?"

Brad didn't respond.

"I know you can see it. What is it?"

He continued to remain silent.

"Tell me what I need to do to make this better and I'll do it," I whispered.

Brad released a long exhale. The intensity of his pain was unbearable. I wanted to place him in my arms to protect and nurture him but I knew this would only make things worse.

"I love you. Nothing has changed for me, Brad. I love you."

I saw his eyes flicker; he wanted to reject my words.

"Don't do that. Don't fob off what I'm saying. I've never lied to you. I loved you then and I love you still."

Finally I saw his lips parting as though he was going to speak, then nothing.

"Talk to me, please. You were the one that told me I was never to hold back from you and yet you're not honouring the same request. I need us to be okay. I love you. Talk to me."

Once again he exhaled. "I used to feel like I had lost you. Now I've come to realise that I never really had you." He swallowed hard and was holding back tears.

"Brad, you never lost me; I'm right here."

"The way you look at him, the way you speak to him, it's real. What you felt for me wasn't the same. Don't try and tell me it was," he said in a broken voice.

"Years ago you said to me your greatest fear was that

I wouldn't fall in love and find someone to share my life like you have with Suzanna. It's taken decades for me to meet someone. I need you to be happy for me. I want you to be comfortable with the reality that nothing has changed between us." I wanted my words to sink in, so I paused between each message.

"You are important to me.

"You are significant to me.

"I love you."

Brad shook his head as he heard my words. "You were never in love with me like I was with you. Seeing you with Bodhi made me realise I wasn't the special guy in your life. I was just another bloke in love with Talia Jacobs."

"That's not true. Please don't devalue what we have. Our bond can never be matched. We made peace with how we felt about one another years ago and created our own paths. You married Suzanna. You guys are amazing together and have such a beautiful family. It's not as though you are available for me, so why are you stuck in this rut?"

He muttered, "I'm jealous."

I reached across and held his hand.

He continued. "I'm happy for you, I really am, Tal, but I guess I never put to bed all my feelings. I always thought that perhaps one day we might have our chance to be together."

"I switched off to the concept of intimacy with you half a lifetime ago. I couldn't move forward without making peace with what was and what was set to be. I knew Suzanna was the better match for you and your dynamic together is something I was in awe of. I looked up to you both in the way you chose to love one another.

You need to find a way to shift from your current frame of mind to accept that I love you deeply and we have a connection that will never be broken. Only we can choose to break the bond, and I promise I never will. You are too important to me."

"Suzanna kicked me out of the house."

I sat up and looked at him. "What? When?"

"Two days ago. I was melancholy and she confronted me. We got into a yelling match and then 'bam!' she told me to leave so I did."

"We need to fix this. There's no hope in hell that you two are going to have problems off the back of my joy at finally finding someone," I said, slightly freaked.

"I know. It's just I said some really shitful things to her. I'm not sure she's ever going to be able to forgive me. I know I certainly wouldn't."

I placed my hands on my head. 'Fuck, do I even want to know?"

"Nope, you really don't, and by the way she may not like you much at the minute either."

I threw my hands up in the air. "Yeah, me," and then lay back down again. This was worse than I had imagined. "Answer the cloud formation question," I said to break from the topic.

"It was a dog chasing a rabbit."

"Correct." I squeezed his hand. "We can fix this. We will fix this."

"I doubt it," he whispered.

"How do you feel about me?" I asked.

"Better."

"You do understand that you're always going be an important person in my life, yes?"

"I know. I just got caught off guard when I saw you

two together. You were perfect and it forced me to realise we weren't. I guess you always knew that, which is why you didn't fight as hard as me to make 'us' happen. I pulled out all the stops and you sought refuge in refrain."

I took a deep breath and exhaled. "I did love you and felt I could fall in love with you if I allowed myself to. There was something pulling me back and the circumstances were always against us, which I saw as a clear sign not to bend the rules to shape us into something we aren't destined to be. It took all my strength at times to adhere to this. You didn't make it easy for me, and yet I still pursued another path because in my heart of hearts I knew it to be best for you and for me. Suzanna is your other. Bodhi is mine."

Brad sat in silence for a while. I honoured his need to delve into his thoughts. This was one thing we had synchronised. Neither of us felt awkward in being present and silent. I continued to search for shapes in the clouds while he worked through his emotions.

Half an hour passed and I saw a vision of what needed to take place. "I'm going to see Suzanna."

"What are you planning to say?"

"I don't know yet, but I do know that in order for her to heal she's going to need to work with me or take it out on me. Regardless, the outcome will be the same."

"What's the outcome?" he said in a flat tone.

"She will realise she loves you and wants you in her life."

"She hates you right now," he whispered.

"It doesn't matter. You just need to readjust to being happy for me that I've found Bodhi and realign to treasuring what you have. She's your other. I was never the one. We had an amazing bond as kids. You were my saving grace. We grew to love one another, to cherish our space, our unique language. We have a bond forged in an unbreakable cast. No one can take away what we had, what we have and what we will continue to share."

I stood up to brush the grass and dirt from my clothes. Brad stood too and slapped me on the arse, just like old times. We laughed.

I looked in his eyes. "Are we good?"

He put his arms around me and drew my body in for a tight embrace. "We are more than good; we're perfect," he whispered.

"Thank you," I said, feeling relieved

Brad stayed at the meadow while I headed to my car. Ruth was sitting on the porch, obviously waiting for me to return. She looked at me with anguish on her face. I could see watching this play out from the sidelines was tearing her apart.

"I need your help, Ruth."

She leapt to her feet. "Anything. Tell me what to do to fix this. Anything."

"I'm going to head home for an hour or so to see Bodhi and then I'm heading up to see Suzanna. I need you to follow me there and gather the kids and bring them back here so I can work through some stuff with Suzanna."

"What if she won't let me?"

"I need you to be strong. Suzanna is going to resist me. I just need you to walk in, take the kids and head off. Leave the rest to me. Brad's going to be fine. He's in a good space now. I just need to have access to Suzanna so I can reach her too."

Ruth hugged me and burst into tears. "Thank you,

Talia. I know this isn't easy for you, but from the bottom of my heart, thank you."

I placed my arms around her and held her in silence until she settled. The truth was, if I didn't exist, none of these issues would either. She was thanking me for correcting what my mere existence had caused.

"Okay, I'll head off now and swing past when I'm on my way. Get everything you need ready for the kids and leave the rest to me." I left her there, jumped in my car and drove home.

When I entered my house, Bodhi was on the couch with his laptop and a freshly made cup of tea. He gave me a delicious smile as I walked in the door. I leaned across the back of couch and kissed him.

"How bad was it?" he asked.

"Suzanna kicked him out. Apparently he said some shitty things. Brad and I are okay now, but it's Suzanna I need to fix."

"Don't you think Brad needs to do that instead of you?"

I smiled and shook my head. "It's not about Brad; it's about me. It's always been about me. Suzanna has been really gracious over the years, but now she feels she's paid her dues and is entitled to have a deeper connection with him rather than it still being Brad and me. No one except the two of us can work through this now."

He shifted his laptop. "I feel uncomfortable about this. What do you mean she wants a connection like you have with Brad? What am I missing here?"

"Please don't freak. I told you Brad and I were close. We have a lot of history and he stood by me through the worst of my experiences in my formative years. It only stands to reason that we would be connected and always hold a profound care for one another. I told you about this."

"I know, it's just that you're mine," he said as he drew me into his arms.

"I am yours and only yours, I promise. This is just something I need to correct. Once everyone is rebalanced this will be put to bed. You don't have to worry. I didn't spend half my life without you to now ruin it. I'm never going to be tempted by another. I only have eyes for you."

Releasing a sigh, Bodhi leaned in and smelt my hair. "Is there anything I can do to help?"

"Yep, hold me a minute." I slid across the lounge suite to fall on top of him.

He folded his arms around me and I rested my head on his shoulder near the crook of his neck. I closed my eyes and breathed in his scent. He always smelt so beautiful.

"I'm probably not going to be able to get back tonight. I can't imagine Suzanna's going to come around quickly, so I'll organise for Ash and Jenna to have dinner with you, if that's okay?"

Bodhi pouted. "I'll miss you."

"You have no idea how much I'll miss you." I kissed his soft lips. "I'd better get organised and go. It's going to be a long night." I stood up and headed across to the kitchen.

"I get the feeling this happens to you a lot," said Bodhi, watching me.

I clenched my hands into fists and lifted them up in the air. "Yeah, me," I said sarcastically as I pulled out some limes, rock salt and a bottle of tequila.

Bodhi smiled. "You're really going for the hard stuff."

I packed the ingredients into a shopping bag. "Yep, tonight we drink. I'm going to find Ash. I'll be back in a minute to say goodbye."

Bodhi pouted again and I couldn't help but make a detour to the couch to lean across and grab his bottom lip and suck on it as I stared into his eyes. As I slowly stood up again he reached for my arm and pulled me across the couch. He caught me as I fell and, without allowing me to catch my breath, he kissed me. I became lost in the delights of his lips and could feel my body sinking into a state of bliss. As he pulled away, he tugged at my bottom lip and smiled.

"Fuck, I love you," I said as he released my lip.

"I just wanted to remind you what you were missing tonight."

"I'm well aware. Once this is over, I won't leave your side. Promise."

"Good. Now hurry up, the sooner you go the sooner you'll come back."

I scrambled to my feet and headed out the door to find Ash. As I wandered towards the stables, I noticed they had made a beautiful vegetable patch out the back. I stopped to inspect their handiwork. It looked really cute, all the plants growing in raised beds with shiny metallic labels for the different crops.

"Do you like it?" asked Ash as she approached me.

"It's super. When did you do this?"

"About a week after you left. It was Jenna's idea. We used all the spare wood out the back to build the boxes, filled it with the compost we've been making from the horse manure and lawn clippings."

"Brilliant work. I love it. Where is Jenna?"

"She's actually in bed, not feeling too good today."

"Is there anything she needs?"

"No, I've made chicken soup and she has all the vitamins there. She just needs to sleep and let her body rest."

"I have to head out for the night. I was hoping you could organise to have dinner with Bodhi. Maybe you could treat him to a good old-fashioned Aussie barbecue? There's plenty of wood out the back so you could create a fire-pit to make some damper for him to try. I have fresh cream and raspberry jam in the fridge. But if you need to stay with Jenna, I'll make other arrangements."

"No, Jenna needs sleep so I'm happy to hang out with Bodhi. He's a really nice guy."

"Yeah, well don't get too handsy. I know what you're like." I laughed.

"When have I ever been handsy?" she said defiantly.

"Just because I was passed out in hospital doesn't mean I didn't know you were holding my hand and rubbing up and down my arm. You were trying to take advantage of me on my deathbed, I know it."

Ash went bright red, just the way I liked her. "Whatever," she said, laughing.

"Let me know if there's anything I can do for Jenna."

"She'll be fine."

"Alrighty, I'm heading off. Remember: hands to yourself." As I walked back towards the house, I could hear Ash's laughter fading into the distance.

Bodhi was in the kitchen making a fresh cup of tea.

"Is there anything you need before I head out the door?"

A cheeky smile appeared. "Well …"

I laughed. "No time, I'm afraid. When I get back – all day, every day – until you're sated."

"Careful. When it comes you, I'm insatiable."

I walked around the island bench and gently kissed him. "Good. Keep it that way," I whispered as I grabbed my shopping bag and headed for the door.

I sent a text to Ruth to let her know I was on my way.

She was waiting on the side of the road in her car. I tooted as I drove past so she could pull out and follow. I didn't want to pre-empt what would happen that night or the dialogue that was to take place. I needed to allow it to flow naturally. So I used the drive time to clear my mind.

Suzanna's car was in the drive so I knew she was home. I waited for Ruth to park her car and we both went to the door together. I could hear footsteps before I knocked. The door opened and Suzanna glared at me.

I looked into her eyes with compassion. It was clear she was in pain and I was her trigger.

"Hey, Ruth's here to take the kids for the night so we can talk."

"What makes you think I want to talk to you?" she asked, clearly annoyed at my audacity to show my face at her home.

I maintained eye contact. "Because if we talk and at the end of this you never want to see me again, I'll honour it, no questions asked. This only comes into effect after we've created a space where we can exchange truths about all that needs to be said and understood."

She rolled her eyes and opened the door wider so we could enter. Ruth bustled around, gathered the kids and left promptly, just as I had asked her to do. I had seen the concern on her brow when I spoke to Suzanna. I knew she would be at home, a frenzy of worry over what was happening here. I hoped for her sake the kids would keep her busy.

When the sound of her car engine had faded, I pulled out the tequila, limes and salt, placing it on the coffee table.

"We need shot glasses, a couple of plates, a knife to cut the limes, and serviettes."

Suzanna stood there for a moment looking at the tequila and then at me. Her arms were folded, her breathing shallow; she was clearly in a lot of pain. I shifted to stand up to fetch the stuff myself, when she turned and headed to the kitchen. Upon her return, she placed everything on the coffee table and sat on the floor opposite me.

"How does this work? I've never had it before," she said.

"It's called 'lick, sip, suck'." I prepped everything and passed across a shot. "Watch me." I demonstrated and she quickly followed suit.

Her face puckered while sucking on the lime. "Hit me again," she said as she slammed the shot glass down.

We did five shots straight down the hatch and then I placed the lid on the bottle. She looked at me.

"Let it take effect and then we can do another series of rounds if you still want to. I need you sober enough so we can talk. This was just to take the edge off."

She nodded.

"Ask me anything you want. I mean it: anything – and I'll tell you, but you need to listen, not judge, not react. Listen to the words and believe what I say is the truth."

"Anything I want to know?"

"Yes. Promise. Go for it."

"Did you and Brad have sex while we were married?"

"No, never."

"What about when he ran off to London to find you. You never had sex then?"

I looked straight into her eyes and said the words slowly, "Brad and I have never had sexual intercourse."

She paused.

"It's not a trick. I'm not playing on words or lying. I have never had sex with Brad. I don't sleep with married men, never have and I never will."

"Did you want to?"

"Yes."

"He was yours for the taking. Why didn't you?"

"Honestly, Suzanna, I knew you were his perfect match. The look on your face on your wedding day told me you loved him with such depth and purity. He was lucky to have found you. Besides, I would never sleep with a married man. It's against my self-religion."

"Why didn't you date each other before I arrived on the scene?"

"We thought we were first cousins. Plus it was complex because Ruth had raised me as her own. There was a lot going on for us back then which didn't create a great foundation for a relationship. There was more agony in our desire than either of us could bear."

"The thing that stopped you both from being together eventually turned out to be no longer an obstacle, so technically I became the obstacle. Isn't that true?" She folded her arms again.

I paused for a moment looking at my shot glass and then returned my eye contact to Suzanna. I drew a deep breath and said, "What I'm about to tell you I've never told a soul. I hoped this would die with me, but I know you need to know to help you get past what you're thinking. I'm trusting you to keep my secret."

She leaned forward towards the coffee table and nodded.

"When it all began unravelling back in our early twenties, after Brad had left me to escape 'us', I did some research into the legality of first cousins marrying in Australia. I found out it wasn't illegal here; we were free to do what we wanted. I never told Brad. I let him continue to search for you. As much as I loved him, there was something always holding me back. I never wanted to hurt him because I do have a profound connection to him and a deep love, but I was never 'in love' with him. It was only when I met Bodhi that I knew the difference between loving someone and being 'in love' with someone. I have never been in love with Brad."

The expression on Suzanna's face changed. I could see this brought her some relief. "Well, isn't that a kicker? Why do you think men are so besotted with you?"

"That, I'm afraid, I can only answer after we do another round of shots. Are you ready?"

"Yes," she said with a smile, sitting up nice and tall.

I poured another four rounds, which we knocked back without too much ceremony. I could feel the alcohol working its magic. I was on the brink of being tipsy and, judging by the look on Suzanna's face, she was already tipsy.

I sighed. "Men and me. Honestly, I believe it's because they think I'm a challenge. If they can score the love of the 'unobtainable enigma' then they feel special. It almost becomes an obsession, a sport of sorts. I exclude Brad from this only because we do have an amazing bond. As kids we were in each other's pocket right from the start. We created our own secret language that we still use to this day. What we have is priceless and I'm forever grateful for his existence in my life. Honestly, if I could have done him the honour of falling in love I would have because I care for him that much, but he wasn't for me. You two belong together."

"Pfft. You should have seen him sulking around here for days after dinner the other night. It was pathetic."

"I'm going to ask you to listen to my words. I'm not trying to justify anything or protect him, but I need you to listen."

"Okay, shoot." She made a gun action with her hand.

I laughed, she was definitely tipsy.

"At dinner the other night, Brad, for the first time since he's known me, witnessed me in love. He automatically questioned the bond we had. Internally he struggled with what he had seen and how he thought 'we' could have been if circumstances had allowed years ago. Brad realised that I had never looked at him the way I look at Bodhi. It destroyed his idea of the past and it made him feel that our connection might be a farce too. It was a shock. I promise you it isn't a reflection on what he has with you. He is and continues to be deeply in love with you. This was never about anything other than him readjusting to a new version of his truth about me."

"Were you ever jealous of me?" asked Suzanna, licking the last drops from her shot glass.

"Jealous, no. I craved to have what you had together. I wanted my other. Watching the two of you when you lived with me reconfirmed how wonderful you were as a couple. I secretly ached to have that for me, but Brad was never part of the longing."

"Don't you think it would be easier if you had told Brad that years ago?" she asked.

"No, it would have made it worse. You know what

he's like. If he's fixated on an idea and you tell him 'no', does he accept it or become like a derailed freight train full steam ahead?"

"You're right. Dumb question. It would have been worse," she said, trying to drag the bottle from under the table.

I casually moved it across so it was out of her reach. "Yep. At least this way he made some great decisions in finding you, loving you, marrying you."

"Why did you walk him down the aisle?"

"He asked me to. At first I was annoyed. I don't like being the centre of attention. Then I realised it wasn't about me. I could see he really wanted me to give him away. It was symbolic of my blessing to say it was okay. It was the least I could do, given how much he had given of himself to me during our adolescence. I remember the moment I saw you walking up the aisle. I thought you were stunning. When I saw the way you looked at Brad, I knew you were meant for each other and he would be loved as he deserved to be."

Suzanna reached across the table, wiggling her fingers. "Can we have another drinky poo?"

"Depends. Are we good?"

She dropped her hand and frowned. "I hated you," she whispered.

"I know," I said with a half-smile.

"No, I don't think you understand. From the moment I saw you at my wedding, I hated you. I knew what you meant to him. I tried really hard to be gracious but underneath I was scathing. Every time he spoke about you he would light up like a Christmas tree. It grated on my nerves and made me insanely jealous. I thought and wished horrible things. Then you came and helped me when I was in labour with

Mia. Your presence, your kindness made me in awe of you. I began to love you and I hated that more." She rested her head on her hands and started to cry.

I got off the couch and went and sat behind her with my legs apart so I could lean her back into my chest and wrap my arms around her. She sobbed heavily and gasped for air as I rocked from side to side. I maintained steady breathing and focused on visualising the release of her pain in exchange for calming healing light filled with warmth and love. I wanted her to let it all go. It was time for new beginnings, for all of us.

Eventually she settled and leaned back into me. I could feel her body soften, surrendering to the calm energy I was projecting.

"I'm sorry, Talia," she whispered.

I squeezed her tight. "Nothing to apologise for."

"Don't you ever get sick of being so perfect?" she asked.

I laughed. "Yep, my presence makes people fall apart, get confused, question themselves, and question each other. I seem to bring out either the worst in people or their very best. There doesn't seem to be an in between. I'm a real angel."

Suzanna propped herself up and turned to look at me. "I know, right? Everyone seems to struggle when it comes to you. I used to envy the affect you had on people but looking at it now I guess it's more of a curse than a gift. That must be shitty for you."

I shrugged. "It's not my favourite experience in the world but I'm used to it now."

She turned to face me and crossed her legs. "All these years I was jealous of what you had, but really it is more of a curse. Fuck, I actually feel bad for you."

I raised my eyebrow and nodded. "Now you're depressing me with my reality. Let's drink." I slid my body across the floor to grab the bottle.

I was surprised at how quickly we had managed to polish off the tequila. For a couple of non-drinkers, we had made light work of the bottle. I knew it was time to put the final steps of my plan into action.

"I'm just going to the toilet," I said as I grabbed my phone and headed to the bathroom.

Suzanna waved to acknowledge me as she lay down on the floor.

I sent a text to Brad:

"It's time. Come over and do exactly what I told you to. Don't be tempted to deviate. Just stick to the words I told you to say. Get Shane to come so he can drive me home. I'm plastered. Make sure he stays outside; tell him I will come out to him. Delete this message and don't you dare ever tell anyone about this or it will backfire."

I pressed 'send', flushed the toilet and walked back into the lounge. I could see that Suzanna needed some caffeine to keep her awake so I headed into the kitchen to make a pot of coffee while I waited for Brad to arrive. It wasn't going to be long before what I hoped would be the start of a new beginning for these two. They deserved to honour each other in totality. I needed Brad to be happy.

As the front door opened, Suzanna sat up. "Talia, are you leaving?" she called out.

I poked my head out the side door of the kitchen. "No, I'm here, just making us some coffee."

Brad appeared in the doorway of the lounge. He glanced at me and then fixed his gaze on Suzanna. I stepped back into the shadows to watch my masterpiece unfold.

He walked across and knelt in front of her. She looked at the carpet. He bravely lifted her face so he could engage her eyes.

"I love you," he said. "I choose you. I choose us. It's always been you. I, Brad Parker, choose you."

Suzanna burst into tears and put her arms around him. He caught her embrace and started to cry too.

I watched as they held each other. I knew they would become stronger for this experience. Suzanna had the insight she secretly craved and Brad, for the first time in his life, was truly free to be completely in love with the right person. It was the best possible outcome and I felt such enormous relief.

I turned the coffee pot off and snuck out the side door so they could have their space. Shane smiled at me as I jumped into the car.

"Thanks for picking me up. I'm sorry about the time."

He leant across and kissed me on the cheek. "You're amazing, Talia. I don't know how you do what you do, but you do it perfectly well."

I laughed. "That had an air of Dr Suess about it."

As he shifted into gear he laughed too. "It did, didn't it?"

"Brad and Suzanna will be fine. Let Ruth know they'll both be stronger than ever before. I guarantee it," I said.

Shane responded, "Like I said – amazing."

It was a quarter to three when I walked in the door. All the lights were out. I quietly entered my bedroom and whispered to Bodhi I was home. He made some grumbling noise to acknowledge me and fumbled about to lift the sheets for me to join him.

"I'II be there soon," I whispered as I walked into the en suite.

I had a quick shower to wash away the emotions of the day, brushed my teeth so I didn't reek of tequila and slipped into some very unflattering pajamas. By the time I was back in the room Bodhi was fast asleep again. I slid under the covers and snuggled up against his toasty warm back. His hand searched around until it found mine, pulling it across his torso. I smiled. Even in his sleep he was demanding. He was too cute.

"I love you," I whispered as I closed my eyes and drifted off to sleep.

I got up early, leaving Bodhi to sleep in. I saddled Rebel and we headed out for a nice quiet meander around the property. Rebel seemed to enjoy it as much as I did. His ears were forward; he had a lovely bounce in his step and showed no desire to head home. It was only in the presence of horses that I felt truly grounded.

It was mid-morning by the time we returned. I didn't have any intentions of being out for so long, but it had proved too enjoyable to have it end early. As I entered the stables, I found Bodhi there, drinking a coffee and chatting to Ash.

"Morning," I said as I dismounted from my trusty steed.

"Howdy," replied Ash.

Bodhi stepped in and kissed me. "Morning, you. Someone got to bed late and snuck off early this morning."

"Guilty as charged." I stole a sip of his coffee.

"How's Jenna feeling today, Ash?" I asked.

"She finds it a bit rough in the mornings but pulls up

better in the afternoons," replied Ash with a twinkle in her eye.

I studied her for a second before I replied, "Morning sickness will do that to you. Who got her up the duff, when is the baby due and are you both going to be Mumsy?"

Ash burst out laughing, looked at Bodhi and said, "Told ya."

Bodhi scratched his head. "How on earth did you come up with that from her one comment?"

"It was obvious. The look on her face told me she had a secret, the glint in her eyes was an indicator she was happy and sickness in the morning reminded me of pregnancy, so I went with my train of thought."

Bodhi opened his wallet and passed fifty dollars to Ash, who proudly snatched it from his hand and tucked it into her pocket.

"You had a wager on me figuring this out?"

"Yep, last night at dinner I told Bodhi. He asked if you knew yet. I said no but it wouldn't take long for you to figure it out. I bet it would take less than a day," said Ash.

I lightly punched Bodhi on the arm. "Thanks for the faith."

They both laughed and Bodhi said, "If it's any consolation, I figured I was backing a losing horse. I just didn't expect you to get it so quickly. It's impressive and kinda scary."

I looked at him and smiled. "Yes, no secrets." Then I turned to Ash. "Speaking of no secrets, spill it."

"Jenna and I decided we wanted to have a baby so we went to a sperm bank, selected a donor and wham bam. The baby's due sometime after Christmas."

"Are you going to put a ring on it?" I asked with a cheeky grin.

"Nah, we don't need to be married. We are married in our eyes."

"Nice cop-out, slack-arse. If she's carrying the baby, then you need to man up and propose," I said with a laugh.

Bodhi opened his wallet and passed across another fifty dollars. I watched in amazement.

"Are you guys fucking kidding me?" I said.

Ash took the money and was giggling her head off as she responded, "Nope, I told him you would start harassing me to propose and that became the other secret bet."

I shook my head. "If you're able to know my every move then holy mother of god I've become predictable."

Ash beamed with joy as she took Rebel away to wash him down and put him back in the yard. Bodhi and I headed to the house to have a late breakfast.

"Sit down. I've made you an omelette."

"Wow, I'm getting spoilt. Thanks," I said as I sat at the table.

"How did it all go last night?"

"Judging by the text I received this morning from Brad, which said 'thank you, thank you and thank you again', I would say everything worked out well."

Bodhi placed a delicious piping hot veggie omelette in front of me and a welcome steaming cup of coffee beside it. "I'm glad. You must be exhausted."

"Actually, I'm not too bad. I was a little emotionally drained yesterday. I didn't know if I could fix it but I knew I had to try. I'm not sure I would be as composed today if I hadn't been successful. They were only having problems because of me."

"You can't take all the credit. They chose to think and adopt what they felt about you." He pulled out a chair to sit at the table with me.

"My existence was the stimulus for the cause and effect," I said, taking my first bite.

"Sure, but you can apply that train of thought to anyone who exists."

"Agreed," I said, continuing to gulp down my food. I was famished.

Bodhi and I spent the remaining five days travelling around Victoria so we could have some time to ourselves in beautiful landscapes. I took him to Mable Gully to see the glowworms in a small cave; we watched the sun rise and set across the Twelve Apostles. I even managed to get us across to William Rickets sanctuary in the Dandenong ranges. We covered some miles in the car but the time spent allowed us to explore one another's minds. Our trip had allowed us to deepen our understanding of one another. I truly loved him.

Constellation
of Truth

I felt a great sense of relief to be back in the US in my apartment. Although I loved spending the time with Bodhi I also appreciated my own space. We spent the first few nights apart. He said he needed to catch up with work and I took the opportunity to reclaim my environment. I had forgotten how all consuming relationships could be. I needed to strike a balance so I didn't tilt either way.

Once I was settled and my jetlag had passed I went into the office to see how everyone was. Much to my delight, when I walked in the door Mable was sitting at her desk with her new glasses and lamp. She was focused on writing a response to one of the many letters stacked high on her desk.

"Morning, Mable," I whispered so as not to startle her.

She rose to her feet and cuddled me. "Oh, dear. You have been missed. Welcome back."

"Thanks. How is everything going with the book and

your responses?"

Mable pointed to a pile of letters stacked in a tray. "It seems I'm getting responses to the letters I'm sending. These ones are addressed to me." She beamed with delight.

"Wow, fan mail already. I'm glad. At this rate you'll need a team of people to support you." I laughed.

There must have been over five hundred letters on her desk. Amazing.

"I'll leave you to it. I have a stack of emails to process myself. I haven't touched a computer since I left for Australia."

"How was the trip?" she asked.

I paused. "The trip was eventful." I tapped on her desk and walked off to my office.

It felt good to be sitting at my desk. I switched on my computer and drew a complete blank over my password. I sat there staring at the screen, trying to recall what it was. I had never done that before. I checked my phone to see if Bodhi had texted. Nothing. I knew he was busy, but he would usually have sent me something by now. It didn't sit right with me so I sent him a message:

"Thinking of you. Is everything ok?"

I called Michael in to override my password so I could do a reset. While I waited I stared at my phone. Bodhi hadn't responded. Once Michael got me in to the system I refocused my energy on processing my emails. I found it impossible to get Bodhi out of my mind, but knew I needed to leave him be. The rest of the day I responded to hundreds of emails, clearing my inbox back down to a manageable size.

Bodhi still hadn't responded by the time I was ready to go home. I was tempted to head across to his office but once again decided I needed to give him his space. I felt lost in his silence. I had expected that he would have made the time to respond by now, even if it was with a brief message. His absence felt personal. I didn't want to get worked up about it so I headed home to take a hot bath and rest. He could come to me when he was ready.

That night I tossed and turned. Bodhi had a key to my apartment so I kept waking at the slightest noise, hoping it was him.

Sadly it wasn't.

In the early hours of the morning I finally fell into a deep sleep. In my dream I was stuck in a cobblestoned laneway with light at the end where I could see the silhouette of a person with their back turned to me. I could tell by the shape that their arms were folded. The more I tried to walk towards the person the further they were from me. I tried to speak but I had no voice. Ravens were circling above, squawking at me, and there was a woman's voice laughing incessantly. I could hear the beat of drums but not the beat I was used to in times past. This was frantic, fast paced angry pounding like a looming threat. The tune had a shrill equal to the sound of the woman's laughter. It was nauseating to listen to. Flies appeared out of no-where and were buzzing around me. I didn't know what was happening. I just felt a compulsion to reach the person at the end of the lane.

In the morning I woke in a pool of sweat. The loss I'd felt in my dream cloaked me like a dark blanket. The room was warm but I was shivering and felt emotionally numb. I checked my phone: still no response. I got out of bed, pulled on some clothes and headed out the door. I needed to speak to Bodhi. What the fuck was going on?

There was no answer at his apartment and the lights weren't on, so I went to his office. As I walked into the foyer, the receptionist greeted me.

"Morning, how can I assist you?" she said with a pleasant smile.

"Hi, I'm Talia. Is Bodhi around? I'd like to speak with him."

"Sure, do you have an appointment?" she said, looking at her computer.

"I'm his girlfriend. He didn't answer my call last night so I just need a quick word."

Her eyebrows rose and her mouth opened in surprise. "Oh, sorry. I didn't realise he had a girlfriend. He is in; I'II just call him for you. One moment. Take a seat." She seemed disappointed.

I stood waiting. It took all my strength not to just barge through to his office. My heart was thudding uncomfortably; my palms were sweating as my clenched fists revealed the whites of my knuckles. I hated the way I was feeling. I could see that the receptionist felt awkward, so I stepped away from her desk to look at the pictures on the walls. Most of them were of Bodhi with bands he had signed up. There was quite a collection. I hadn't known his business was so large.

"Excuse me, Talia. He said now's not a good time; he'll call you later." She had an apologetic look on her face with an underlying smirk.

I pulled out my phone and sent him a text.

"I'm not leaving until we speak. Now please, ten minutes. NOW."

I heard the ping on his mobile so I knew he had it switched on and had received the text. I waited.

"Talia."

I turned to see Bodhi. He gestured for me to follow him, and then walked down the hall and into the first available conference room. Bodhi positioned himself on the other side of the large oblong table and was looking out the window, back turned to me, his arms folded. I stared at his body language and fell into a deep sadness. This was just like my dream.

"Just tell me," I whispered. "The silence is killing me. I deserve better than this. Tell me, what's going on?"

With his back still turned, he said with a harsh tone, "I lost two really big opportunities while I was gallivanting in Australia with you and I'm really pissed off."

"You're punishing me because a business deal fell through?" I asked, trying not to raise my voice.

He turned to face me and maintained his arms in a rigid fold. "I only went to Australia because it was important to you. I shouldn't have gone. I should have been here running my business instead of standing on the sidelines while you played nursemaid to your 'special' relationship with Brad."

I ignored his snipe. "I asked you when you were free to travel. I didn't dictate a time for leaving. I left that up to you. Why are you taking this out on me? What's this really about? Have you changed your mind about how you feel about me, about us?"

He dropped his head to look at the carpet and stood in silence. I glanced out the window and saw a flock of ravens coming towards the window. One by one they landed on the sill and proceeded to squawk and tap on the glass with their beaks. I knew something wasn't right. My ravens were my guides and protectors. I had no idea what they were trying to tell me; my mind was split into fragments of thoughts. I couldn't believe this was happening.

Bodhi ignored the ravens, it was as if he couldn't see or hear them. He raised his gaze to return mine. His eyes were vacant. "My work is important. Not all of us have lazy millions sitting in the bank to fall back on. I have responsibilities to myself, my staff. They all rely on me to keep this venture successful. I can't sacrifice all that I've worked for to play nursemaid to your whims."

Nothing about this sat right with me. There was something else driving this. I couldn't even recognise the man before me. He was rigid, distant and cold as ice. I felt like we were no longer connected.

"Is there someone else, Bodhi?" I asked, cringing at how he may respond.

"No," he snapped.

I knew instantly that meant 'yes'. This wasn't just about his work; there was someone interfering and at the moment I was hedging my bets it had to do with another woman. My heart sank. It took all my strength not to burst into tears. I didn't want to give him the satisfaction.

"This was a mistake. I had a romantic notion and moved too fast. I need to reclaim some space. I need to think," he said, looking away once again.

I felt dead inside. I wanted to crawl under a rock. It felt as though we had an audience but there was only us in the room. Aside from the ravens, Bodhi and I, you could have heard a pin drop in the rest of the office. Yet my instincts were screaming out messages that we weren't alone. I knew I was missing something.

"Bodhi, you know it's impossible to lie to me. Who is she? Is this about Lex? Why are you treating me like this?"

"Well, you're wrong this time. God forbid the great Talia Jacobs has made a mistake. Keep Lexie the fuck out of this," he yelled.

I knew he was trying to bait me so I would lose my temper. He was hiding something and I wasn't leaving without knowing. If this was to be our end then I wanted closure so I didn't spend the rest of my days wondering.

"Can you please tell me the truth? If you do this, I'll walk away and you will never hear from me again. I'm not leaving until we talk this through. Your choice, Bodhi."

He kicked the table leg with his foot, releasing a grunt of annoyance and said, "Lexie came over the night we got back from Australia. When our eyes locked, I realised that it was her I truly loved. All these emotions came flooding back and I knew she was my soul mate. She's back to being the woman I fell in love with. I was kidding myself about the romantic notion of you and I. You're not capable of falling in love. That's why you struggled all your life to feel anything for anyone. I'm sorry, but that's just the way it is. Are you satisfied?"

I stood there stiff as a board. The words spilling out of his mouth as he continued to purge his feelings burnt marks into my heart. The ravens were in a frenzy, some leaving little splatters of blood on the window. All I could do was listen, yet inside I was screaming 'stop' over and over.

When Bodhi finally finished talking I muttered the words, "So it's over."

"It never really began," he whispered.

I looked at him one last time. "As you wish," I said, and turned and walked out the door.

He didn't try to stop me.

I wasn't even sure that he watched me leave. It didn't matter. I knew his position and was going to honour his request, because in its purest form free will was the governor and if this was his truth then I would respect it regardless of what I wanted. I struggled to smile at the receptionist as I politely thanked her and then exited the building.

The cool breeze heightened the sense of cold as tears streamed down my face. I couldn't stop my body from shaking. I was distraught and for the first time in my life felt what it was to be completely lost. I had nowhere to go. I switched off my phone so I wasn't tempted to send or receive any calls. I no longer had a voice or a coherent thought in my head. I wandered the streets aimlessly, watching the world go about its business while I felt the edge of death cloak my being.

I unconsciously gravitated into a phone shop and purchased a new sim card. The consultant transferred all my numbers across and cancelled my old number. I paid for it to be silent so I couldn't be found. I went home, made a few calls, sent a couple of emails to the office letting them know Blake was in charge until further notice, packed a small bag and was out the door.

At the airport I waited to board my plane. My eyes stung as I sat down and sent a single text to Brad.

"This is my new number. I promised you – no secrets. I'm going to walk the earth for a while. I need to get lost among strangers. Don't ask; I'm not ready to talk. I'm headed to China. If you tell anyone or try to find me I will throw away this phone and no one will have access to me. I just need some time. Don't reach me unless it's a catastrophic event. Don't even reply to this text. I want silence. Let the others know I have gone travelling, nothing more. Please assist Ash if she needs anything. Don't break my trust in you; it's all I have left. Talia."

I switched off the phone and placed it my bag. I didn't want to think anymore. My mind had been reeling with flashbacks of us in the tree. The words Bodhi had said. I questioned whether any of it had been real. Why would he spend his life searching for me and then discard me as though it meant nothing? The pain of his words was unbearable. I couldn't get the image of him so distant and cold out of my mind. He had fought to wake me from my emotional slumber and then left me to feel the depth of one's loneliness. If this was to be my karmic lesson then I had learnt it well.

"Excuse me, miss, we're boarding. Are you coming on this flight?"

I looked at the airhostess and smiled. "Yes, sorry. I was lost in thought. I'll come now."

She looked at my tearstained face and offered me a kind smile. I could see she related to my evident sadness. I boarded the plane, placing my bags in the overhead locker before sitting in my window seat. Everything felt surreal. It wasn't meant to be like this. I had started to believe in fairy tales. Stupid, stupid me. I was such an idiot.

I disembarked in Hong Kong. I needed to get a visa processed to get into China so I stayed for a few days while my application was being sorted. I hadn't wanted to do it from the US. It was unbearable being in that country and I certainly didn't want to chance seeing Bodhi again. He had asked for distance so I was giving him what he wanted. His lesson from me was 'be careful what you wish for. I'm prepared to grant it'.

I stayed in my hotel room for the entire duration of my stay. I had no energy to interact with the world. Keeping my room mostly dark and silent, I left only the bathroom light on so I could find my way around, but in truth I hardly moved from my bed and fought to take one breath after another. I couldn't bear to witness others seeing my angst and pitying me while I felt so emotionally vacant.

When I received the call that my visa was ready I booked my flight and headed off to the airport again. It had been days since I had eaten anything. My clothes were falling off me. I could feel myself wasting away from the inside out. I slowly sipped on some water before boarding the plane to China.

Three hours later I was in Beijing. I grabbed my bags and, once out of the terminal, I flagged down the driver I had arranged to take me to my destination. I passed across the address, which was written in Mandarin, he nodded his head and we were on our way.

The landscape melted into a fusion of colours as we travelled towards the Daoist temple where I was to reside for the coming months. Shaolin monks who specialised in training visitors in martial arts ran the temple, which was said to be thousands of years old. It had been on my bucket list to visit for years.

When I arrived there was no one around to greet me. I paid the driver and watched him leave. Standing alone in the middle of nowhere, I felt empty. My heart was replete with echoes. The heat of the day seared above me. I shifted closer to the entrance to stand in the shade so I could rest a moment and find my bearings.

"Hi, are you Talia?" said a smiling man in an orange robe.

"Yes, hello."

He bent down to grab my bags. "Welcome, we were expecting you yesterday," he said as he walked off.

I followed. "I had to get my visa processed in Hong Kong so it took longer than expected. I'm sorry; I should have called to let you know. It slipped my mind."

He took me to a building lined with doors at the back of the monastery and placed my bags outside one. "This will be your quarters for the duration of your stay. The communal wash facilities are at either end of this building. When you have settled you can meet me in the building over there. I will introduce you to the others. Wear something comfortable. Your training starts today."

I nodded and went inside the room as he left. In the corner was a small bed with some basic sheets and a blanket. There was a grey metal locker and a small side table, no window. It was depressing and reflected perfectly how I felt. I placed my bag down beside the locker, sat on the bed and burst into tears.

It was time to pull myself together. Emotionless, I changed into my gym gear, put my runners on and headed to the washroom to clean up before meeting the crew. When I looked in the mirror I was shocked to see my reflection. I was gaunt, my eyes were sunken in, swollen and red from crying, and my hair lacked lustre. I was a mess. I washed my face – no improvement. I took one last look to remind myself what I had allowed myself to become and headed off to the communal area.

As I opened the door I saw twenty or so people actively training. I stood quietly near the entrance and watched. The room was large and had a myriad of traditional martial arts weapons on the wall. The group that was in training consisted of all ages, shapes and sizes. I could see by their form that they also had varying levels of fitness. I had little time to consider my own fitness level for this endeavour. I imagined the first few weeks were going to be an awful shock to my system. It had been a while since I had engaged in regular exercise.

The monk who had met me at the entrance looked across. "Talia, come over here, please."

I walked across. All eyes were on me as I stood next to him and faced everyone. It felt like the first day at school in Haiti all over again. It was such a cruel flashback to experience, given the circumstances. I couldn't look anyone in the eye and diverted my gaze to the floor, hands nervously clasped together.

"Everyone, this is Talia. When you get a chance, make yourselves known. Now get back to training," he bellowed.

All of a sudden the room was a hive of activity again and I was left standing next to the monk, who was waiting for me to lift my gaze. When I looked up at him he inspected me from head to toe. "Come," he said as he walked off, leaving me to silently follow.

He took me into another large room adjacent to the workout area. This had rows of tables and bench seats.

"Sit," he said and then disappeared behind some doors.

When he returned, he was holding a bowl of steaming hot noodles. He placed them in front of me, passed across some chopsticks and waited.

I picked up the chopsticks and started to eat. He continued to watch until I had eaten a fair amount of it.

"Eat it all. Then go out the front gate, take a right and travel on the path for five miles until you reach the great lake. There you will sit and meditate. Let everything that has brought you here go. When you come back, it is only you that can walk through the gates. Get some rest. Then tomorrow we will start training."

I nodded. He took one last look at me and then walked back to where the others were training.

My stomach grumbled as I finished the last of my noodles. I drank the soup and then placed the bowl and utensils on a bench near the kitchen before taking the side door marked 'exit' to head out as instructed. At first I walked down the path and then found myself in a light jog, which migrated into a frantic run. I continued at full speed until my body betrayed me. As I stumbled to a halt and leant forward, gasping for breath, I could feel my head pulsate with pain. I was so unfit.

I walked the remainder of the way and eventually reached an opening which afforded a view of the great lake. It was spectacular. Large, rugged mountains loomed on both sides. The trees were in flower and the waters calm. I walked to a spot near the edge of the lake and sat, drinking in the visual splendour. I had no idea the region possessed such beauty. It felt serene in comparison to the turmoil that was bubbling under the surface of my skin.

Knowing I was unable to suppress my thoughts, I decided to mentally step through what had happened and used my rational side to guide me. I knew that I couldn't change anything that had occurred. I needed to accept it and allow myself to move into a space of nothingness. I continued to talk inwardly for hours until I was over the sound of my inner voice. The only option was to let it go. I chanted it like a mantra as I rocked back and forth. It became the only thing that saturated my mind.

Satisfied that this was the best I could achieve, I rose to my feet and slowly walked back to the monastery. It was dusk by the time I reached the doors. The monk was standing there waiting for me, assessing me as I approached. I stopped when I was in front of him. He looked me in the eyes and I returned his stare. After a couple of minutes he nodded and stepped aside so I could pass. I went straight to my room and crawled into bed. I don't even remember my last thought before I transitioned into slumber. I was beyond exhausted.

A bell was being rung in the courtyard. Waking in a daze, I listened to the noise as it became louder. I had lost my bearings and forgotten where I was momentarily. The room was dark so I had no idea what time it was. I assumed it was still black outside. I ran my hand along the wall to find the light switch. As I turned it on, there was a knock at my door. I sat up.

"Come in."

The door opened slightly and a voice spoke in a heavy accent. "Ten-kilometre run start in pipteen minutes. Warm-up for morning training." The door closed.

I never wore a watch and my mobile was switched off, so I had no idea what time it was. All I knew was that I had 'pipteen' minutes to get my arse into gear for a decent-size warm-up run. I put my clothes on and headed across to the communal washroom to brush my teeth and wash my face in an attempt to wake myself up.

"Morning," I said to the lady brushing her teeth at the basin next to me.

She gave me a toothpaste-filled smile.

I was tempted to jump in the shower but knew there was no point, given I was about to go for a run. I washed my face, brushed my teeth and tied my hair back. More ladies came in and out of the bathroom; it was a hive of activity. They all seemed really nice. I headed back to my room to put my toiletries away and then proceeded to the common room.

People were stretching, doing star jumps in

preparation for the run. I decided to use a skipping rope to warm up my body. It was a shock to see how quickly I lost my breath. Fifty skips in and I started to sweat, puffing like a bastard. Oh, my. This run was going to be eventful. As I sat on the floor to kick off some stretching, a lady beside me leant in.

"Hi, I'm Nathalie."

"Hi. Talia." I said as I placed my hands around my toes to stretch forward.

"It does get better. The hardest part is the first two weeks. Your body needs to get used to all the training. Pace yourself in the first couple of days and then start to push as hard as you can so you get fitter quicker."

"Okay, thanks."

I knew the regime was high intensity. It was exactly what I wanted, perhaps needed at this stage. Eight hours of training a day, leaving only time to eat and sleep. The absence of thinking was welcome. I was hoping my mind would be consumed with supporting my body during this physical onslaught; there was no point in thinking about Bodhi and me – even though I couldn't get him off my mind.

A monk entered the room. He opened both doors, calling out, "Everyone to the front gate and down the path. You know the way. Those that don't, follow the others."

People formed groups to run in. They must have figured out previously who matched their pace. I went behind a cluster of people and kicked off my run with a light steady pace. This would be my first true jog in years, so I had no idea whether I would be able to make the distance. Finding a steady rhythm, settling into a pattern of breathing and relaxing, was the key.

Some tension rose as people passed me. I needed not to be the last person to return from the run. I'm not sure what drove this aspect of my nature; I just knew I didn't want to be left behind. I picked up my pace and started to overtake some of the less skilled runners. I readjusted my speed and completed the run easier than I had expected.

Upon our return, people went off to shower and then have breakfast. I wasn't hungry but knew I would need to put something into my system. It was going to be a big first day. The queue for the food moved quickly. The system seemed to work efficiently: you held out your tray and people served some food onto it, and then you shuffled along to the next item. I had no idea what they were putting on my plate.

At one station, I looked at the lady serving and said, "I'm a vegetarian. Can you tell me what this is?"

I pointed to a dollop of what looked like slimy translucent worms.

She smiled to acknowledge me but didn't respond.

The man ahead of me turned. "It's seaweed. If you haven't had it before, you'll need to get used to it. The workouts you do here will demand more from your diet and this green stuff is packed with vitamins and minerals like iodine, calcium, iron, to name a few."

"Okay, thanks. Is there anything on my plate that's not a vegetable?"

He laughed. "It's strictly vegetarian here, so you're fine. Anything mysterious on your plate will be vegetable-based."

"Handy to know. Thank you. I'm Talia."

"I'm Russell. Follow me. We can sit at my usual table. I'll introduce you to some people."

"That's nice of you, thanks."

We walked across to a table filled with an eclectic mix of people from across the globe. A portly man with a cheery disposition caught my eye as he shifted across, gesturing for me to sit next to him. The edge of his barrel belly pushed up against the table and he wore a headband that made him look more like he belonged in the audience at a tennis tournament.

As I sat down, Russell introduced me. I nodded to acknowledge them all as they greeted me. I was fascinated by the diversity of people who were attracted to taking part in developing their martial arts' skills. The training was said to be gruelling so I hadn't expected to see so many out-of-shape people in attendance.

"So what brings you here, Talia?" asked Mr Headband.

"I just needed a break from reality. Sometimes you need to step outside your life to be able to witness it with clarity. I've had this place on my bucket list for a while and decided it was time. What's your excuse?"

"My wife dragged me along," he said as the lady beside him leaned forward and waved.

"How hard are the training sessions? Is there anything I need to worry about?" I asked.

In a symphony of laughter they all simultaneously replied, "The rope."

I raised an eyebrow and smiled. "Sounds a little S and M. What exactly is 'the rope'?"

Russell laughed. "The main outdoor workout area is thirty-foot high and only accessible by ropes. You're expected to climb up. Don't worry; it sounds harder than it is."

"What happens if I can't do it?" I asked, now feeling a

little concerned.

"You get escorted through to the secret stairwell and you do the walk of shame like me and a few others," said Mr Headband.

"Ah, at least there is an alternative," I said, feeling relieved.

"Yes, there is, but new people aren't supposed to know that. It deters them from trying," said Russell, glaring at Mr Headband.

I chuckled as I playfully nudged Mr Headband, who was doing a hand action of zipping his mouth and throwing away the key.

"The secret's safe with me," I said with a smile.

After breakfast the masses headed out to the ropes. I followed and watched people climb up to the top, while others were escorted to the secret passage. I waited until the last of the crew climbed before making my first attempt. Russell stayed back.

"The trick is to never look down, find an angle that you can have your feet against the wall to support your body and then just place one hand after the other to get yourself up. Watch me." He grabbed the rope and proceeded to climb. After a few steps up he gestured towards the rope closest to him.

"Okay, here goes nothing," I said as I placed one foot on the wall and grabbed the rope.

I slowly started the ascent. It was easier than I had expected but hard enough to get my heart pumping. The height was daunting. I was greatly tempted to look down as I steadily used all my strength to climb. At the halfway point sweat was dripping into my eyes and I could feel my grip loosen. The drop was far enough to do some damage so I had no intention of letting go.

"It's okay, Talia, you can do it. One hand, one foot. Keep going," said Russell, who maintained my pace.

The edges of my hands were turning white and the rope was burning my palms. I could feel myself starting to psych out but the pressure of having Russell beside me and people at the top watching and yelling words of encouragement left me no option but to continue my ascent. Three quarters of the way up there was a ladder. I grabbed hold of it and climbed up the remainder of the way.

At the top, the students gave me a round of applause. I smiled, doing a half-bow as I wiped my sweaty palms on the sides of my track pants. I felt dizzy from anxiously holding my breath most of the way up.

Russell patted me on the back. "I knew you could do it. Most people fail the first few times," he said with a wink.

I shook my head. "I was psyching myself out halfway up. I thought I wasn't going to make it."

"Ah, but you did. Tomorrow it will be easier and by the end of the week you'll wonder what all the fuss was about."

I nodded, still trying to catch my breath.

"Come across and join the class."

I followed him to the workout area where people were following the instructor's tai chi moves. I took my position beside Russell and loosely followed the movements. Flashbacks to Thailand came to mind as I felt my body shift into the rhythmical pattern. It felt familiar, a sense of home.

The class took forty-five minutes and I, like everyone else, had sweat pouring off me. We were melting away under the sun's rays. Segmented oranges and cool water were provided between the classes. The instructors didn't offer us much of a break. Less than fifteen minutes passed before the next instructor arrived up the rope to take us through the motions. This class was focused on mental strength and balance. The instructor had us climb upright poles where we were to stand still with one leg out. I found I was okay until I saw another person wobbling. Losing my focus, I started to shake and eventually fell to the ground. The instructor just glanced and waited for anyone who fell to get back onto the pole. After my sixth time falling I had little strength to climb up again. I stood facing my pole, wondering how I was going to do this again.

"You must never give up. Stand on the pole, balance, focus," said the instructor.

I clumsily climbed up once more. He stood in front of me as I looked straight ahead.

"Focus on the still of the horizon. Clear your mind and extend your leg. Find your balance," he said in a reassuring tone.

I took a deep breath, found a focal point, extending my leg once more. It was hard not to acknowledge the pain running through my body. Nothing about the position was natural or comfortable. The ball of my foot holding the weight of my body seared with a burn that threatened to ignite. Once again I could feel my mind trying to take over to psych myself out. As I started to wobble, I calmed my breath and upon exhale placed my hands out front in a praying position. I closed my eyes and visualised the horizon. Slowly the pain started to dissipate and I felt strength in my position.

The last class before we broke for lunch was about

striking the blocks of wood in front of us. Each time the instructor called out a name in Mandarin it would represent a different strike. I watched the others, doing my best to copy their moves. They all seemed to be acquainted with the various actions so I was going to have to play catch-up. At the end of this class my arms were numb. I could hardly gather the strength to jiggle a finger.

I walked across to Russell. "Do we have to climb down the ropes? I can hardly move my arms."

He laughed. "No, we take the stairs. This is it for training in this area today."

"Thank god for that."

Russell smiled. "Come on, let's get some lunch." He placed his hand on my shoulder.

I was surprised at how hungry I was. I had hardly touched my breakfast but working out for over three hours was certainly taxing on my body and my appetite. It was the first time I had ever gone back for seconds. The food was not my usual staple but the pickled vegetables, seaweed and rice were a delicious combination. The clear broth they served was my favourite. It looked like cloudy water with some soya beans, pickles and seaweed floating in it. It was packed with flavour. I had three small bowls of it before I decided I had had my fill.

After lunch everyone dispersed to have some free time. I decided to walk back to the lake. When I arrived there, the monk who had greeted me at the entrance was sitting near my stone. I walked across and sat beside him.

"How was training, Talia?" he asked, without turning his head.

"It was challenging. I'm assuming it will get easier."

"If it does, then you are not doing it right. The

stronger you get, the harder you must push."

I thought about this for a moment. "Yes, I understand."

He nodded as he raised his hand and pointed to the lake. "Tell me what you see, how you feel when you gaze upon her."

I looked out to the lake and the distant mountains. "I see the mountains are divided on either side but they yearn to be together. The water separates them and it makes me feel sad. I want them to be together, as I feel they once were." I didn't know where my thoughts had come from and spoke as if I was outside myself.

"The legend says the mountains were once together but they let a rift divide them and hence the waters came to fill the void. They were two lovers who allowed life to get in the way of their destiny and now they are forever divided by what they chose to break them," said the monk with steady tone.

My stomach sank as the parallels were not lost on me. "So what I see is true."

"What you see is true for the mountains. Stubborn and rigid in their ways. You need to focus less on them and more on the free flow of the waters that touch their edges. If the mountains were not so stubborn they would see that the waters do not separate them but reconnect them to one another. In life you must be like the water, Talia, not the rock. The waters mould to any place and to any circumstance. If the mountains were not so rigid in their focus they would feel the connection has not altered; it is enhanced by the energy of the water's flow."

I took a deep breath and nodded. How fortuitous to hold a conversation about a legend that reflected my own journey perfectly. In the first moment of pain I turned myself to stone and walked away rather than be present and work through the turmoil. Bodhi and I were divided with no waters between us. At the first test of our love I accepted him pushing me away instead of holding true and fighting for our love. I chose to adopt his words as an excuse to rebuild my armour and made myself unattainable once more, defaulting to refrain to falsely manage my own pain.

"Thank you," I whispered.

The monk raised himself to his feet and walked back towards the monastery without uttering another word.

I decided to skip the afternoon classes. Every fibre in my body was already screaming in pain. I would aim to execute a full workout the next day. I sat there until dusk, staring out at the waters. My mind was once more focused on Bodhi. There was a part of me that wanted to leave and find him, but I knew I had much to learn. My journey in this mystical place was unfinished. I rose to my feet slowly and walked back to the monastery in the darkness, feeling torn.

I stood outside the monastery entrance as the monk approached. He once again stared into my eyes and I returned his gaze.

"The pain you feel, learn from it. Use it. Your training and time here is not over until the calm of the waters flows through you. Stay."

I nodded and proceeded past the entrance. I went to my room and fell asleep in silence. My spiritual journey was in its infancy. It had only just begun.

Reality Bites

Come on, Talia, switch on your fucking phone. How can she just leave without a word and think this is okay? Fuck. I've sent her hundreds of texts, got the caretaker to check her apartment, work, no one knows where she is. This is driving me insane. It's been over two months. Enough already. Fuck, fuck, fuck. She's really pissing me off right now.

"Hello."

"Hi, Billy. It's Brad. DON'T hang up again. Please, I need to speak with you. It's important. Talia's missing."

"What do you mean: she's missing. For how long?"

"Just over two months. I'm destroyed with worry. I need to know what happened between you two. There might be something she said that gives me a clue on how to track her down."

"I'm sorry she's missing, but I don't want to talk about it," said Bodhi.

"Listen, pal, we can do this on the phone or I can come to you. Either way, it's going to happen. I promise you, nothing good will come of you and me being face-to-face right now."

Bodhi was silent.

"It's your choice. I'm not bluffing," said Brad, hoping to god he would speak.

"Okay."

Brad released a silent sigh of relief. "If you know where Talia is, I need you to tell me. I have to find her. It's been months. She hasn't contacted anyone in the office, she hasn't been home and her phone is switched off. I'm going insane. I need to find her."

"Sorry, I don't know where she is."

Brad gritted his teeth. "What did you do to her? I've seen her walk away before but the message she sent freaked me out. I've been sick with worry and know that she's on the edge of disappearing, which means we could all lose her permanently, thanks to you. What the fuck happened?"

Bodhi paused for a moment and then spoke, his voice cold and distant. "When we got back home I found out I had lost a couple of stellar business opportunities. My life has been devoted to building my business and these were two gems that could catapult me to the next level to compete with the big players in the market. I flipped out, got angry and ignored her, and then said a few things that made her walk out. That's it. Oh, no, wait. And I got back with my ex-girlfriend the night I returned from Australia."

Brad couldn't believe his ears. He could feel his blood pressure catapult as he headed towards a blind rage. "What the fuck is wrong with you? How can you profess to be completely in love with her and then all of a sudden flip a fucking switch? Do you have any idea of what you have lost, you cock-sucking piece of pond scum?"

Bodhi's voice shifted to a more chipper tone. "What can I say? The heart wants what the heart wants. I have to go. I'm late for a meeting. Nice chatting to you."

Brad was left staring at the phone in shock. What had just happened? Who the fuck was this guy?

"AHHHHHHHHHHHHHHHHHHH!" he screamed as he ripped the phone from its socket and threw it across the room.

He sat on the couch, his hand cradling his face as he burst into tears. He shook with rage.

"Brad, are you okay?" Suzanna shook his shoulder.

Through pursed lips, he struggled to speak. "Sit down. I have to tell you something."

Suzanna quickly sat beside him and started to cry, assuming the worst. "Brad, please tell me the kids are okay. What is it? What? What?"

"Talia's missing."

She gasped as she placed a hand on her mouth. "Oh, my god. When? How? I can't believe this."

Brad removed his hands from his face and turned to hold Suzanna's. "Don't get angry at me. Talia sent me a text two months ago saying that she was going to China and that she wasn't going to be in contact. She told me if I tried to contact her she would ditch the phone so she could never be reached."

"Okay, but why China and what happened with her and Bodhi?"

Shaking his head, Brad proceeded, "You're not going to believe this. I finally got through to him after trying for weeks. That cocksucker told me that he got back with his ex-girlfriend the night he returned from Australia and then said, 'Oh, well, the heart wants what the heart wants.' He even sounded happy about it." Brad stood up as he raised his voice. "Can you believe that absolute fucking CUNT?"

He swivelled around and punched the wall, breaking the plaster and splitting his knuckles.

Suzanna jumped to her feet and grabbed his arm as he was setting up to do it again. "Honey, no. This doesn't solve anything. I just don't get it. They were amazing together. Nothing seems to add up. Poor Talia. She must be totally heartbroken and she's out there all alone."

Brad whispered, "I know. As if she hasn't already experienced enough heartache and loss in her life." He started to sob as he turned and buried his head into the crook of Suzanna's neck. "I'm so scared that she's done something stupid. I just can't bear to think of her in pain. I don't understand why this stuff keeps happening to her." His sobs grew louder as Suzanna gently stroked his back and cried silent tears too.

This was a complete disaster.

Eventually they both took a seat on the couch.

"We have to think of a plan to find her. I just don't know where to start," said Brad, peeling the skin off the edge of his fingertips.

Suzanna wiped the last of her tears away and blew her nose. "Contact the Chinese embassy and ask them what the procedure is to report a missing person and have it broadcast around China. I'll make us a pot of tea and hop online to get some ideas about what to do when a person is missing in a foreign country." She patted Brad on the knee and stood up.

"Um, okay. I'll need your mobile."

"Just use the home phone. It will be far cheaper," she said as she continued towards the kitchen.

"I would, but in my rage I ripped it out of the wall and threw it across the room," he said, shrugging his shoulders.

"Okay, well use your own mobile."

"Nope, threw that too. It smashed the window on the way out."

Suzanna shook her head as she looked at him then she gave a half-smile. "It's in my bag."

The next few weeks were consumed by family obligations and researching what could be done to assist in searching for Talia. Brad was transferred from department to department. He had been hung up on more times than he could count and eventually when he managed to speak to someone they confirmed that he needed to refer the matter to the police. Needless to say, reaching the right person in the police department was equally difficult. Their phone company was set to have a high sales month as Brad continued to smash phone after phone.

Suzanna eventually found some information and gleaned ideas from what others had done. She organised for flyers to be placed in shop windows in as many towns as she could locate people to do it. They placed advertisements in most of the local papers and on social media sites. As more time passed, horrible thoughts crept into their minds. Emotionally they were both exhausted and felt completely inept.

Suzanna looked at Brad sitting on the porch with a vacant expression, cigarette in one hand and a glass of whiskey in the other. He had lost over ten kilos in two weeks and had seemed to go grey overnight. She placed a hand on his shoulder. Brad didn't budge.

"Go to China," she whispered.

He slowly turned his head and looked up at her with tear-stained eyes. "Really? You're okay with that?"

"Yes. We've tried everything we can here and it's getting us nowhere. I've shelled out thousands of dollars to strangers in good faith that they will post the flyers, but we don't know whether it's been done. Someone needs to go, and you have the best shot of finding her. Who knows? Maybe the bond you two have will make you accidently cross paths with her." She paused. "Go. I'm sure."

Brad tossed away his cigarette, jumped to his feet and embraced her for the first time since this had all started. "Thank you. I love you so much. Thank you."

Suzanna smiled as she stroked the back of his head. "You're welcome. Make sure you don't come back without her. We all need Talia."

Mountains Divide

It had been three months of constant training. Mentally I had finally reclaimed my balance. I felt whole again. As I heard the call signalling 'pipteen' minutes before the morning run I reached for my phone for the first time since I had arrived. I needed to connect again. It was a milestone, given that when I arrived I had no intention of surfacing ever again.

The light from the mobile stung my eyes as it booted. I waited to see if there were any messages. None came through. I felt a little disheartened. I knew that I had asked Brad not to contact me, but Brad being Brad I expected that he would try. There was nothing. I stared at the phone and considered calling, but I didn't know what I would say.

Staring at the phone wasn't going to give me a different result so I decided to head out for the morning run. I had grown accustomed to the feel of the cold morning air burning my lungs. I liked finding the rhythm of the movement in my pace. It no longer felt foreign. I was strong and fitter than ever before. Unlike the first couple of weeks where I struggled, I now was part of the lead pack. It felt great to have some visible rewards for all the physical effort.

The day went by fast. A sense of restlessness grew within me. In fact I could feel a desire to reconnect surfacing. After dinner I returned to my room: still no messages. My stomach flipped as I sat on my bed and stared at the screen. I wanted to call Brad but couldn't bring myself to dial the number.

An urge to leave suddenly overwhelmed me. The thought produced goose bumps that cascaded down my body. It was time to shower and pack my things. I loved being there but it had served its purpose. I wasn't going to be any more centred than I currently felt and it had already exceeded my expectations. As the water from the shower spout poured down I closed my eyes, soaking up the warmth of the liquid. I saw an image of the lake and the two mountains appear on the back of my eyelids. I had to go visit them one last time.

That night I slept like a newborn baby after its first feed. I felt whole again, nurtured, safe from all harm. The dank room that I had loathed when I arrived had become my cocoon. Everything inside these four walls was simple. I needed to ensure that when I left I maintained the essence of the simplicity it had offered in all aspects of my life.

In the morning I woke early to take one last walk to the lake as planned. I wanted to give my thanks to her for all she had shown me. When I arrived, the monk was perched in a squat on a rock. I walked across in silence and sat beside him, staring out into the darkness. First light would arrive soon. I looked forward to its reveal.

"You are leaving us today." He kept his eyes closed.

"Yes."

"Good. It is time."

I nodded my head as I replied, "I will be sad to leave this place."

"You take this place with you. No one can come here and not be claimed by her waters. She gives to you and you offer a portion of yourself in return. She will always be in your mind and your heart."

I liked the thought of that and hoped it was true.

We sat in silence as the first light crept across the sides of the mountains and shone onto the crystal blue waters. It was a breathtaking sight to behold. I found myself mesmerised by the soft light. The rays seemed to extend at an angle, bouncing off the edges of the mountains to cross one another so they fused in streams of pure light.

I sat upright and pointed. "Look, the mountains, they're touching. They use the light's rays as hands to connect once more."

"Yes." He nodded. "You see, every morning they embrace the light, which embraces them."

Tears streamed down my eyes as I watched the light weave its magical union. The ache for connection was now a tidal wave rampantly flowing through my veins. I reached my right hand out to touch the rays that were creeping closer towards us. I wanted to be part of the mountains' join. I welcomed the warmth on my hand as the rays danced across the tips of my fingers. It felt like the process of emergence.

"It is time, Talia," said the monk as he rose.

I scrambled to my feet and looked at the lake one last time. She was beautiful. I turned and followed the monk quietly back down the path once more. Everything seemed peaceful. The birds must have decided to sleep in. The only sound was our footfalls on the path. As we reached the entrance to the monastery, the monk turned to me and stared into my eyes, as he had done on the day of my arrival. I returned his gaze and smiled. His face was round with perfectly smooth shiny skin.

"You are ready," he said, then bowed and walked inside.

I retrieved my bags and headed back to the front to wait for my driver to arrive.

"Talia!" Russell jogged towards me.

"Hey! Morning, Russ."

"What's this?" He pointed at my bag.

"I'm just waiting for the car to arrive. I'm heading off."

"You were going to leave without saying goodbye? No way." He stepped in to stand in front of me.

"Yeah, I'm not good at goodbyes. They always seem too final and it makes me sad."

"Give me your number. I would love to catch up with you when I'm in the US next. Is that okay?"

"Sure, I'll text you now." I pulled my phone out of my pocket to send the text and saw I still didn't have any messages. My lips pursed as I shook my head, releasing a big sigh.

"Is everything okay? You look really sad." He placed a hand firmly on my shoulder.

"I'm fine. I was just expecting to hear from someone and they haven't contacted me yet. I guess I'm a little disappointed. That's all."

"Okay, so long as you're fine. If you need to talk, I'm a great listener." He paused to see if I would respond but I just gave him a half-smile to acknowledge his offer. "Here, give me the phone. I can never remember my number unless I type it."

I passed my phone across to Russell.

The car arrived and the driver jumped out to place my things in the boot. I turned to Russell and smiled as he passed the phone back.

"I guess this is it," I said, stepping in to give him a hug.

He gave me a warm embrace and smelt my hair. "We're going to miss you. It won't be the same."

"Take care of yourself and say goodbye to the others for me."

"Will do."

I jumped into the car and headed off down the road without glancing back. I never liked looking back. Instead I raised my hand and waved in good faith that Russell was standing there watching me leave. I spent the whole trip alternating between looking out the window and staring at my phone.

The driver took me to my hotel, where I settled for the night. My dreams were presented in images with stardust particles surrounding them like magic fairy dust. They were snapshots of treasured times past. Bodhi and me as kids, him as an adult, our first embrace in the coffee shop. I lay silent as I watched the presentation on the back of my eyelids transpose. I felt calm until I was transported back to the dark dank cobblestone laneway of the dream I had had months prior. Everything was still the same. The ravens were still squawking, the incessant laughter echoed through my mind and that incessant manic drumming was like razor blades. I could feel my heart sink as I witnessed the silhouette of a lone man still standing with his back to me.

The only difference was a piece of paper floating down from between the two buildings. When it landed on the ground I walked towards it. The closer I got the louder the laughter was until it rose to a deafening shrill that started to peel the skin from my body. There was a force trying to push me back from the paper. I knew it was important. I had to reach it. After much struggle I bent down. My now skeletal hand stripped of all flesh grasped the paper. The moment I mouthed the words written the shrill and drum beats vanished. I looked up to see the man turn and slowly make his way towards me. Tears filled my eyes when I realised it was Bodhi. His arms weren't folded as I had first thought. I felt horrified as I looked at his pale sickly grey complexion; his body was encased in a straightjacket and his mouth bloodied from the stitches, crisscross-woven shut by a red velvet ribbon bowed at each end. I gently removed the ribbon, unthreading it from his skin to free his mouth from the bind. A single blood-filled teardrop from his eye landed on my hand as he mouthed the words, 'I love you now and forever.'

Jolted by the shock of his words, I woke, gasping for air. Sweat dripped down my brow as I felt my heart beating so hard if felt like it was trying to escape from my chest with every pulse. I reached across to touch my aching ears. They were still ringing from the shrill of insane laughter, causing a sharp pain to thunder through my brain. I needed a pen and paper. I leapt out of bed and fumbled through the drawer to scribble down the words I had read in my dream. When I finished writing it, I stared blankly at the words.

"Okay," I whispered, feeling sorrow in my heart as I accepted the message. Bodhi needed my help.

My appetite distracted me. I was as hungry as a savage bear. I ordered a fruit platter and a black coffee. This would be the first cup of coffee I had had since arriving in China. It was surprising how good it tasted. Each piece of fruit glided down my throat and into my grateful stomach. Today was going to be a big day.

When I walked into the bathroom I caught my reflection in the mirror. I looked fit. I smiled and touched the glass where the reflection of my face was. My eyes widened in disbelief as I realised my hand was covered in blood splatter. I inspected my body but couldn't find anywhere it could have come from. I placed my face closer to the mirror and then I saw it. I had been bleeding from both ears. The shrill of that voice somehow crossed planes to affect my physical body. This confirmed what I believed was happening. Why didn't I think of this before? Urgh! I could have kicked myself. In the light of a new day, it was so obvious.

After showering and dressing, I took the piece of paper with the details and headed out the door. The address was located in a rough part of town. The driver refused to take me any closer than the bridging point. In his broken English he blurted out some directions while constantly looking around to see if anyone was approaching, and then sped off down the road.

I shook my head as I watched the taxi disappear. As I turned to walk in the direction he had suggested, I noticed a man in my peripheral vision step out from an open doorway to my left. He had what looked like nun chucks in his hand. Then another man stepped forward, then another. There were five in total, all covered in intimidating gang-like tattoos, all holding weapons of various descriptions, smiling and tapping them in their hands while staring at me.

This is it; I'm fucked, I thought to myself. I could handle one, maybe two – but five? I could see nothing good was going to come of this. Where's Jackie Chan when you need him?

The man with the nun chucks yelled something to his mates in Mandarin and then raised his hand to gesture to move forward. I didn't bother looking for a weapon to defend myself. I knew there was no point in running. I would have to stand and try to fight. Internally I felt disheartened that my life path seemed to be presented with neverending battles. When does it all get better? It was the first time I had felt compelled to succumb to asking myself the question Why me?

The leader of this motley pack stopped directly in front of me. The others stood behind him in a scattered order. He looked me up and down while exaggerating the way he chewed on the toothpick in his mouth. I remained still, looking straight at him.

He removed the toothpick from his mouth. "You not scared?"

I was surprised at how clean his English was. He had an accent but his pronunciation was perfect.

"Should I be?" I asked, staring back at him.

He turned to the others and translated my words. They all started laughing as he turned back to face me again.

His expression contorted in attempt to look scary and he widened his eyes. Leaning forward, growling through gritted teeth, he said, "Yes. We are killers."

I was so over the drama and bullshit of my life. I was ready. If this is how I am destined to die then I would make it a good death. I would kill as many of these sons of bitches as I could. I continued to watch him while ever present to the rush of my adrenalin surging through my core.

All of sudden his face lit up with a smile. "Just joking. You are Talia. Grandma sent me to protect you and take you to her house."

"Li Jing is your grandmother? She knew I was coming?" I said, the anxiety dissipating, now replaced with a sense of relief and curiosity.

"Yes, Grandma Li," he said, excited that I knew her name. "She has been expecting you and sent us to wait. We check every day for the last week."

"Ok. Thank you. Can I ask your name?" I did a slight bow. My mind was reeling with questions.

He bowed in return and when he rose he tapped his chest. "I am Jackie Chan."

I smiled. *Of course you are.*

"Follow me. Keep close," he commanded. "This is a rough motherfucker place. Don't worry; we Kings," he screamed at the top of his lungs, spinning in a circle with his arms expanded. His crew all nodded, smilingly their approval at his theatrics.

I quickly learnt that he wasn't exaggerating.

I'm not sure about 'kings' but I was certain, as I heard doors slam and people call out in warning and then run, that these fellows were greatly feared. Six blocks later we arrived at Grandma Li's house. Jackie told the others to stay outside while he escorted me into the house.

When we entered, the thick smoke of incense and cigarettes wafted into my mouth, causing me to choke. As I bent forward, Jackie slapped me on the back while laughing and yelling out to his grandmother. In a matter of moments she appeared as Jackie swiftly left without saying a word.

Grandma Li was no more than four foot tall. Her cheeks were so big she didn't seem able to open her eyes.

In fact, I wasn't sure how she could see at all. Her hair was an exquisite shade that reflected hues of grey-blue in the shifting light. She had what I would call chicken legs: pencil thin, with a rotund midriff supporting the base of her ample bosom. I instantly loved her energy. Grandma Li emitted a vibration so strong I could detect a barely audible hum when I was standing beside her.

She did a token bow, turned and walked into the next room.

I tried to muffle my laughter as an image of her bowing too far forward, causing her to topple over because of the weight of her belly and ample breasts, popped into my head.

She gestured for me to sit then walked off into another room. Hands on lap, I assessed my environment. I surmised, based on the multitude of jars with weird-looking creatures suspended in fluid, that she might be a healer. The air in the room was thick with smoke. I found myself suddenly gasping for air. As I stood up to walk to the blackened window, she reappeared.

She placed what looked like a shrivelled up apple core flush under my nose and said, "Breathe."

In blind faith I asked no questions and did as instructed. I inhaled as deeply as I could and instantly felt better. She gestured for me to hold the item and smiled as the expression of amazement landscaped my face.

"Sit." She gestured to the chair.

I waited in silence while she hovered around the room, randomly selecting items from her disorganised shelves.

The more I stared at the jars with the floating enigmas the more I started to believe they might be alive. My eyes seemed to be playing tricks on me.

I raised my hand and pointed to them. "Excuse me, Grandma Li, what are those?"

She turned to see where I was pointing and laughed as she slapped her chicken leg.

"Foetuses: human, monkey, tiger, jackal, rabbit." She resumed gathering items.

When she had finished, she piled them all on a small three-legged table in front of me. I was relieved to see none of the jars she had placed there contained floating objects. I watched as she bobbed her finger up and down, taking stock of what was on the table. She then tapped her finger on her lip while she thought.

Hands raised in the air, she said, "Ah, yes," and then turned and walked to the dreaded shelf.

Glancing up and down, looking at each row carefully, she selected a jar.

Fuck me; nothing good can come of this. I watched her place the latest jar on the table at the closest point to me.

She glanced at me, or at least I think she did, as she released a chuckle. I nervously smiled as I leaned in to take a closer look.

"What is it?"

"Elephant foetus."

As soon as she said that I could see the malformed outline of a little trunk. I sat back in my chair and continued to watch her as she buzzed about. When she re-entered the room she was holding a cup of tea.

As she passed it to me, she said, "Must relax. Must be relax, for cross."

I nodded and took the tea.

I sniffed it before I took a sip. It had no smell. *Was it green tea or some variation thereof?* As I took a decent gulp, an expression of horror appeared as the liquid slid down my throat. I wanted to vomit. If I hadn't known better, I would guess I had just drunk watered-down liquid shit.

When Grandma Li came into the room, she looked at the expression of disgust on my face and burst out laughing, once again slapping her leg. "First is horrible. After one no taste. Must drink. Must relax. No relax, no cross."

"I'm sorry. I just can't." I pushed it away.

My insides were churning and I was certain I was about to projectile vomit at any moment.

She gently placed it back in my hand again and said, "Talia, must drink. Want help boy, then drink."

I stared at the deceptively innocent looking cup of liquid. I took a deep breath and raised the cup to my lips while she watched. If I was going to do this it made sense to skull. As I emptied the contents into my mouth and swallowed, preemptively grimacing, I was surprised to discover it was now flavourless. How bizarre and thank fuck.

She reached across to take the cup, patting my left knee. "See? Grandma no lie." Then out the room she went again.

I was torn. Should I sate my curiosity by asking to know the ingredients of the tea, or should I leave be? Should I, shouldn't I? Should I, shouldn't I? I looked across at the items spread across the table. When my eyes landed on the elephant foetus I thought it wiser to leave the composition of the tea a mystery.

I wasn't sure now how long she had been absent. All I knew was I had to fight to keep my eyelids open. Each time I blinked it felt harder to lift my lids.

"Eh, eh, eh eh," she said as she ran towards me waving a fan in my face.

She waved the apple core thing under my nose again.

As I inhaled, the veil of drowsiness immediately started to dissipate. I looked at her with a questioning expression.

She placed her hands together and waved them. "Ahhh, work too fast. Too much relax too quick."

I nodded and smiled, wondering what was next.

"Make potion, must relax." She muttered some other words that sounded like gibberish to me as she gathered various items from the table and crushed them with a mortar and pestle into a fine powder.

The whole process took her about an hour.

When she had finished, she handed me a hair tie. I automatically grabbed my hair, placing it in a bun. She fetched a stool and sat directly in front of me.

"Careful listen. Woman evil black heart no soul hate very strong. Break spell, must fight demon. Fight good, win," she said, pushing a clenched fist in the air.

I repositioned myself to sit up straight. "What demon?"

"Shhhhht. Shhhhht. Listen." She paused. "Demon must conquer. Use mind." She paused for a moment. "Okay, use mind."

"What do you mean? That's all you know?"

She stood up to leave the room again.

"Wait! I have questions."

She paused and looked at me.

"In my dream last night a woman screamed loudly and there was this horrible drum beat. When I woke up my ears were bleeding. How is that possible?"

She sat back down and held both my hands. "You no faith, lost hope. Make you danger. No protection Marlee give when girl gone, weak. No faith, no protection."

"Wait, you know Marlee? How?" I was astonished to hear her name spoken.

"Yes, old friend. She come visit Grandma Li. She say Talia come. Tell Grandma everything. She help prepare." Her expression became serious. "If not conquer demon then death and spell on boy never broke. You must win."

I nodded, while wondering why Marlee had never chosen to visit me. I missed her so much. I wished she was right there with me. I could really have used a friend.

She raised her index finger and tapped it on my skull. "Use head." Then she tapped my sternum. "Trust heart." Grandma Li shuffled to her feet and left the room again.

I had no idea what that meant but I had to have faith that I would be able to figure it out. There were two options: leave things be and let Bodhi stay under an enchantment spell which falsely bound him to his ex, or cross over the planes yet again, except this time go forth and battle with some demon where the only weapon I had was my head, my heart and faith as a shield. I used to think my karma was jokingly associated to me killing a Sherpa in my previous life, now I was starting to believe I had slaughtered the whole village.

There was no joy in living if I didn't have Bodhi as an integral part of my life. The image of him in the straightjacket haunted me. It was possible that his core essence was trapped in purgatory while his physical body was here. The whole situation was totally fucked up. How anyone could choose to do this to another person they professed to love was beyond me. The motives were selfish, weak and heartless. I had to try and fix this. I would have regrets if I didn't. Even if Bodhi came out of this with no desire to return my love, knowing he was free was enough. He meant everything to me.

As Grandma Li re-entered the room I could see she was hiding something behind her back.

"Ready?" she asked.

"Yes."

Quick as a whip she produced a piping hot cup of tea, attempting to pass it to me. "Good. Drink this. Must relax."

I almost fell off the chair trying to get away from it as I yelled out, "Fuck, no! Not a hope in hell. That stuff tastes like elephant shit."

She raised one eyebrow remarkably high. For the first time I could see a small section of her pale blue eye. "You taste before?"

My face contorted at the thought. "You're joking? Tell me you're joking?"

"Not joke. Drink. Must relax." She once again tried to pass it to me.

I waved my hands, turning my head. "No way."

She shrugged and placed the tea on the table. "Okay, no relax, no cross over."

"Don't you know another way? There must be options?" I pleaded.

"No. To travel must drink. Door open. No drink, no door."

I looked at her and then back at the tea. Great. My last supper is elephant-shit tea. That should be a useful icebreaker when I'm at the pearly gates.

"Ahhh, fuck it." I reached across, grabbed the cup and threw the whole brew down my gullet. "Oh, my god, I think this brew was worse." I covered my mouth to stop myself from vomiting. As the cramps started, I doubled over, holding my tummy.

Grandma Li was almost on the floor laughing hysterically. She was trying to speak but couldn't get the words out. I was feeling too sick to be irritated by her enjoyment. It was taking all my strength not to throw up. I feared that this would only result in me having to drink more tea. I was in hell and I hadn't even left yet.

Ten or so minutes had passed before Grandma Li was able to regain composure. She came across and started plastering the paste she had made earlier onto my face like a mask. So internally I had elephant shit swilling in my intestines and now elephant foetus on my face. Oh, Lord, please tell me this gets better?

"You know tea taste bad on first sip and then no more?" said Grandma Li.

"I'm well aware of this delightful little fact."

"Why you not sip? Suffer less, drink tea no problem?"

My eyes widened as I looked at her. "Why didn't you tell me to do that?"

"Not so funny," she replied and then went into another frenzy of cackling laughter.

By the time she was finished I was well on the way to losing myself in the crossover. The last words I recalled were to sniff the shrivelled apple core thingy she placed in my hand to return.

My heart raced as I landed with a loud thud on a small ledge in a cavern. As my eyes adjusted I could see the ceiling adorned with stalactites. It was beautiful. There was water running below and the place seemed empty. I sat on the ledge and heard pieces of it crumble and fall to the floor. It was a fair way down.

'Use your head, trust your heart and have faith,' was the only information I had to go with. My head contained my mind, so this battle must be mental rather than physical. My heart meant it needed to be true and faithful. Well, I guessed I had to trust myself and have faith that good would reign over evil. As I looked around to see if there was anything I could use as a weapon or shield I heard a voice whisper the word 'staircase'. Carefully I leaned forward to peer over the ledge to see if one existed.

Nothing.

I only managed to disturb more of the loose rocks. This ledge I was almost certain wasn't going to hold.

I closed my eyes to visualise a staircase from the ledge to the floor. I repeated the word 'staircase' as I solidified the visual. When I opened my eyes the room was unchanged. My instinct told me I was on the right track. Instinctually I felt I needed to approach it differently. I could hear the curdling calls of a demon beast echoing through the network of tunnels. This thing knew I was there and was coming for me.

The words *Om Namah Śivāya* flashed across my mind's eye. It was a mantra taught to me by a Hindu holy man when I was travelling around India. *Namah Śivaya* was believed to have great powers. The intonation of these syllables was set to cleanse the soul from the binds of the mind and reinforce one's clarity of intellect. *Namah Śivāya* was revered as the most powerful mantra of them all.

I closed my eyes, cleared my mind and started to silently chant the words. In the background I could hear the shrill coming from the creature. Its call sent goose bumps across my body. There was pain in its horrific calling that led me to distraction. The more I chanted the louder the cries of torment became. The sounds reverberated off the cavern walls, multiplying the depth of its noise. As I relaxed my body and cleared my mind once more I allowed the chant of the words to consume me. Drifting down the rabbit warren of a trance I could sense the walls of the cavern shuddering. I broke from the chant to look down. There before me was a three-headed creature with a single body. The faces were horrifically disfigured. With red eyes they stared up at me as they released their screams of anguish.

My palms started sweating as I realised the three heads were the Haitian men who had raped the little girl I had saved. Thoughts of my parents flooded in and I could feel my hatred for them consume the core of my being. The head in the centre released the sounds of incessant laughter. It grated at my nerves. I hated him most of all, for he was the one who had murdered my parents. In a fit of rage I jumped to my feet. I wanted to scream and visualised jumping off the ledge onto them, ripping their puny melted heads off their elongated necks. Death would be the only kindness afforded to them that day. I possessed no fear in my heart; I wanted blood.

The more enraged I became the larger they grew, cackling louder, which fuelled my insanity. They were now at the wall, starting their ascent towards me. It wouldn't be long before they reached the ledge. Tears rolled down my face as my body shook from adrenaline and loathing of this putrid abomination. It was clear they grew stronger, feeding off my state of mind. The anger had to cease. I knew now the only way to conquer was to give them absolution from their sins, to surround them in white light. This was one of the unscripted laws of the universe. An eye for an eye would just make everyone blind.

The depth of my frustration was unbearable. Without warning, I reefed my head back and released an almighty scream. I took one last look at them as I drew breath and, upon the exhale, I chose to release the pain. As I did, they slowly started to shrink, confirming my instinct. Each breath brought the same result. I stepped back and repositioned myself so I could sit down. Closing my eyes, I did my best to block out their calls and restarted the mantra.

Gently I rocked back and forth as I chanted the words *Om Namah Śivāya* loudly so it would echo throughout the network of caves. I symbolised the increasing intensity of the beast's shrill as absolution, returning it to the three trapped within through energy transference, and projected white light to bind their lost souls to the light. They fought hard against its receipt, slamming their body at the wall, causing my ledge to continue to crumble. Holding steadfast to my purpose, I continued the chant, feeling its strength grow as they weakened. Hours passed as they relentlessly fought to free themselves from my projections. The approach seemed only to contain the beast, not destroy it. I knew the moment I ceased the demon spawn would be once again free. At the deepest point of the trance I saw Bodhi appear before me. I was overwhelmed by the presence of the enormity of love we held for one another. As I infused our love's purity with the white light I projected this out to the beast in lassos of love. In my mind's eye I could see it falter as its wretched body gave way and fell to its knees. Bodhi intertwined his hands in mine, placing his head on my forehead.

"I love you, Talia," he whispered.

A shift in energy saturated the environment in a magnificent burst of light that was now being generated from both of us. The cavern was filled with a blinding spectrum of colours as the light refracted from the stalactites dripping from the ceiling. The creature released its final series of bloodcurdling screams before falling to silence.

When I opened my eyes, Bodhi was gone. I was standing alone in this space of confrontation. I carefully shifted closer to the side of the ledge and peered down to see three deceased human figures on the floor before me. It was over. I had won.

Closing my eyes once more, I visualised a staircase. When it appeared I carefully made my descent down its steep narrow steps. I stood quietly over the three lifeless bodies, feeling removed from any emotion. It was in that moment I realised the absolution was not for them; it was for me; my weakness had been my loss of faith and it was in the presence of these men and our associated experiences that I had cursed God and turned my back on believing in the good of man.

I knelt before them and manifested three single perfectly formed long-stemmed blood-red roses, placing one on each of their sunken torsos, whispering, "Go with God, may you rest in peace as shall I."

I had finally forgiven myself and could feel a quiet sense of peace for them and for me. As I stood up I took one last look around the cavern before pulling the apple-core thingy from my pocket and raising it to my nose to inhale deeply. It was time for me to go home.

My head was pounding as I opened my eyes and realised I was lying in a bed. I tried to sit up, but the pain seared my brain like a hot poker.

"Head hurt?" asked Grandma Li, who was walking into the room.

"Yes," I muttered.

As I lay my head back down on the pillow I could hear her footsteps leave the room as quickly as they had entered. The pulsating thump consumed my brain, causing unbearable pressure. I felt like I was dying.

My body shook, the pain surged, piercing the back of my eyes as the presence of Grandma Li once again in the room had startled me. She was holding a cup filled with piping hot liquid. Squinting my eyes, I aimlessly stared at the steam free-floating whimsically towards the ceiling.

"Drink," she said as she leaned over me.

She placed the straw against my bottom lip. Slowly, I sucked on the liquid, hoping to God it didn't taste foul. By the third gulp, the pain was already starting to dissipate. I was starved and the welcome fluid felt like it was spiralling down an empty drain. Within minutes the pain was almost gone. I sat up and looked at Grandma Li patiently watching over me.

"Thank you," I said, feeling eternally grateful for the receipt of relief.

"You win?"

"Yes, it is done," I whispered, still feeling disassociated.

"Use mind?"

I looked at her and mustered a half-smile. "I harnessed the power of the mantra *Om Namah Śivāya* and the philosophy of Omnia Vincit Amor, meaning love conquers all. I started channelling white light and then love presented itself to complete what had been started. The monster was in the form of three men from my past."

"One demon? You lucky. Demons eat angry. This power. You must clean to free. Demon dead, you free. We break spell," she said.

"Why didn't you tell me what I needed to do?"

She bowed her head and played with her fingers. I could see she was reflecting on something that made her feel sad. "Not allowed. Fate punish if try."

"I understand. You mentioned now we can break the spell. Bodhi appeared in the cave and it was his love, the love we felt for one another, which delivered the final end to the demon's wrath. Doesn't this mean my man is free from the spell?" I asked, hoping the answer was a succinct 'yes'.

"Hmm, boy there?" She placed her finger to her lips as she tapped them. "Love pure," she said, tapping on her chest, "very strong love. This good." She gave me a big reassuring smile.

"Is that a yes, he is free from the spell?"

"No. First clean soul. Make protection strong. Now break spell. We do now. Okay?"

A dreaded thought washed over me. "Do I have to drink that tea again?"

Grandma Li covered her mouth as she chuckled. "No tea."

"Then I'm ready," I said as I shuffled across the lumpy mattress to get myself out of bed.

I followed her into the room we had been in before. I sat in the chair and patiently waited on her instruction. The table had been cleared of all the items she had previously used. In its place there was a fountain pen and yellowed parchment paper. When Grandma Li returned she was holding a knife in one hand, a bowl in the other. She gestured for me to give her my hand. I shifted forward in my chair and held out my right hand, suspecting she wanted to cut me to get some of my blood.

Ruthless in her execution of the incision, she dragged the knife diagonally across the length of my open palm. I grimaced as I felt my flesh tear. Profuse amounts of blood gushed out. She flipped my hand over the bowl while patting it. I was thankful that whatever she had given me to fix the pain in my head was also assisting me to not feel the cut without a magnitude of discomfort. After a few minutes, satisfied that enough had been drained, she handed me another drink for the management of the pain as a top up. I sipped on the tea while she skillfully bandaged my hand. She had clearly done this before.

"You must write love letter from the heart. Make three copies exactly the same. One we burn for universe, one you keep, one we send."

I shifted the table across so it was now in front of me. Reaching across to pick up the quill, I realised now my left hand would have been the better choice for the cut. I adjusted the quill in my bandaged hand and dipped it in my blood. Crimson red droplets fell on the page as I placed the quill in position. At first I was compelled to express how I missed him, what it felt like to lose him. I went on and on for pages as I cried. I was doing this for me. I needed to let all that I had left bottled inside out so I could be free to tell him how I really felt in my heart of hearts.

When I finally started writing my letter to him the words just oozed from my soul.

Your voice reached my ears like a delicious melody, pounding with lustful rhythm aching in my heart. I can't seem to get you out of my mind. Flashes of our passion keep bubbling to the surface. It feels like you are present with me, touching … kissing … The way you make me feel mobilises my senses into rapture. My thoughts remain motionless, as if trapped in a frozen moment. Internally I can feel these deviations are awakening my deepest desires for you. Crave me with fervour, my love. Together we can elevate each other, taking a journey on passion's eternal high. You're all of everything and anything in between to me in my mind's eye.

In the blessed hour of our next meet, when the clock strikes true, my commitment will from that moment forth be devoted to the perfect execution of our dreams in life and all your most intimate fantasies. It will be a slow seduction of raunchy intent. I will set every inch of your body ablaze from your head to your toes. My soft lips will enslave themselves, caressing you. My tongue will lavish and violate your sacred spaces. With mastery, my hands will investigate every curve of your poetic canvas like an unquenchable beast. My sole ambition will be to leave you always torturously aching for more. I want our appetites for all aspects, body, mind and spirit, to be feverishly insatiable.

Make me reef in anguish as you pleasure me, my love. Your enchantments will dominate my vessel as you tease and make me your willing slave. Command me to touch your naked flesh. Guide me to taunt your tender lips, kissing away our burdens. I will demand to feel your body grinding hard against mine. I want to see your eyes mirror my passion, filled with a blazing fury that will put Dante's inferno to shame. Seduce me in ways that make me fall to my knees, expressing every emotional element you have so our gossamer threads of devotion are euphorically intertwined to become one.

I love you ~ Always ~ Talia Jacobs *Reach* +86 444 4444 4444

~ xXXx ~

I called out to Grandma Li. It didn't take long for her to respond. She had a tray of food in hand that she placed on the table. She picked up one of the letters and proceeded to read. I watched as her cheeks flushed red, she fell back into a chair and started fanning her face as she continued to read my words. Finally it was my turn to laugh at her.

When she was finished she collected the letters, making no comment on the content. She just nodded her head and left the room. The smell of the food had my full attention. I was starved. Every mouthful of the noodle soup felt like heaven. I couldn't recall the last time I had eaten.

When Grandma Li re-entered the room she was wearing a traditional Chinese outfit made of fine silk threads with intricate pictures of people and places that no doubt depicted a scene from the archives of ancient Chinese history. She somehow looked taller. As my eyes gravitated to her, I realised her hair was now placed on the top of her head in a rotund bun. This gave the little munchkin the visual deception of greater height.

"You have four letters?"

"I want to send one to his work and one to his home. Just in case it gets intercepted at home by her and she destroys it."

Grandma Li nodded. "I finish spell. You have photo of girl?

The receptionist at the hotel had helped me source an image of Lex from Bodhi's Facebook page. She had kindly printed a copy of it for me before I left to go to Grandma Li's.

I used my left hand to get the crumpled piece of paper out and passed it across. "Here you go."

I knew Grandma Li was going to place an irrevocable binding spell on Lex so she could never do this again. The idea of this journey being almost over allowed relief to wash over me. There would soon be an end to Lexie's poisonous reign of terror. Thank God.

"You sleep. Morning it ready."

I smiled, thankful to understand my contribution to

this experience was complete for today. My body felt as though I had run a marathon completely unprepared. I slowly rose, executed a slight bow and left in the direction of the bedroom before Grandma Li had time to change her mind. I needed sleep.

The divine smell of roasted coffee beans sauntered through the air. I wanted to sleep more but my need for sustenance was far greater at that point. I fumbled my way through the network of little corridors, using my sense of smell to guide me to the kitchen where I found Grandma Li whipping up a storm for breakfast.

"Morning."

"You sleep?"

"Yes, really well."

"Good, eat." She passed across a plate of hardboiled eggs, seaweed, and inoki mushrooms with a side dish of hot noodles. I didn't care about the hazards of maybe burning the roof of my mouth; I was famished. My time at the martial arts training centre had me using chopsticks like a native. Without hesitation I picked up my sticks and started barrelling down mouthfuls into my pit. I gladly consumed the plateful and unashamedly went back to receive seconds. It seemed all the experiences of the past few days had made my appetite ferocious.

Lights Embrace

With the letters posted, I had nothing to do except wait. Luckily for me I was beyond exhaustion so I spent the next few days sleeping and waking to intermittently check my phone for messages. I started to wonder whether my phone was even connected to an active telco network. As I fumbled through the settings I realised the WiFi and network button was set to offline. Frustrated by my own stupidity I selected WiFi and network activate to 'connect' and rebooted the phone. It seemed like I was staring at the small screen forever as it searched to download the messages. All of a sudden a stream of texts started to come through. I was delighted to know Brad was true to being Brad. He had ignored my request for silence and texted anyway. God I missed him. The phone was beeping madly as each new message was received. I felt myself sink when the phone hit full capacity at five hundred texts.

What have I done? Brad must be beside himself to have tried so many times to reach me.

I didn't want to waste any time reading the messages. I needed to call him.

Still not knowing what I was going to tell him and feeling an enormous amount of guilt over choosing to disappear, I dialled.

"Talia? Talia? Is that really you, Talia?"

"Hey, Brad. I'm really sorry. Yes, it's me."

"Fuck sorry. Are you okay? Where are you? I've been worried sick about you," he blurted as he burst into tears.

I could feel myself choking up at the sound of his sobs. "I'm still in China. I spent the last few months in a monastery learning various martial arts styles while I was trying to heal my heart."

"I fucking hate him for what he did to you. I've been sick with worry. I only got back from China yesterday. I spent weeks putting up missing person posters, registering you with the local enforcement agencies."

My heart sank. I felt ashamed of my selfish behaviour. "I don't know what to say except I'm so sorry, Brad. I had no idea you were freaking out. You shouldn't have worried. You know I can take care of myself."

"We all need help, Talia, even you. When I finally got through to that cocksucking piece of scum and he told me what had happened, I was a mess. I can't even begin to imagine how you felt. I know you really loved him. The thought of what he did to you just wrecked me."

"There's something I need to tell you …"

It took a little over four hours to recount the details blow by blow. Brad struggled to accept what I was saying and fought with fervour against the possibility of Bodhi and I being reunited. I understood where he was coming from but continued to work with him until he came to terms with my truth. I loved Bodhi and nothing was going to stop me from being with him. If it was in my power to influence, I would. He was my one true love.

Post the call, I sat on my bed emotionally depleted from having to recount the experience. Reciting the ordeal sounded surreal even to me. I felt compelled to remove all evidence of the past. Text by text I painstakingly read through the messages, followed by 'delete'. At first, every time I cleared a message, another would come through. I started to believe I would never reach the end. Determined to get the job done, I managed to clear my inbox by 5 am. My eyes felt like sandpaper and I was consumed by sadness. I missed Bodhi and ached for him to be near.

I woke to the sound of a text coming through. My heart thumped. This one had to be from Bodhi. I nervously flipped open the screen.

"Contact your local service provider for hot new deals 1800 service."

My heart sank. I was ready to burst into tears. What if he never receives the letter? Should I go back to the US? Grandma Li had said not to go to him; he 'had' to contact me. Fuck, waiting for a call that may never come is nothing short of torture. I was so frustrated in my feelings of longing meshed with interwoven layers of helplessness. I hated waiting. I got up and had a shower to wash the stink off my dehydrated skin. I leaned my head against the cold tiles, allowing myself to release the well of emotions swelling inside my belly. As the water poured down on my body I contributed with tears as I bawled like a child.

As I dressed, I decided I had to get out of the hotel room. I was going stir crazy. I grabbed my wallet and phone, put my shoes on and started to head out the door when I saw I had a new message. I took a deep breath and clicked the 'open' button.

"Talia, it's Bodhi. I got your letter. I know you probably hate me right now and you have every right to, but I need to speak with you. It's important. Please I'm hoping to God you are still in China. I'm here. If you're still here too, I need you to meet me at Tiananmen Square today at midday. I need to see you. Honestly, Talia, it's important. I know you don't want to hear this right now but I'm saying it anyway: I love you. Bodhi."

My body was shaking as the tears flowed from my eyes once more. I was so relieved to see the message. I felt the weight of the world melting away as I read the words 'I love you' over and over. It had worked; the spell was broken. That psycho bitch would never be able to harm him again.

I looked at my phone and wondered what I should say. I decided to keep it simple and replied: *"Tiananmen Square 12 noon today, okay."*

To kill time, I decided to take a walk around town. I found the square and hovered in its vicinity, anxious as midday drew in on me. I purchased a coffee and sat on a bench to bide my time. It felt as though my life revolved around waiting. The people walking by seemed to be as lost in their thoughts as I was in mine. A little boy caught my attention as he dropped his ice cream and burst into tears. The child's mother swiftly picked him up and gently swung him from side to side. I smiled. Such small events provided momentary trauma in the mind of a fledgling, who knew no worse a tragedy than the loss of his cone.

I went across to the foot of the bridge, which led into the magnificent red building. I thought about the massacre that had taken place there years before when students chose to protest, wanting to promote pro-democracy. This massive space gave the illusion of expanse, openness, but to me it held secrets, the residual essence of many memories of revolt, pain, bloodshed and the tragic wasted loss of life. It was a strange choice to meet here. There were so many other wonderful places to choose from, but here I stood, once again waiting.

As the time approached noon I sent Bodhi a text.

"I'm here near the footbridge to the entrance of the building."

To an observer I looked like anybody else just out for a walk. Inside, my stomach was churning. It was a balance of butterflies and nerves. I had no idea how this would pan out. I was usually intuitive about things, knowing well in advance how life would unfold, but when it came to Bodhi I was flying completely blind. All I knew was this was going to be one of the most significant days of my life.

In an attempt to distract myself I searched the visible expanse of the square and noticed a divine elderly man in beautiful traditional dress approaching. He had an elegant lady beside him, who was also dressed in traditional attire. The people behind followed closely in an orderly queue carrying instruments. I watched as they advanced directly towards me. When they drew nearer I realised they were performers, possibly part of a Chinese traditional theatrical group. Their thickly layered make-up was wonderfully dramatic and hauntingly surreal.

Much to my surprise, they stopped directly in front of me. The lady and old gentleman did a slight bow and then the band members spread out into position. I smiled and kept still, watching and wondering what on earth was going on. In a compulsion, I diverted my eyes to quickly survey the landscape, looking for Bodhi.

He hadn't responded to my text and it was now ten past noon. I was a little annoyed, given his emphasis on this being important. I simply hated waiting and, yes, this was significant, which is precisely why he should have been there on time.

The music started, diverting my attention back to these lovely people. My body instantly responded to the beauty of the sounds resonating from their instruments. The little hairs on the back of my neck stood up as the traditional melodic tune reached my ears and surrounded my core. I watched with a smile of appreciation as the elderly man opened a scroll and spoke in Mandarin with a gentle confident tone. The lady who had been by his side had now stepped closer to me and began to translate.

"My love, I search for you, once again travelling through space and time to find my elusive other. I am not whole without you as I know you are not whole without me. We are yin and yang. You are the light to my dark. We are interchangeable, complete together and no one can understand the 'we' between you and me.

"Our love is set to be boundless, limitless and worthy beyond compare. I am yours. You are mine. I am no one if I cannot be allowed to be within your arms. I want for nothing more than all you have to offer. I, in turn, give you my world. Our hearts are synchronised to beat as one; our souls emerge to be fused to dance for all of eternity. I will fight an endless battle to be proven worthy to stand by your side once more. Neither the devil nor the wrath of the gods could deter me from what I know is real. My love for you is pure and true.

"How can I go on feeling less than whole? The day you departed you took my soul. I am empty, hungry for images of your smile, the sound of your laughter and the touch of your

soft lips against mine. No one and nothing can replace such beauty to my eyes.

"Would you have me stand here in the wake of the reality that I am your humble slave? You have mastered my heart as it only beats for you. I succumb to all that you wish of me, from me, to me; do as you will. Anything you want that I can offer is already yours for the taking.

"Love me like no other. Be my best friend, my soothsayer, my lover. My life is presented before you as yours to do with as you will. I am in love with you and cannot bear another moment to pass without knowing you still love me too. I feel as though I am a grain of sand in an ocean of rocks that has found, against all odds, a place where I hold purpose and union. You are my home.

"Intertwine your desires, hopes and dreams with mine and we shall rise above the visible skies to create a spectacular display of enigmatic proportions. Our love is beyond the comprehension of the gods. We are unmatched in our loves purity and will be the envy of all who dare to take witness. Choose to release thy love once again without reserve to be mine and I shall forever more be thine.

"I love you, Talia Jacobs; know this to be true – Yours always Bodhi Reynolds.

The music faded into silence as the man rolled up the scroll and passed it to me. I accepted it and did a slight bow as thanks. Tears rolled down my cheeks. My heart inconsolably ached once more. Bodhi's words swam through my mind and reopened the pain in my heart that I thought I had shelved forever. The lady who had interpreted tapped me gently on the shoulder and pointed. Through glistening eyes I looked in the direction indicated and saw Bodhi approaching.

The theatre group quietly returned the way they had

come. As their figures grew smaller with distance, Bodhi became larger than life standing before me.

"Hey," was all I could think of to say.

He reached across and wiped a falling tear from my eye with his thumb and then placed it in his mouth. "Salty," he said with a half smile.

I was so moved by what he had written that I remained speechless and could only focus on staring into his beautiful eyes. Finally having Bodhi present was silently overwhelming me. It felt like a dream and if it was I never wanted to wake up again.

As he stepped into my personal space he grabbed my face with his hands and stared right back into my eyes. "I'm sorry. I don't know what happened to me. It was like I was possessed. All those things I said to you spewing out of my mouth like poison. I don't know where it came from. Inside I was screaming, writhing in pain, trying to free the truth of what I was feeling, but for some reason I just couldn't stop. You have no idea what it was like to be forced to watch you walk away and not have the ability to move my legs. I wanted to chase after you, to tell you I had a lapse of sanity, but I just couldn't." Bodhi paused for a moment, closing his eyes to fight back the tears. "Talia, I can't offer you an explanation and don't want to create excuses. All I know is when I had to watch you walk away armoured with the pain I had caused, a part of me instantly died inside. The longer you were lost to me the more I felt I was losing myself. I became a shell of a man. I had to fight to breathe because I simply didn't want to. In your absence I started to think I was losing my mind. I would have these dreams where I was a puppet on a string and someone else had the controls. I could hear their laughter in the darkness but never saw who the puppet master was manipulating my strings. I would wake up in a pool of sweat, manically patting down my body to see if I was attached to anything. The dreams felt so real. It was horrible. I know this is all too hard to believe. I couldn't believe it and it was happening to me. Then one day I received your letter. I read it over and over to feel you near. I cried hysterically like a fool. It was the first time my mind and body complied with what I wanted. The next day I woke early and knew something had shifted within me. I was different. Whatever had plagued me before was gone. Just like that. It was the strangest experience of my life. The fog had lifted from my brain and I was able to be me again."

I remained silent, caught up in my thoughts about what had transpired. My poor Bodhi had been through so much. The images of him in the straightjacket trapped in the dank alley were still visually present in my thoughts. The truth behind the whole experience could never be revealed to him in case he became consumed by emotions of betrayal against Lex. It would place him at risk, as there was a possibility she could feed off his anger to weaken the binding incantation placed on her. This was a cross of knowledge I would have to bear. Brad knew the whole story, but I trusted he would respect my wishes for silence on the matter.

"Talia, say something … Please?"

Bodhi found he couldn't wait for my response. "It will never happen again – promise. Please forgive me. I can't lose you again."

I took a deep breath and released it. "It's okay, Bodhi. I believe you."

He immediately leapt forward and embraced me. I leaned my head on his chest to listen to his heartbeat.

I was so implicitly sad. I found myself mourning for the time we had lost that could never be recovered. All the hurt from what we had experienced could never be removed, just accepted and with the will of the gods one day released. I knew none of this was his fault, but it didn't stop the pain of his harsh words, the rejection feeling real. I closed my eyes and focused on harnessing the energy of our love for one another.

"Don't let go of me, Talia, I need you to hold me, please," he whispered through my hair into my ear.

I didn't move. I continued to listen to his heartbeat.

"I'm so sorry. I fucked up. I'll never forgive myself and will spend the rest of my days trying to make it up to you. I never want to let you go. I want to hold you in my arms always."

Tears streamed down his cheeks, matched by my own. I released a loud howl of anguish as my body shook with my cries. He wrapped his arms tighter around me and wept heavily too. I was limp, filled with a thousand unspoken sorrows. Flashes of the saddest moments of my life swam before my eyes, forcing the intensity of my pain to be released through tears as I gasped for air.

Between gasps, as my body heaved for air, I managed to mutter, "I love you."

Bodhi's hand held my head as he pressed it firmly against his chest, rocking me gently from side to side. "Thank you, baby. I'll do anything to make this right again. I know I hurt you. I'll never forgive myself. I swear; I love you more than anything. Just stay with me forever."

I continued to cry as I thought about the mother picking up the child who had dropped his ice cream cone. There was comfort in being encased in Bodhi's arms while being nurtured. It almost felt as though I was in a cocoon once more. Safe, being loved and, most importantly, allowed time to process my flood of emotions.

I eventually calmed down. My eyes were swollen and my head hurt. I needed to lie down. This was all too much for me to process. Nothing could have prepared me for seeing Bodhi again, let alone that I would be standing there wrapped within his masculine arms. I didn't want to move but knew I had to. We couldn't stand like this forever and the square was becoming crowded. I needed to rest and have some time to process everything.

I slowly lifted my head to look at him. "I need to lie down. I'm going back to my hotel."

"Can I come with you? I don't want to leave you, not like this. I don't plan on ever leaving your side again."

"Yes." I intertwined my fingers with his and started to walk back to the hotel.

The presence of our looming sadness must have been felt as I noticed people stared at us as we passed. My eyes were visibly swollen and red, my posture slumped. I must have looked a treat.

When we arrived at the hotel room, I looked at him and smiled as I opened the door, while releasing his hand so I could go to the bathroom. Closing the bathroom door without saying a word, I sat on the toilet and cried. I thought I had finished with all the sorrow but realised that I hadn't truly begun. I needed the space to try and release it all. I wasn't going to be able to reconnect with Bodhi unless I let go of how I was feeling, and this seemed to be the only way I knew how to do this.

After a while Bodhi knocked on the door and entered. My body was folded over with my hands covering my face, still manically sobbing. Quietly he knelt before me, shifted my rigid hands to encircle his neck, before picking me up and carrying me to the bed. As he gently placed me down, he positioned himself beside me and partially lifted my torso so I was across his body with my head once again resting on his chest. He stroked my hair as he listened to me cry until I drifted off to sleep, beat from emotional exhaustion.

I woke a few hours later to his snoring. My arms had pins and needles and the room was dark. I had no idea what time it was. I reached across for my mobile and saw a message from Brad.

"Are you ok?"

I replied, *"Yes, sleeping. Bodhi is here. Thank you … I will call you later."*

It was 5 am. I quietly moved off the bed and headed for the shower. I had been sweating overnight so I stunk to high heaven. I peeled off my clothes and stood under the warm water. I had no more tears left in me to shed. I was exhausted and feeling a depth of sadness greater than I had ever felt in my life.

I dried myself off and wrapped my body in the hotel robe. I towel-dried my hair and then went to dress in some fresh clothes. As I was putting them on, Bodhi stirred. He rolled over, stretching out his arms.

"What time is it?" he whispered.

"It's about 5:30," I replied.

"Come back to bed." He gestured with his finger.

I looked at him as I pulled on my T-shirt. "Okay. One sec. I just want to get a drink of water."

I walked back into the bathroom and poured a glass from the tap, drinking it all down. When I went back into the room he was holding up the blanket for me to crawl in, so I did. He wrapped it around me as I snuggled close and then placed his beautiful arms around.

"How are you feeling?" he asked, staring into my eyes.

"I'm okay. How are you?"

"I'm better now that we're here together. You have to know how sorry I am." He brushed his nose against mine.

"I know you are. It just hurt. It still hurts."

"I know." He gently kissed me on the lips.

I closed my eyes and leant forward, advancing on his withdrawal, transitioning his consoling kiss into one of passion. He shifted his body so it was half across mine as we continued our lip interlock. I released a small sigh and pushed hard against his mouth. I wanted him to feel my intensity of grief. Tears welled up in my eyes once more. I needed to shift this sombre veil that cloaked my being. I reached across and took off my T-shirt so my bare flesh could be against the warmth of his skin. I ran my hand down his torso and unbuttoned his jeans. He lifted his hips as I slid them down his legs. We shuffled to undress while maintaining eye contact. The moment our clothes were removed Bodhi positioned himself on top of me, parting my legs with his knees, and then entered me slowly. I groaned as I felt his first deep thrust. My hands braced against his shoulders as he rhythmically moved in and out.

I lifted my hips to allow him to plunge deep inside me. His bony hips pushed hard against my inner thighs as he continued to pull in and out. I ached with delight as he tortured my nipples with his tongue. Goose bumps ran up my torso and across my breasts as his cold breath greeted the saliva he had left on the tips of my nipples. I released a long groan as he started to bite my neck and tug at my left earlobe with his lips. Completely turned on, I found myself reaching down to stimulate my throbbing clitoris. I could feel I was getting close as my body stiffened in preparation for an almighty shudder that wracked my body. Electric pulses of pleasure lit my senses up like the fireworks on the eve of a 4th of July celebration. I continued past the first and embraced the delivery of a second more intense orgasm. The delight in the raptures of visceral sensation had my entire body activated in spasm before surrendering back into being soft and limp again. Bodhi quickened his gyrations as he stared into my eyes. When he came, his face contorted as he bit his bottom lip. He lowered his body onto mine, panting.

"That was intense," he whispered.

I didn't respond. I just shifted myself so he was now beside me with his head on my shoulder.

"Are you okay?" he asked.

"Yep, just a little tired. I think I need to sleep some more." I was suddenly consumed with thoughts of Lex. She had been making love to him all these months. I couldn't get images of them exchanging intimate moments from my mind. The concept made me feel ill.

He shifted the blankets and placed them on me, his arm across my torso. "Get some sleep. I'm going to shower. We can go get breakfast after that if you want."

"Okay," I said as I snuggled into the warmth and closed my eyes.

I fell asleep while he showered and dressed, by the time he returned to my side I was snoring. He gently stroked my face until I woke again. I opened my weary eyes and mustered up a half-smile as I looked at him staring at me.

"Are you ready? You need to eat something."

"Okay," I said as I stretched my body and slowly sat up.

He stood and waited by the door. I rose, dressed, ran my fingers through my tousled hair and headed towards him.

As we walked out, he smiled. "We're going to be okay. I know it's been a rough few months, but I'm never going to leave you again."

I nodded and grabbed his hand, squeezing it to acknowledge his words. There was a part of me that wanted to explain what really happened. Give him a full appreciation of the impact this experience had on me. I knew my silence was the only option. The secrets must find a home within my mind, never to surface, for the cost of risking otherwise was too high for all involved. I had to let it go.

The hotel had a scrumptious assortment of breakfast options. I selected poached eggs on toast and Bodhi ordered the full hot breakfast. We sat and slowly ate the food while watching the people outside scurrying to work.

"It's nice not to have any plans," I said.

"Yes, well we do need to get back home at some point soon, yes?" asked Bodhi.

"Yes, I guess we do need to get back."

That afternoon we made love in the park. We had found a spot near a manmade lake surrounded by reeds. He laid his jacket down and gently placed me on it. I stared up at the cerulean skies as he positioned himself on top of me. I loved feeling his body press against mine. I was never going to tire of his eyes gazing with longing expectation.

Later that evening, we organised our flight out for the next day and packed our bags. It was time to go home.

Reunited Souls

My apartment smelt of stale air and a layer of dust coated everything in sight, but it was good to be home again. I was exhausted, emotionally and physically. Bodhi headed straight to his apartment from the airport so I had some time to gather my thoughts and relax. I decided to call Brad. I needed to hear his voice.

"Hey, you, how are things?" I asked doing my best to sound upbeat.

"Thank God you're alright. How are you? What happened between you and Bodhi?" asked Brad in a chirpy voice. I was expecting him to still be pissed.

"I'm doing okay. Bodhi and I are going to be fine. It was tough seeing him again. All the pain resurfaced and it just wrecked me. The way he explained his version of the experience only added to my anguish in regards to the whole debacle."

"I've spent some time thinking about everything that you told me. It's so bizarre that it's hard to believe but in saying this and knowing it was you who told me I decided it must be true. I even did some research on the Internet. There's some seriously crazy shit happening out there. I've actually shifted to feeling sorry for the guy. I think if I was in his shoes I would want to know the whole truth about what happened. I know you told me the reasons why he can't ever know, but Jesus. If you don't tell him he's always going to blame himself when none of it was really his fault."

"I know. I'm just scared that knowing will make him bitter and angry. I thought maybe if he didn't know and we had a happy life together he would become at peace with it. It's not the easiest pill to swallow."

"Yeah, I hear you. I don't know, Tals. You'll have to go with your instinct on this one."

"I'm leaning towards not telling him. It must remain our secret. Please don't give me reason to regret my trust. Tell me you haven't spoken about it with anyone?"

"Just Suzanna. Sorry, I had to explain why I was so manic. She pulled out all the stops to get you on the missing persons' list and allowed me to go to China to look for you. Telling her was the right thing to do."

"Jesus, Bodhi, really? What was her reaction?"

"Surprisingly, she thought it all made sense. She's never experienced anything esoteric but she believes it exists, so from her perspective the truth provided her with relief."

"Wow, I never saw that coming. Like I've always said, she's a real catch. How are you both going?" Inside I was feeling disappointed that he had gone against my wishes. It was a sign that I could no longer trust him with my secrets he once craved to know. I understood his reasons for deviation but he did this naively, unaware of the potential true cost of such knowledge being released in Chinese whispers. I should have known better. This one was on me.

"Stronger than ever. We are so in love. She's amazing."

I was genuinely relieved for them. "I'm so happy for you, Brad. You deserve the best and you got it."

The tone in his voice changed. "You have to promise me you won't ever do anything like that again. I'm not sure I could cope. Seriously, I was out of my mind with worry. It nearly destroyed me. I need to know that you'll talk to me, tell me what's happening, let me help you."

I closed my eyes and I leaned into the phone. "I know. I'm really sorry. I never meant to have this affect you guys. It caught me off guard and I found myself so empty inside I was fighting to breathe. I didn't know how to process the enormity of pain so my only solution was to disconnect. I was completely lost. You can't imagine the shock I felt from being on cloud nine to complete emptiness. Within the single beat of a heart my perspective on love had shifted from its endless potential to nothing. I honestly felt like I had died and I guess emotionally I allowed myself to."

"If he spoke to you the way he spoke to me on the phone, all cold and distant, I probably would have punched his lights out. I understand why you reacted the way you did. I do. I just don't want you to do that anymore."

"I hope to hell nothing like this ever does happen again, but if it does I promise I will do my best not to shut down again."

"Thank you. Okay, don't make it too long before you come home. We've forgotten what you look like," he said as he released a hearty laugh.

I smiled; it was nice to hear him laugh.

"I'll aim come home in the next couple of months. I just want to settle in here first and then I'II be ready to roam again. Promise."

"Okay, I'll let the others know you're back from your travels. I love you, crazy girl."

"I love you too."

I felt a little sad when the call ended. I was homesick and missed them all. I wanted the kids to jump on me again. They would have all grown so much by now.

Keys rustled in my door and my beautiful man entered.

"Hey," he said as he leaned in to kiss me.

"I wasn't expecting you to come over so soon."

"I know. I missed you so I grabbed some things to stay overnight. I hope that's okay with you."

"Sure, of course it is. This place is a bit of a dust bowl. I thought I might give it a clean-up."

"Cool. I'll give you a hand."

"Nope – I want to potter so you settle in and find something else to do, okay?"

He looked at me with a wicked smile. "The only other thing I had plans for involved you. Do you have a maid's outfit handy that you could wear while dusting?"

I laughed as I swanked my way into the kitchen to fetch a duster. "You wish."

He sighed. "Yes, I do."

When I returned he was already settled on the couch with a blanket across his lap and his laptop on the coffee table. I made him a piping hot cup of tea and started my dusting frenzy. I couldn't believe how much there was to do. Happily lost in my thoughts I stripped all the shelves bare to clean each of the items. It was a rather therapeutic exercise.

"What would you like for dinner?" asked Bodhi, his phone in hand.

"Hmm, dumplings. I would like some Singapore noodles and dumplings."

"Okay, I'm onto it. Do you feel like watching a movie tonight?"

"Sure, pick one from the shelf. Your choice; I've already seen them all."

I pulled out the vacuum cleaner to give the floor a once-over and then jumped into the shower. I was covered in a thick layer of dust and my left nostril was blocked with muck. It had been a lukewarm day outside so the apartment was the perfect temperature for me to wear a light summer frock. I felt whimsical wearing it and decided to put my hair in pigtail braids while it was still wet so that when I released my hair in the morning it would hold a nice crinkled wave. I looked like an overgrown child.

Bodhi had set out all the food on the coffee table. He then went into the kitchen to collect plates, cutlery and open a bottle of red wine. While he was busy playing host, I turned out the lights and placed candles everywhere. I had missed my candles. There was something wonderful about getting lost in the flickering luminescence.

"Wow, you look adorable." He lifted my arms to inspect me.

I curtsied and said, "Why thank you, kind sir," in my best southern accent.

Raising an eyebrow, he said suggestively, "You know, we could always skip the movie."

"Nope, I've decided I want to watch *Ever After*. Have you seen it?"

"No."

"Good, it's a beautiful fairy tale. I'm sure you'll love it. It's a must-watch."

"Okay, but I still think my idea is better."

A wicked thought crossed my mind. "I'm thinking my outfit isn't complete. I'll be back in a second." I headed into the bedroom again while Bodhi assumed the position back on the lounge.

When I walked out this time I was wearing make-up, white opaque stockings that finished above the knee in a lace trim and my tan leather boots that ended just below the knee. I slowly walked across to the lounge room and watched Bodhi's jaw drop as he inspected me from the ground up.

"Holy fuck, Talia. You look amazing. Are you trying to kill me?"

"No, just reminding you why you should never leave," I said with a cheeky grin.

After switching on the TV I slowly bent down so he could see the outline of my lace knickers cupping the edge of my arse. I placed the DVD into the player and then settled down on the floor with my back against the couch. I knew he was watching in silent awe.

Bodhi sat up, placing one leg either side of me.

I pressed 'play' on the remote and reached for the food. "Let's eat. I'm starved."

We both filled our plates and consumed our meal while watching Drew Barrymore play Cinderella. I loved this story. The way Leonardo da Vinci was depicted was divine. It made me want to believe in fairy tales.

I pushed the last of the food on my plate away and leant back against the couch again. Patting my tummy, I took another sip of shiraz. "I'm stuffed. I could curl up and go to sleep now."

Bodhi leant across, placing his empty plate on the table, took a sip of his wine, returning the glass back to the coffee table before resting both his hands on my shoulders. He started to give me a neck rub. I was tense and could feel his nimble fingers pressing against the prominent knots under the surface of my skin. I sighed as the tension started to ease. I leant my head back to look up at him and he greeted me with a gentle kiss. I could taste the remnants of dinner on his lips.

His face was serious as he delicately ran his right hand down my chest, pressed against my full tummy and then nestled his fingers between my legs. Bodhi placed his index finger under my lace stocking, touching the inside of my thigh. He held his gaze as I opened my legs slightly in gesture for him to proceed. Shifting his hand sideways he delicately glided up the length of my milky white thigh before positioning his hand so he could burrow his fingers underneath my lace knickers.

I exhaled, whimpering, "Kiss me."

He tilted his head slightly and placed his lips hard on mine as he inserted a finger. I arched my hips forward so he had more access to plunge deeper. I could feel a surge of heat rise from my loins to my face, making me flush with desire. I ran my hand down the length of his arm and pushed his hand with mine to guide his intentions. He used his other hand to masterfully knead my breast and pull at my nipple. All the while I was wriggling as his thumb started to massage my inflamed clitoris.

"You don't play fair," I whispered into his mouth as he continued to kiss me.

He shifted his head to suck on my neck and the edge of my ear lobe. "Neither do you."

The intensity was overwhelming. I adjusted my body so I was on my knees facing him, looked into his eyes as I unzipped his pants. I stood up, allowing him access to slip my knickers off. As I stepped out of them he parted my vaginal lips to expose my clitoris. Using his tongue he plunged deep into the crevice and back out again. His hands held my hips as he rocked me back and forth. Electric pulses of pleasure shuddered through my core with each lashing. I was so worked up I could feel the beads of sweat dripping down my spine. He knew precisely where to place his magic tongue. The depth of his strokes sent me into raptures of pleasure.

I climaxed, my head swung back, thrusting hard against his face, screaming, "Oh, God, yes, just there. Just there, don't stop. Fuck. Just … oh … don't … stop …"

His hands stilled my hips as I quivered. Bodhi continued to relentlessly massage my clitoris long after I had come. His eyes were closed and his face was soaked. I could see he was in a frenzy, wanting more. Shifting his hands, I leant down to lick his lips. I loved tasting me on him. Slowly he reinserted a finger inside me as I groaned and then teasingly placed it in my mouth, watching with excitement as I gently sucked on it like a lollipop, playfully rolling my tongue around.

Pulling down his jeans, I tossed them across the room. His erection jutted from his Y-fronts, commanding my attention. I shifted the soaked fabric down to unleash his manhood and positioned myself on top as he braced his arms around my torso. Gently I hovered over his penis so it was just above the entrance to my vagina. As I kissed him I lowered myself onto the tip of his cock and then lifted to release him again. On my third attempt Bodhi tightened his grip like a vice and without warning lifted his hips to thrust the length of his hard shaft deep within me. I released a yelp as he continued to guide my torso down onto him as he simultaneously pushed up to meet me halfway.

Consumed by the fire roaring in my belly, with eyes closed, I called out, "Come inside me; fuck me hard."

He grunted and released an elongated moan as he continued to push my torso down to greet his hips thrusts. Resistance was futile; I had to succumb to the rhythm of his compulsion. My lower body ached with expectation as I felt myself building towards another orgasm. I placed my hands on his face and stared into his eyes. He quickened the pace and arched his back to deepen his access into my dripping pool of delight. I squealed as the rush of familiar warmth overtook my body. Shivering from the electric pulses shuddering through my core, I threw my head back, releasing a series of blissful groans. Bodhi leaned his face onto my torso as he shifted into a position that allowed him to thrust quicker. I could feel his breath change, he started to pant heavily and then came inside me. He grunted as he held my body down so his shaft was fully enveloped. I gently rock back and forth to feel his cock press against my vaginal walls. He yelped as he used his hands to still my movement. Leaning across, I placed my head on his shoulder to rest, savouring the blissful moment.

"That was out of this world," I said, releasing a loud sigh.

"You made me so fucking crazy. I thought I was going to blow after the first three pumps. Fuck."

I laughed as I slid off him to sit on the edge of the couch. "Guess now I know the secret. Stockings and boots," I said, reaching down to unzip my shoes.

"No, you're my weakness. You drive me insane. The way you smell, the way you look at me, the way you walk, talk – and don't get me started on the way you taste. It's everything about you, Talia. You make me want to fuck you senseless all the time. I've never experienced that before. It's amazing. You leave me speechless every time."

I smiled as I touched the side of his face. "You were naughty. You didn't wear any protection."

He shifted to pull his underpants back up. "I know and that 'come inside me' line drove me into a fucking frenzy."

I leant across and kissed his swollen red lips. "That's why I said it."

"You're wicked."

"Yes, that I am," I said, feeling very smug.

That evening we slept like babies. I didn't stir once. When I woke the room was so dark for a moment I thought I was back in my cocoon room in China. The thought immediately brought me a sense of comfort. There was something wonderful about feeling contained, safe in a space of no expectations.

I was looking forward to heading into the office later that morning. It had been too long since I had seen the crew. I jumped into the shower and got dressed. Bodhi was still fast asleep when I leaned across to kiss him on the forehead. He clumsily reached out, grabbing me, and threw me on the bed.

Laughing, I whispered, "I'm going to head into work."

"No," he said, nestling his face into my chest.

"You need to get up and go to work too, don't you?" I enquired.

"I don't want to leave you. I don't want to share you with anyone. You're mine," he replied in the cutest voice.

I kissed the top of his head. "Yes, I'm yours and you're mine."

He squeezed me tight.

"I'm going. I'll see you tonight. Do you want me to come and stay at yours?"

"No, I want to stay here again. I like it here better."

"Really? How come? Your place is so much bigger and the lighting is spectacular."

"Yep, but your place has character, warmth and smells of you. I sleep better here than I do at mine."

I thought about this for a moment and realised it was more likely because he and Lex had been living there together. The residual memories were still too fresh for him to deal with. I could understand that. "Okay, I'll see you tonight." I attempted to shuffle off the bed but Bodhi was still holding me tight.

"Nope, I'm serious; I'm not letting you go. I don't want to share you with anyone."

I laughed as I resigned myself to staying a little while longer.

"Is there anyone in particular you're worried about or is it the general populous?"

"I'm suspicious of Michael. I think he likes you," said Bodhi in a muffled voice.

"No, he's gay. I know he loves his job and likes me as a person, but that's it. He's more inclined to be crushing on you than me."

Bodhi lifted his head so I could see his face. "No, I'm sure he has a thing for you. Gay or not, he's crushing on you in a big way."

I laughed and kissed Bodh's perfect soft lips. "Whatever, it doesn't matter. It's how I feel that counts and I only have eyes for you."

"I know," said Bodhi unconvincingly.

"Do you feel better?" I asked.

"No, not really. The thought of you sharing time with anyone is driving me a little crazy. I want you all to myself. If I could lock us in this room forever I would do it in a heartbeat. You have no idea what I went through during the last three months. I never want to be without you ever again."

I shifted my body so mine was flush against his. "I know," I whispered. "You just have to ensure you never ask me to leave again and I promise I never will. If you push me away I will feel unwanted and always comply with your wishes. Love and be loved is the only way I'll ever allow myself to be present."

"I'd sooner die than ever ask you to leave me. That's what haunts me now. I don't know why I did what I did and I'm petrified that it might happen again. I was not myself," he said.

I gently stroked the back of his head as I listened to him cry. "I know. Shhh, I know."

It was clear that we both still had a journey of healing ahead of us. I knew exactly how he felt. I may not understand his pangs of jealousy, but in my heart I didn't want to leave him either.

Foundation

When I walked into the office all eyes were on me. Michael was in disbelief as he ran up to greet me with a hug.

"We missed you," he whispered.

"I know. I missed you guys too," I said, beaming as I returned his embrace.

"How is everyone?" I asked the team.

"Great," replied Silvia.

The others nodded, smiled and waved as I looked to acknowledge them all. I walked across to Mable's desk noticing it was cleared, instantly a sadness wash over me. I touched the desk with my left hand and wondered.

"Excellent, I'm glad all is well. I guess it's time for me to get back to work. Michael, come and give me an update on what's been happening."

"Okay," he said with a skip in his step as he followed me to my office.

I sat in my chair and switched on my PC. I didn't forget the password this time. I had made it easy to remember. "BillyBooXXX." It's the pet name I had given Bodhi. Billy because that's what people called him, and

Boo because he is my bootiful boyfriend. The triple X represented the dirty thoughts I constantly had about him.

"So what's up, Doc?" I asked.

Michael sat in the chair and folded his arms. "Where have you been?"

"Ah, I was in China training in martial arts at a monastery."

"Wow, really? No wonder we couldn't find you. You look amazing, by the way."

"Thanks, you tried to find me? Why?" I said, suspecting I knew the answer.

"We were worried about you. I know you like to travel and disappear but this was different. You didn't say goodbye. Your brother Brad kept calling looking for you. We got in touch with Bodhi and he told us you two had broken up." Michael dropped his head and played with his hands.

I could see that he had been genuinely worried.

I cringed at the thought of everyone knowing my personal affairs. "Yeah, I didn't say goodbye to anyone, not even my family. Bodhi and I had a huge fight and broke it off. I was completely lost so I disappeared. I needed to find myself. I'm sorry if I made you worry."

"It's okay; I understand. I would have lost my mind if that had happened to me. I could tell that you really loved him. I hate going through break-ups. It feels like you're dying a slow emotional death. How are you now?"

"Great. Bodhi and I are back on track. Everything is as it should be."

Michael's expression shifted to surprise as he clapped his hands in delight. "Oh, thank god for that. You two are made for each other. I swear I have never seen a more perfect match."

I smiled at his words. We were made for each other.

"So what's been happening that I need to know about?" Still awaiting the news about Mable.

Once again an expression of worry washed over his features. I watched as he shifted his hands to his lap and clasped them together tight, leaving his knuckles white. "The good news is Mila finished the autobiography and the book titled *Walter and Mable Philosophies of Life and Love* hit the shelves three weeks ago. It's been in the top-ten bestsellers' list for the last two weeks."

"Really? I was supposed to proofread it before it went to print. It's already on the top ten sellers' list? Wow, how good is that? Awesome! Get me a copy; I want to read it. Where is Mable? I noticed her desk was cleared."

He looked down at his hands. "Um, that's the bad news. She passed away in her sleep a week ago. We had the funeral yesterday. We found a letter addressed to you on her desk. It's there, near your keyboard."

My heart sank. "How did she pass? Was she with someone? She wasn't alone, was she?"

"I was supposed to take her out for breakfast that morning. I went to her place. When she didn't answer, I got the building manager who lives next door to give me access to her apartment. She looked like she was sleeping. I panicked when I realised she was dead. It was like I had lost a family member." Michael paused as he started to shake and cry. "She was family to me. I loved her."

I walked across and gave him a consoling cuddle. "We all loved her. She was divine."

Michael continued between sobs. "I didn't know what to do so I called Blake and he stepped in to help. Together we organised the funeral, charging everything to the company. I thought you would want to pay for it. I hope that's okay."

"Of course, I'm glad you did. Do you want to make arrangements for grief counselling? Anyone from the team is welcome to use the services. It's important we embrace the beauty of knowing her, even if it was for shorter than we desired."

"No, I think we'll all be okay. I miss her. She was such a delight in my day."

I could see by his demeanour that he was regaining his composure. "Alright, ask the team in case there's someone that feels the need to talk to a counsellor. If there isn't anything else, I really want to read this letter. I'll chat to you later."

"Nope, that's it for now." Michael stood and walked out the door, closing it behind him.

I walked back over to my desk and picked up the letter to open it as I whispered, "Ah, sweet Mable. I'm so sorry I missed being with you on your deathbed." There, in her perfect olden-style handwriting, was her final message to me.

To my angel Talia,

I have no idea where you have gone but know that my heart and thoughts travel with you. In all my time I had never dreamed of being shown the kindness that you have bestowed upon me over the past few months. I believed that my sole purpose was to live my remaining days aching for the love I had lost. You showed me my time could be utilised to remember what Walter and I had shared. You helped me to once again relive the treasured times we shared along with the words of dear Walter's wisdom. For this alone I shall remain forever grateful.

The book is complete. Mila did a splendid job of capturing the essence of our lives. I am so proud that I beam with joy each day, knowing it may help others to seek and share their own divinity with one another. I couldn't have done this without you. You believed in me and I want to tell you here that I believe in the significance of you too.

I often wonder what it would have been like to live your life instead of mine. I cannot imagine living my whole life believing that I was destined not to locate my partner to share it with. I am talking about that deep profound connection that we all secretly crave and a lucky few receive. I saw a change in you when you were reunited with Bodhi. He was able to reach out and touch your heart effortlessly like no other. You understood his language and he yours. You felt the warmth of his intentions and instantly knew no harm would come in the space you both created for one another.

All that once seemed impossible became possible just by knowing he existed. I could see you wanted to be with him, to share everything, leaving no stone unturned. You stood before him emotionally naked with no expectation or judgement. It reminded me of how I felt when I met my Walter.

Bodhi is your other. He is connected to you. His gossamer binds are intertwined in the fabric of your being. He could want for no more than all that you have to offer and in return he will provide the same. I could feel the importance of your union.

It's with certainty in my heart that I know you will walk the same path of mutual desires and exchange the intensity of your divine love. He will want to create a life with you, for you. I know that you are hurting right now and believe that all is lost. I don't know why you broke up, but I just know that this is not the end for you two. You have to have faith and believe.

Bodhi is yours in totality and you are his. I hope that

you can see this and know that it forms part of your life's purpose. It is only a matter of time before all eyes will witness what mine have been blessed to see. Your embrace will synchronise your hearts to a rhythm that will carve a new future together.

Never doubt this: he loves you. If I am right in saying that you love him too, then don't give up on love. Fight for what you deserve and reclaim your destiny. Thank you for being my friend. Dare I say that you are the daughter I would have been proud to call my own. I will be endlessly indebted to you for awakening my vigour for life.

Always. - Mable

I read the words over and over as the tears streamed from my eyes. The words were written with passion and eloquently placed her thoughts into my heart. I felt incredibly blessed to have been a small part of Mable's life. I was going to miss her greatly. She had brought out the best in us all.

I wiped the tears as I walked out my office to see the team. "Guys, go have a long lunch on me. Celebrate Mable's life and exchange stories with one another about how she made an impact on yours. Lest we forget the multitude of gifts she bestowed on us all."

The team nodded and organised to go to the local watering hole. I wanted to read Mable's book, so I stayed behind with the copy Michael had obtained for me. Once they had gone, I made myself a cup of tea and settled in to read. The cover was perfect. It showed her hat sporting a lovely weeping orange gerbera. I was surprised to see that it contained over three hundred pages. She clearly had a lot to say. I smiled as I read the dedication.

For my love, to my love, the memories of your words of

wisdom are contained within the pages of this book that represents a window into the lives of two soul mates who, against the odds, found one another and had the fortitude to embrace what eludes many. I will love you from this life till the next and beyond. Eternally yours – Mable.

I thumbed through the pages, reading snippets of their life story. I was delighted to see some of her old photographs were in there too. Mila had really outdone herself. The book was wonderful. What an amazing legacy to a life that had been.

I was interrupted by a text on my phone.

"Lunch? Nowish?"

"Sure, meet you in ten. My office?"

I had been so distracted that I had forgotten about how I had left Bodhi that morning. He had fallen asleep and so I had taken the opportunity to sneak out, leaving him a note to reassure him of my love. I hoped this was enough to make him feel a little better. I wanted him to be secure, but I understood that my propensity to place myself in a form of exile had instilled a very real fear in him that I would need to allay somehow.

Bodhi entered within five minutes of receiving my text. His face beamed as he walked into my office.

"You look awfully chipper."

"Yes, I just closed a really big deal that will take me to the next level. It's the one I thought I had lost when I was in Australia with you."

"Wow, congrats. What does this mean?"

"Well, longer hours, more travel and, from what I can glean from the contracts, about a thousand new bands to sign up, which means the promotions and tours will go into overdrive."

I stood up and gave him a cuddle. "That all sounds

amazing and very draining. Are you going to be okay managing all this?"

"Nope. I told you: my priority is you now. I'm going to open some positions so that it doesn't all fall on me."

"Are you sure? You don't seem like the type who easily gives up the controls. I need you to be happy. We don't work if you're not happy." I stared into his eyes.

"I need to be happy, yes. I'm happiest when I'm with you. I meant every word I said this morning. I want to be with you always."

"Think about it first before you change anything."

"Nope. I'm sure. It's you and me all the way, babe. I want to create a life with you. I want to marry you, have children. We can live wherever you want. I don't care so long as I wake up beside you."

I kissed him on the lips and pressed my forehead against his. "The idea of children scares me."

"I know, baby, but we can work through those fears together when you're ready. I really want to have a family with you. I want a little girl and, God willing, a little boy too."

I laughed nervously as I grabbed my purse to head out the door.

"Where is everyone?" asked Bodhi, looking around the deserted expanse of the outer office.

"I sent them to the pub. Mable passed away. Her funeral was yesterday. I wanted to give them some time out to celebrate her life. She was an amazing individual. She left a profound mark on us all."

"Talia, I'm so sorry. She did seem like a darling," he said, pouting his lip.

"Don't be sorry. She lived a great life and left a wonderful legacy in the autobiography she published.

Her memories will live on for all to see. I'm led to believe that she passed in her sleep. It's a perfect end really."

Bodhi reached across and held my hand as we left the building. It was a mild day with not too many people roaming about. We settled on a sandwich bar down an alley. Bodhi ordered the triple-stack BLT and I grabbed a salad roll. I couldn't believe my eyes when his meal came out. It was like the leaning tower of Pisa. The amount of oil dripping from the sides made my blood coagulate.

"Really? You're going to eat that?"

"Yep, every last bit." He licked the oil that had dripped onto his hands.

"Good luck."

"Thanks. This is going to get ugly."

"Indeed it will," I said with a chuckle.

"I have a client's launch party tonight that I need to front. Do you want to come with me?" asked Bodhi, chewing with his mouth open.

"Depends. Who is it?"

"He calls himself the Big C. The party is at his warehouse across town. I need to go but I won't stay long. Come with me, please?" He pouted as tomato sauce dripped from the side of his mouth.

"Okay, but I really don't want to stay long. I'm still a little jetlagged."

"I know. I don't plan to be there long either."

That evening Bodhi arrived in a cab. I had decided to make my eyes look smoky to match my steel-grey satin halter-neck backless dress that clung to my form. His jaw dropped when I walked towards him.

As he opened the cab door for me he mouthed, *Wow.*

"Thanks, I thought I might need to make an

impression with Big C tonight," I said with a cheeky grin.

"I'm sure you'll leave quite an impression on him and everyone else there tonight. OMG! Look at you, Talia. Seriously, you're going to be the death of me, girl."

I placed his hand on my knee as I whispered, "Satin."

Bodhi's leg started to jiggle as he bit his bottom lip and stared at his hand touching my leg. Using my index finger, I traced the outline of his hand and ran it slowly up and down his arm, while he silently maintained his gaze.

When we arrived at the venue a bellhop greeted us. The building was a converted warehouse that had an art deco feel to the interior design. It was out of place for the neighbourhood, which was dominated by old Victorian double-fronted terraces.

"Excuse me, I heard this building has a VIP elevator. Can you show us where it is?"

With a glint in his eye the bellhop pointed to double doors just inside the entrance. He pressed a button, opening the doors to reveal the opulent décor of a purple room with a velvet upholstered day bed. The walls consisted of smoky glass reflective mirrors.

As we entered, the bellhop gave me a wink and said, "Enjoy."

The doors closed and a female voice said, "Welcome to the VIP fuckervater. You have thirty minutes to complete your mission. Pants down, please. Time to get it up."

Bodhi held eyes of astonishment as he looked around the elevator. The mirrors changed to screens displaying various porn scenes. The music playing was called *Pony* and it repeated the words you can ride it, get on it over and over. His hands were now on my hips.

"I guess we have thirty dirty minutes to kill. Whatever could we do?" I said in my sweetest innocent voice.

Bodhi leant in and kissed me, pushing me gently against the left side wall. I ran my hands down the length of his spine, using my nails to scratch him. I knew all about this elevator. I had googled Big C and this building had come up in a feature article about this quaint little room of lust. It was one of the reasons I had dolled myself up. It's not every day a girl gets to seduce her man in a fuckervater.

I turned to face the wall. Bracing my hands on the railing I teasingly bent over and positioned my legs slightly apart. Through my satin dress, Bodhi ran his hand up my thigh and massaged the outline of my perfect peach-shaped arse. I could feel him separating my cheeks and then releasing them, trapping the cold satin in the crack of my butt. I bit my bottom lip, arching my back further to pronounce my derrière.

Bodhi shifted my dress to one side to expose me to the elements. He groaned deeply when he realised I was without panties. He ran his hand between my legs and with ease slipped his index finger inside me.

"You're so wet," he whispered.

I pushed hard against his finger as he glided in and out of my hungry vagina. He shifted his position so his other finger could stimulate my clitoris as I continued to sway back and forth to work against his pressure. I wanted Bodhi to lose control tonight. The thought of his arousal made me quiver with expectation. I could feel his engorged penis pressing hard against my thigh. I wanted him inside me. I was burning with desire.

My body was turgid with passion, overwhelmed by the torment of his ever present erection throbbing against my leg. I could no longer hold back the surging waves of pulsating flux that washed over me like waves of electric modality. My bottom lip was now bleeding from me biting it so hard. Bodhi grabbed my hair and reefed my head back, accentuating the arc of my spine. I squealed as I felt myself shudder from the throes of a climax that was to reset the very core of my womanhood to a space beyond reason and satisfaction.

"Fuck me. You have to fuck me now," I said with an exhausted breath.

Bodhi unleashed his cock from his pants and slammed it with missile precision deep inside me. My head almost hit the railing as he repeated his thrusts, alternating between slow and steady and then hard and fast, shifting the pace to align with the release of his groans now freely expressed with each delicious plunge. I found myself compelled to commentate and removed inhibitions so my noises of ecstasy echoed as they bounced off the walls. Heightened to my sensory pleasures, Bodhi was consumed by his need to reach the ultimate release of his sweet juice inside me.

I could feel his knees shake as he attempted to push deeper. There was a gentle breeze from his balls as they slapped against me. I reached down and squeezed them softly, rolling them between my fingers. He screamed as he came to a climax, thrusting short and swift before collapsing his torso onto my back, panting for breath.

"Oh, my God, Talia. Fuck me."

I giggled as I slowly shifted to an upright position. "I believe I just did honey. Does this mean you like the elevator?" I said with a wicked grin.

Bodhi sat on the day bed as he pulled out a hanky to tidy up before adjusting himself and doing up his zipper.

"I'm speechless. You sent me over the edge with your dirty talk."

My face flushed crimson. I had surprised myself with some of the things that had flowed from my mind during our passionate exchange. "What can I say? I felt inspired."

Bodhi reached for my hands and pulled me across to sit beside him. Using his index finger, he moved the strands of hair from my face as he gently sucked on my bleeding bottom lip.

He pouted. "Ouchy?"

"No, it felt kinda nice. I knew I was bleeding but I couldn't stop biting it. I think it increased the intensity of my orgasm."

Bodhi shook his head and smiled. "You never cease to surprise me, Talia Jacobs."

"I'm glad," I said as the elevator doors unexpectedly opened to a sea of watchful eyes.

We both stood up. I readjusted my dress and we walked out hand-in-hand. People clapped, laughed, pointed and patted our backs as we passed by them. I found it rather amusing to know they knew what we had been up to. Bodhi squeezed my hand and led me to the bar. We ordered a couple of dry martinis and headed over to say hello to Big C.

"Hey, you made it." He was dressed in a large fur coat and sporting a purple velour top hat.

"Hey, Big C. This is Talia."

"Mon cheri." He bent down and kissed my hand.

I smiled and did a little curtsey in response.

"So, what do you think of the fuckervater, my man?" he asked Bodhi.

I decided to cut into the conversation. "Why do they call you Big C?"

"I'm a curator, I'm a cultivator, I'm a contributor, I am BIG C. Yo."

"Okay, that seems crystal to me. Bodhi, go ahead and answer Big C's question." I stepped back and sipped my martini, amused.

Bodhi glanced at me and then looked back at Big C, who was waiting for a response. "It was an unforgettable experience."

"The way your fox is looking I bet it was the ride of a lifetime."

"It doesn't get better. I can assure you we're both very satisfied."

"That's good, my man. Enjoy the party, mingle. I'm going to find me a woman to ridddde," he said, pulling a face and executing a pelvic-thrust motion.

We both chuckled as he walked off. "Wow, he has a big personality and don't get me started on his magical dress sense," I said.

"Yeah, he is great at what he does and has a huge following, but he's missing something. I'm not sure what it is yet. When I do I'll fix it and market the shit out of him. He'll make millions."

"You're sexy when you talk business," I said as I played with the buttons on his shirt.

Bodhi pulled me towards him and ground his hips into mine. "Careful, missy. I'm almost ready to take you again."

I bit the bottom of his ear lobe. "You wish." I turned and swanked my way back to the bar for another martini.

I could feel Bodhi's warmth pressing up against me. "Make that two, thanks." Bodhi held up two fingers to the bartender as he whispered, "Did you take your pill this morning?"

I closed my eyes and shook my head. "No, I ran out a few days ago and keep forgetting to fill my script. Bugger." I felt anxious. It hadn't even crossed my mind.

He nuzzled his face into the back of my neck. "So technically we could be pregnant."

I turned to look in his eyes. "Technically, you just made me petrified."

"No, you being pregnant would make me the happiest man in the world. I want to see that belly grow. I want to feel our child kicking. You will make an amazing mum. I promise you."

I turned to get our martinis off the bar. "Here, drink. You're starting to get nesty."

"I have been for a while. I just didn't want to freak you out."

"Okay, so you don't think you're freaking me out now?" I said, nervously laughing.

He smiled as he slapped me on the arse. "Toughen up, princess. You'll survive."

I followed him to the dance floor, where we carved our way closer towards the centre. Hip-hop wasn't my thing to groove to, but Bodhi seemed to have some moves. I shuffled my feet from side to side as he executed his air gyrations, swivels and turns. I enjoyed watching his dance technique unfold into more exaggerated moves. He seemed so lost in the music. It was nice to see him happy.

When we returned to my apartment we both fell into a heap on the bed. It hadn't been a late night, but the extracurricular activities in the fuckervater had taken their toll on us. My back was a little sore from the tension of arching. I curled under the covers and fell asleep almost instantly. There was something comforting about being wrapped up in a blanket and having your head surrounded by feather down pillows.

In the morning I heard Bodhi rustling in the kitchen. I did a massive cat stretch and slinked to his side of the bed to snuggle with his pillow. I could still smell his scent. I kept my eyes closed as I heard his footsteps come towards me.

"Morning, Sunshine," he whispered, placing a cup of hot tea on the bedside table.

I squinted my eyes and smiled. "Morning."

"I don't have to be at work until the afternoon so I thought we could have breakfast and then spend the day together."

"I have work," I said, pouting my lip.

"No, you don't; you never have work. You can go in later." He kissed my lips.

"Breakfast will be ready in ten. Wakie-wakie."

I rubbed my nose and stretched my arms above my head as I yawned and released a high-pitched squeal. I sat up and took a sip of the tea. There was something wonderful about that first mouthful. You can feel it glide down your throat, the aged leaves of steeped oolong leaving a distinct flavour that leaves you wanting more.

I slipped on my bed socks and headed to the kitchen. The food smelt great. Bodhi already had the table set with freshly squeezed orange juice, toast, eggs, warm baked beans, sautéed mushrooms and slightly roasted tomatoes.

"Wow, this is amazing. My compliments to the chef."

Bodhi took a bow and then sat at the table to eat. I loved the morning sun in the kitchen. It was warm and welcoming. Even in the winter months the sun seemed to shine in here at first light, if only for an hour. We split the newspaper. Bodhi read the business and sports section while I looked at the travel and entertainment portion. Oh, yes – and the comic strips. I had a thing for reading the comics.

Resigned to the fact that I wasn't going to work, I settled onto the couch in the lounge to finish reading my section of the paper. Bodhi headed off to the bathroom to get ready. I wasn't sure where we were going that day but I suspected that he had something planned. My preference was leaning towards having a lazy day at home where we could read, watch a movie, fuck, sleep and then wake to do it all again. Seemed ideal in my mind.

He walked into the lounge and sat on the floor with his hand resting on the couch near mine.

"Do you want to get ready?'

"Where do you want to go? I thought we could stay here and have an indulgent day of rest and relaxation."

"Perhaps tomorrow. Today I want to take you shopping," he said with a sparkle in his eye.

"Shopping? You have the wrong girl. I don't like shopping – ever. You know that."

"I do, but it's for a special occasion."

I looked at the expression on his face and knew now he was definitely up to something. "Tell me where first and I'll think about it."

"It's a surprise."

"Hmm, nope. You know I hate surprises. Tell me?"

"Talia Jacobs, you are impossible at times, you know that?"

"I do."

"Good. Hold that thought."

He shifted to sit perched on his knees, gathered my hand in his and looked in my eyes. "Marry me," he said.

I threw the paper over the back of the couch onto the floor and rolled around to face Bodhi. He reached down and kissed my hand while he stared into my eyes.

"I'll marry you, Bodhi," I whispered, still in shock at his proposal.

He kissed me passionately as tears rolled down his face. I could feel him shaking. I placed my arms around him to still his shivers.

"Does that mean we can have a PJ day and stay home?" I said with wishful thinking.

"Nope, it means we're going shopping for your wedding ring."

"Yikes – a ring? No, really. I'd rather you design a tattoo and I'll place it on me anywhere you like. How's that for the ultimate symbol of devotion?"

"I'll take you up on the tattoo idea, but I am buying you a wedding ring and an engagement ring. I want everyone to know that you're mine and no other's."

I lifted my hands and did my best re-enactment of jazz hands. "I don't wear jewellery. I wear tattoos."

"I guess you'll have to get used to it. The good news is that you can pick the rings. I want you to be happy with them and I'll be happy that you're wearing them. As for the tattoo, I'll design something and have it placed where the sun don't shine," he said as he patted my upper inner thigh, laughing.

"Oh, that sounds nasty."

"It'll be worth it. Also, if it's okay with you, I really want you to use my surname when we're married. It's important to me."

I pulled a face that clearly indicated I didn't like the idea. "How about if and when we have kids they take on your name and I leave mine the way it is?"

"I'm a traditional man. I want my woman to have my surname, wear my ring and bear my children under wedlock."

I cringed. "Please don't tell me you want a traditional wedding," I said, my hands covering my eyes, shaking my head at the thought.

"Nope, the wedding is your domain. Anywhere you want, anything you want, I'll do. Just no Vegas."

"Really? Oh, man, my ultimate wedding fantasy always revolved around an Asian Elvis celebrant being present while we exchanged vows in a traditional makeshift white chapel, shortly followed by getting divorced the next day by a Mexican Marilyn Monroe. It's on my 'things to do' list."

"Very funny. Not a hope in hell. Which brings me to my final point of negotiation."

"There's more? What?"

"Pre-nup. I want us to have a pre-nup in place so you don't think I'm marrying you for your money."

"I don't want a pre-nup. It's not needed. All the money is held in trust, so you don't have access to it regardless of our relationship status. It serves no purpose," I said, not liking the idea of a preemptive preparation for a possible exit before we had even begun.

"I want one anyway. You can have everything of mine. I won't ever want anything of yours, not even when you pass. I want this to be solely about you and me."

"Bodhi, that's the whole point: it is just about you and me. Do you see how I choose to live? Look around at this place. I've never felt a compulsion to live lavishly, even though I have the means at my disposal to do so. Money only holds a value to me for a comfortable life and to assist in ways that are aligned to the potential betterment of the world and people at large. I'm telling you there's no way that you can gain access to the money because of how it's been structured. We don't need a pre-nup and, more importantly, I trust you. The whole idea makes me feel like you already have an exit plan in case this doesn't work out. I have to say, all jokes aside, to me, if I get married, divorce isn't an option."

Bodhi squeezed my hand. "Honey, I have no intention to ever let you go. Divorce isn't an option for me either. I still want the pre-nup. Can you just agree with me on this?"

I released a big sigh. "I'm telling you, it's a waste of time, but I'll get my lawyers to draft something. If it makes you happy, so be it. Is the business portion of this deal over now?"

"Yes," he said with a beautiful smile.

"Okay, I'll jump in the shower. Give me a few to get ready. Apparently we're going shopping," I said, wiggling my fingers.

"Talia."

"Yes?"

"Are you disappointed that I didn't give you an extravagant proposal?"

I touched the side of his face. "No, this was perfect. I don't need a fuss. I need you."

"You don't know how happy you've made me. I'm going to devote the rest of my life to making sure you're the happiest woman in the world."

I kissed him and then headed off to the shower. It felt surreal to be talking about marriage, wedding rings, pre-nups. I still felt like a teenage girl only on the cusp of womanhood. I knew nothing about the concepts he had raised. I was, however, profoundly aware of my depth of love for him and my desire to spend the rest of my days by his side. This to me was enough. Mable was right about Bodhi and me. God, I missed her.

As I wiped down the mirror to remove the steam, I opened the drawer to get some make-up. Bodhi walked in and grabbed the pill dispenser that was on top of the bench.

"One more thing. I want you to stay off the pill. I really want us to try for a baby. I know it freaks you out. It scares me too, but I want it so bad. I don't see a reason to postpone this part of us."

I took a deep breath and turned to face him. "You are a demanding creature this morning."

"I am." He placed his arms around my waist and his head on my chest.

"The idea of children scares the shit out me. I'm not sure I'm going to be able to cope," I said.

"You will. I know you will. It's important to me. I want to start our family sooner rather than later. Some people take months, even years to fall pregnant. It's not as easy as everyone thinks."

"I need some time to think about it," I said, stroking his hair.

He raised his head to reveal an expression of disappointment. "Okay, but don't take too long."

"I won't. Promise. I just need to have it feel right. I don't know if I can even explain it. I want to know within myself that I'm ready," I said, shrugging my shoulder.

Bodhi leant in and softly rubbed his nose against mine. "I'm ready and when the time comes you'll be ready too. I know you will."

"God, I hope you're right. This is something neither of us can afford to fuck up."

"Us, fuck up?" He laughed. "We won't, not with this. Promise."

"Okay, give me a minute to dry off my hair and put a face on. Go finish reading the paper and stop thinking. No more demands; I've hit my saturation point," I said, threatening to tickle him.

Bodhi laughed as he left the room.

We walked the streets to scout all the known jewellery stores. I was going out of my mind with all the bling that was on offer. Talk about a sensory overload. None of it was what I considered the ideal design. They all looked the same to me, nothing stood out as *the one*. I could see Bodhi had his heart set on one design in particular. It was nice, but it had a price tag that was a small fortune. I knew money wasn't the issue. I just felt a little uneasy; it seemed like a waste of money to me.

As we continued down the street, I tugged on his arm.

"Let's go into this store." I pointed to an old vintage-wear shop across the way.

"Talia, even if they sell rings in there, I'm not buying you a second-hand ring."

"If I have to wear it then you'll buy me the ring I want, yes?"

"Sure, but second-hand?"

"Don't be such a snob." I poked him in the ribs.

I grabbed his hand as we crossed the road. Inside the place was dank and cluttered with items. It was the perfect visual display of chaos, with items stacked high and leaning in a way that threatened to topple over at any given moment. I loved it. Under the glass counter top I spied a row of rings. Immediately I saw one which held my interest. I slid open the side window and tried it on.

Just as I was holding my hand out in front of me to get a better look, a lady appeared from behind the clutter.

"Nice choice, dear. This is a miner's faux ring. It's metal and shaped to look like it has a row of clustered diamonds. It was designed by the poor to create the illusion of wealth."

I looked closer at the ring and realised she was correct. It was cleverly designed to have raised edges so it looked like a row of diamonds. I flashed it at Bodhi.

"Talia, no."

"Yes, it's perfect. We'll take it. How much is it?"

"I'm afraid this one is a hundred dollars, my dear. I know it's only metal, but the design is rare these days."

"Perfect, thanks." I turned and looked at Bodhi.

He grudgingly handed over his credit card as he stared at my hand. "Are you sure this is the one you want?"

"I'm sure," I said, beaming.

"Okay, the lady gets what the lady wants." He shook his head, smiling.

I knew he was disappointed.

"Lovely," said the sweet old woman as she completed the transaction.

Once out on the street again Bodhi grabbed my hand to look at the ring. "Okay, time for a new compromise. This can be your engagement ring, but I get to choose your wedding ring. It's not up for negotiation."

I laughed. "So much for a compromise. This really pisses you off, doesn't it?"

"Well, kinda. You chose a poor man's ring over all those beautiful pieces you saw in the store. I think you did it to spite me."

"I knew it. You're pissed off. Trust me, I wouldn't

buy a ring I didn't want to wear for the rest of my days. This is the one I felt drawn to and believe suits me best. I really like it and I'm happy you bought it for me. Promise."

"Well, I still don't like it. I think I might downgrade it to a friendship ring and buy you an engagement and a wedding ring."

I burst out laughing, "No a chance in hell. You agreed that I could choose. This is it. I love it and I love you. Now stop it."

He released a big sigh. "You're impossible, you know that? Fine. You can have it your way, this time."

I chose to ignore the words *'this time'* and did a little leap of glee, clicking my heels together. "Yippee, thank you."

We headed back to the apartment, where we remained for the rest of the day, making love, sleeping and then waking to do it all over again. Neither of us made it to work. It was the perfect day.

Universal Union

Michael was the first to volunteer his services to help me organise the wedding. The concept was still all too surreal for me to entertain alone. My head was riddled with ideas, which surprised me. I had never imagined I would one day walk a path of union with another. Bodhi stepped aside and relinquished responsibilities, leaving all the planning to me. In some ways this made it easier and at the same time infinitely harder.

I spent the first month painstakingly looking at venues. There were professional scouts that gave me an endless list of places to explore. They all seemed vanilla and lacked imagination. If I was to do this then the venue would need to be enchanting. It had to be unique so it became the wedding no one would ever forget.

It took the better part of two months to find the perfect place for the ceremony. It was high in the mountains, deep within a tree-lined forest filled with majestic old redwoods. Michael had locked in a celebrant and organised the design of the layout. I wanted to keep the invitation list to a minimum. I shuddered at the thought of people watching me walk down the aisle.

An old friend who had forged a career as a renowned Australian fashion designer was making my wedding dress. I had her model the dress after the one Drew Barrymore wore in *Ever After*. It was the perfect dress for me. I even organised the outfit that Bodhi was to wear. He refused to know anything about it. He insisted he wanted it all to be a surprise. I was inspired by what the mad hatter had worn in the *Alice in Wonderland* series. I thought poor Bodhi might regret his decision when he saw the outfit. I hoped he liked the colour purple.

The florist provided me with samples of bouquets. I decided pale pink roses would be the perfect accompaniment for my grey dress. I loved that it was all coming together so nicely. Michael organised several marquees for the event so people would have a sheltered space to relax and enjoy the evening's entertainment.

We had locked in Valentine's Day, 14th of February, as the date. Even through all the coordination activities, the proposal, buying the ring, nothing made it as real as the date being set. I, Talia Jacobs, was going to be married.

There was nothing more to be done. Michael had been outstanding in his role. On the night before the wedding we all stayed at a local hunting lodge. The place was a bustle of activity as everyone arrived in grand spirits. I did my utmost to ensure all our family and friends were settled into their rooms as quickly as possible. I loved seeing everyone so happy. The atmosphere was electric. Bodhi joined me beside the open fire and smiled. I knew he was excited. I, on the other hand, felt a little nervous.

He shifted the hair from my face. "Tomorrow you will be my wife."

"And you my husband."

"Yes, the proudest moment of my life."

"Me too. I do want to ask one favour, if I may," I said.

"Anything."

"Meet me at the beginning of the aisle. I don't want to walk down it alone. I need to have you beside me. No one has the right to give me away. I'm yours."

He kissed me. "It would be my honour."

Hearing these words gave me instant relief. The idea of aisles and me just didn't mesh.

That night I didn't sleep a wink. My mind was weighed down with thoughts. I wanted the day to be perfect. I kept running through a checklist of all the things that needed to be done, all the while wondering if Bodhi was getting any sleep. I had wanted to have him with me, but he had insisted on maintaining the tradition of being apart the night before the wedding. I thought it was a waste not to be together on a night we both could have shared. The next day was to be the official beginning of our future together. I wished my parents could be here, and Marlee too. I missed them all palpably.

Brad was the first to come to my door. He was a sight for sore eyes.

"Here I bought you a cup of tea."

"Thanks, did you sleep well?" I said as I took a sip.

"No, I kept waking up. Our mattress was really lumpy. How did you sleep?"

"I didn't. I'm so nervous I stayed awake thinking about today."

"I bet," he said as he winked.

"Ruth and Suzanna were up at first light to check and make sure everything is in place and set to be perfect for

your special day. They're both super excited. We all are."
He paused for a moment to look at me. "You're going to
look absolutely beautiful."

"Thank you."

"Okay, well you have your tea. I'm going to head
out to see if they need my help. You don't need to worry
about a thing. Just focus on getting dressed and being
there on time. Leave the rest to us. I'II see you later." He
kissed me on the cheek and promptly left.

I closed the door and drank the rest of my tea on the
deck. The morning sun was shining and thankfully it
was set to be a beautiful day. After my tea was finished
I hopped in the shower to get ready. I left my hair down
and kept it wavy. Bodhi liked me to look natural. I only
accentuated my eyes and placed some gloss on my lips
before I slipped my dress on. It was divine. A perfect fit
for a perfect wedding.

As the time drew near I found myself increasingly
overwhelmed with nerves. I stepped out onto the deck
to feel the warmth of the sun's rays on my skin. I quietly
recomposed myself, released a final sigh and ventured
out the door to face the crowds of eager ever watchful
eyes. As I walked down the narrow hallway I could feel
my knees were weak, threatening to give way, and I was
weighted down by a multitude of butterflies playing
havoc in my stomach. Brad was waiting for me in the
foyer. He looked amazing and was beaming with pride.
Relieved, I smiled as he put his arm out and held on tight
while we walked down the path towards the whispers.

"You look spectacular," he said.

"Thanks. You scrubbed up nicely too."

We travelled the rest of the way in silence. My skin
was the only thing containing me from going everywhere

at once. My body was sending pins and needles to different random parts of my body. I started to think I might be heading towards an anxiety attack. I had never experienced this before. It was funny to think after all the horrors I had been through this was what made me feel unhinged. I was a strange creature indeed.

Bodhi, true to his word, was waiting at the start of the carpet we had laid out to form the aisle. He looked regal. The top hat completed his outfit. Just seeing him made my fears abate. I was now allowing a calmness to wash over me as Brad tenderly kissed my cheek and passed my hand to Bodhi.

"Are you ready?" Bodhi asked.

"I am," I whispered.

"You look incredible."

"So do you," I whispered shyly.

The violins started to play as everyone stood up. I smiled, trying to acknowledge as many people as I could while we slowly walked down the aisle together. It felt like the longest distance. The flowers strewn on the carpet whirled around, massaged by the gentle breeze. Looking around, I felt relieved. The venue was set perfectly, better than I had imagined. It was indeed enchanting.

We stopped in front of a big redwood and stood beneath the archway formed by its expansive network of branches. I was up first. Beads of sweat formed on my brow as I nervously struggled to remember my vows. I reached down to pick up the two plaits that Marlee had made from our hair as children and then untied the length of rainbow-coloured ribbon from my hand, placing the end of it in my left hand, together with the two plaits nestled in my palm. I then positioned Bodhi's open left hand against mine and began to diagonally wrap the ribbon around them. This was an act of binding, a symbolic commitment between two souls to unite as one. The belief was that if either person wanted to end the union they would need to cut the bind in half. It was an irrevocable break that would unlink the souls' connection. When I had finished wrapping our hands together, I tied the end and began my vows.

"You are my all of everything and I offer you me in totality. You are mine and I am yours. I will love you from this day to the next. Until my last breath, it will be your name that I whisper to the universe as thanks. My soul is bound to yours, intertwined to the fabric of our being. I will love you like no other; you will be my best friend, my husband, my lover. I will want for nothing more than you offer. It is divined in the presence of these people and God that I will be yours for eternity. None other shall pass through my heart or make it beat as it does for you, my love. I offer you my life." I paused, tilted my head as I looked at our bound hands. A tear formed in the corner of my eye. "I am ready to have our babies."

Bodhi was crying. "You are?"

I pouted. "I am. I want us to start our family. I'm ready."

I was no longer conscious of the crowd. It was just Bodhi and me staring into each other's eyes.

The celebrant cleared his throat in a not so subtle attempt to move the proceedings along.

Bodhi wiped his tears and started. "Talia, you were the one I was searching for my whole life. You are the one who completes my essence of being. I know no other way to love than with enormity. I offer all that I am to you. I will be your best friend, your husband and your lover from this day to the next, until our days' end and beyond. I have never wanted for more and will be forever grateful that you chose to bind our souls in an endless dance of light and love. You are mine and I am yours. I give you this ring as a symbol of our commitment to love one another. It is my gift of everlasting eternity."

I slipped the ribbon off our hands and tied it in a bow around the two plaits. When I was done, Bodhi gently slipped the ring on my finger. It was spectacular. The square diamond was set on white gold that had scroll etchings and small ever sparkling white diamonds nestled neatly within their bed. It was truly beautiful. I would always treasure it because it came from him.

Brad stepped forward to pass me Bodhi's ring. As Bodhi presented his hand, I placed it on his finger and then clasped his hand, placing it on my heart, mouthing the words, I love you.

The crowd stood and clapped wildly as we sealed our vows with a kiss. He held my face gently to his while our lips danced in celebration. I could have stayed in that moment forever. We turned, raising our hands in the air.

"We did it," I yelled.

The small crowd once again roared with approval, releasing countless streamers into the air. The kids jumped about laughing as they energetically scurried to catch the falling coloured strings.

Hand in hand, we walked back down the path, crossing over a traditional wooden handmade broomstick. In an old Wicca tradition, a married couple would commit to marriage by stepping over a broomstick. It represented a clean sweep of all past woes. The two who crossed over were gifted new beginnings in their union. It also provided the binding protection of the sacred matrimony. No other could interfere with the bond. If it was destined to break it was now only possible through a couple's own undoing. The broom would be hung on the inside of the doorway of their home so all who entered were bound to abide by the pact, unable to influence or interfere. As we walked over it, I squeezed his hand.

"I'll explain later," I whispered.

We continued down the path towards the reception area.

His masculine hand shifted to hold my arm tight. "Do you have any idea how incredibly beautiful you are?" he said.

I felt myself gushing, "Thank you."

The marquee was set and the banquet underway. We had everything running off a spit. There was lamb, pork, chicken and beef. The salads extended across two tables and the assortment of desserts took up another three. Everyone's bellies were set to be filled that night. Bodhi took me straight to the dance floor for our first dance. He was charming and polished in his execution of the classical waltz. I followed his lead with grace, feeling as though I was floating on air. As I turned to my left I could see Walter and Mable dancing with us. Walter smiled at me and gave an approving nod as he looked at Bodhi. A tear rolled down my cheek as I felt the warmth of their love. Mable and Walter being present to me was a sign that Bodhi and I were blessed.

The evening's festivities were enhanced by the performance of various acts. I had arranged for snake charmers, belly dancers, flame throwers, acrobats and singers. Bodhi and I walked around and spoke to all our family and friends. When we reached Ruth, she couldn't stop crying, almost driving me to start crying too.

"Talia, you look so beautiful. You look like your mother."

"Thank you, Ruth. That means the world to me."

"The ceremony was positively charming. The vows were moving; it was perfect," she continued.

Brad came up behind and tickled me. "Hey, beautiful."

I squirmed as I turned to face him. "Hey, I did it."

"Yes, you did. I'm proud of you, Talia."

I gave him a cuddle. "Thanks, Brad. I love you."

He squeezed me tight, breathing in the scent of my hair, and then released me. "Right back at ya, kiddo."

Ash was next in line for a cuddle. She looked amazing. Her hair was straight; she was wearing a dress and had a little bit of make-up on.

"You look divine – what happened?" I said in jest.

She shrugged. "Jenna picked the dress, not me. She insisted, so I'm doing as I'm told."

"Well, you look stunning. I looked for you last night but couldn't find you. I wondered if everything was all right. Where's Jenna? Couldn't make it?"

"No, she stayed home with Rose. It's a big trip flying across here. We decided it was best not to try. Bubs is just getting over an ear infection and looks like she's about to start teething."

"Of course. Fair enough. I still can't believe that you're a mother now."

"I know. It blows my mind too. It's the best thing that's ever happened to me."

"I'm glad, Ash. You deserve to be happy."

"Well, I owe it all to you. I wouldn't have met Jenna if you hadn't interfered with your love-match attempt."

"True. Well done me." I patted myself on the back in jest.

Suzanna and the rest of the family all huddled around to compliment me on my dress and the wedding in general. I felt so happy my cheeks were starting to hurt from smiling. I never knew it was possible to feel this wonderful. It felt like a dream, my very own fairy tale with Bodhi as my Prince Charming. All these years of not believing had been magically dissolved by this experience. I was the luckiest person alive.

When I finally got around to seeing the crew from work, I laughed at Michael, who was being his flamboyant self. It was clear that no one was assigned to be his wingman. He had even managed to pick up Bodhi's third cousin. I cringed slightly at the thought of being related.

The fireworks I had arranged capped off the night. Everyone had gathered outside to look into the divine night sky. The sound of the fireworks being launched gave me goose bumps. It didn't take long before the darkened skies were illuminated with a multitude of exploding streams of coloured lights. It was a spectacular end to the best day of my life.

Michael had organised to have our honeymoon suite alight with candles. There was an open bottle of champagne, complete with strawberries, and rose petal leaves were strewn everywhere. Bodhi carried me over the threshold and gently placed me on the bed. I lay there as we stared at each other.

"You are too perfect for words. I never want to forget this moment. You are my wife, Talia Reynolds."

I stretched out my hand. "I am your wife and you, my dear, are my husband."

Bodhi's face lit up. "Wait one second." He moved over to his suitcase and pulled out a piece of rolled up paper with a ribbon around it. "Here." He passed it to me.

I sat up and looked at him sheepishly. "What did you do?"

He bounced up and down on the bed like a little boy. "It's a surprise; open it."

I unravelled it and saw that it was a deed to a house. "You bought us a house?"

"Not just any house. It's the house of our dreams." He clapped his hands in excitement.

During the past few months, Bodhi and I had discovered we both loved to look at real estate. Sometimes at night we had scrolled through the web sites to see what was for sale. We had both had our eye on this amazing property, the best I had ever seen, perfect in every way.

"Do you mean to tell me you bought the house we loved?"

Beaming with pride, he responded, "I sure did."

"When?"

"Two days after we saw it online I went to have a look. I bought it on the spot. I knew the minute I walked inside that it was our home."

"I don't know what to say." I pouted. "I never even thought to get you something and you've bought us a house."

Bodhi leaned in and took my bottom lip in his mouth. In a sultry tone, he said, "That's not true. You said 'yes' to having our baby."

I felt a rush of heat surge from my belly. "Thank you for this. It's amazing. I want to give you some money towards it."

"Not a hope in hell, honey. This one's on me."

I looked at him, trying to decide whether to push the point. I didn't want to taint the perfection of our wedding day, so I concluded it was best to let it slide. I knew he could more than afford the place, but that was beside the point. I really wanted to contribute.

I released a big sigh, smiled and said with excitement, "When are we moving in?"

"We already are. I arranged for shifters to pack all our stuff and take it to the house so we only have to worry about unpacking. If we don't feel like it I'll call them back to help us." He winked.

I shook my head. "You're amazing. I'm so lucky. Thank you. It's the perfect present. I love you," I said as I leant in and kissed him.

"I know," he whispered through joined lips.

Bodhi flung his top hat across the room and crawled over the king-size bed to lie beside me. We stared into one another's eyes as the candles flickered. That night we made slow torturous love to one another over and over until our bodies could take no more.

Meanwhile our family and friends celebrated through the night and into the early hours of the morning.

The breakfast room was filled with guests weary from the night's undertakings. I did the rounds, going from table to table to chat with those I hadn't managed to talk to the night before. The stories of their antics made me smile. I was pleased; no one was going to forget this wedding.

After breakfast Bodhi packed our bags, we said our goodbyes and headed off to the airport. I had purchased tickets to Malta. Originally I had planned to hire a villa in Saint Barth's but decided that Malta would be a quieter alternative. The island was small enough to travel around in a few days before we settled in a spot overlooking the sea for the remainder of our stay. I had heard so many wonderful things about it that I couldn't resist.

As I suspected, the people were welcoming. Once settled in our accommodation, Bodhi and I went to explore the area on foot. The weather was lukewarm, the water tepid. The absence of a breeze made the sun feel warmer on my skin. I was wearing open-toe sandals, a skirt and singlet top. Bodhi wore three-quarter cargo pants and plain white T. I loved his arms, his strong masculine arms.

We settled down at the edge of a footbridge, allowing our feet to hang over the edge. The amount of marine life was astounding. I watched a manta ray dance below, its wings ever so graceful. I don't recall a time when I felt so relaxed. I leaned into Bodhi's shoulder and soaked up the sunshine. I hoped all the days were set to be like this. We were truly blessed.

On our way back to our accommodation we stopped at an ice cream parlour. I had a watermelon gelato and Bodhi selected passion fruit. The flavour was out of this world. If I closed my eyes I could have sworn I was eating a watermelon. I planned to return once a day to sample every flavour.

Our room had a spectacular view of the ocean below. It was modest in size, containing all the basic creature comforts one needs. I put the overhead fan on and jumped on the bed.

"Read to me." I passed Bodhi Mable's book.

"Okay.' He settled in beside me and started.

I closed my eyes as he read the words, smiling at the image of Mable adorning her beautiful straw hat as I drifted off to sleep.

When I woke it was late in the evening. I went out onto the balcony and could hear the ocean crashing against the rock walls. The stars were out in full display, as if to show off to the moon. Bodhi came up behind me and wrapped his arms around my waist.

"Let's make a baby," he whispered.

I turned to face him and kissed his neck softly. He stood still as I lifted his T-shirt over his head and took off his pants. He undressed me in the light of the moon, then picked me up and carried me to our bed. I watched as he used his fingers to trace the outline of my form. Goose bumps followed his trail. I arched my back as he nuzzled into my breasts and kissed them.

"You are going to be an amazing mother."

"You will be an amazing father."

He parted my legs, positioned himself between them and entered me.

"God, you're beautiful. Wrap your legs around me," he whispered as he nibbled on my earlobe. "Hold on tight, baby, I'm so turned on right now that I just need to be inside you."

My body responded to his words, releasing droplets of nectar down my thighs. I lifted my legs, scissoring them tight across his heaving back. He released an ecstatic groan as he thrust harder. The arch of my back heightened the sense of him inside me. My body shuddered as I grasped the edge of the sheets on the bed. Knuckles white, I held tight as he rode me hard. The sensation of his body heat rubbing against mine sent pulses of electric bolts up my thighs and buttocks, bared to the dark. Trembling and moaning, I felt my body melt as the sweet sensation of orgasm took over. I loved how easily he could command my body to reach the pinnacles of pleasure. My legs remained locked around his torso as he languidly opened his eyes to gaze into mine, before releasing an elongated groan of pleasure. His body shuddered with blissful familiarity. I always enjoyed watching Bodhi come.

"Fuck, I love you," he said as he moved to lie beside me.

"I know, baby. I love you too," I whispered, shutting my eyes.

He wrapped his arms around me and nuzzled his head into the crook of my neck. We lay like that until we drifted off to sleep once more.

Twin Flames

When we arrived at our new home Bodhi carried me over the threshold. I squealed and giggled like a thirteen-year-old schoolgirl. When he put me down I was in awe of the beauty of the place. It had cathedral ceilings, marble tiles, and intricate fretwork on the enormous double staircase. The images we had seen on the Internet were impressive but didn't do it justice. This place was a masterpiece.

"Well?"

"Bodhi, it's stellar. I can't believe its ours."

He nuzzled into my hair and whispered, "I'm glad you said 'ours'."

"Yes, well I still would love to give you some money for it."

"Shh. Come, I'll show you around."

We spent the next hour ooing and ahing at the beauty of our not so humble abode.

In the end we decided to call back the crew to help us unpack. It took a couple of days to find the right place for everything. By the end of the home stretch I was losing my will to live. I absolutely hated moving house with a passion. When the last book was placed on the shelf I released a long exaggerated sigh of relief.

"Done," I said, smiling at Bodhi.

"Not quite. There's one more thing we need to do to make it complete."

I looked around. "What is it? Everything's unpacked. I'm sure of it. All the boxes are empty; I checked them twice."

He walked across and kissed my neck. "We still have to christen the place. I'm thinking, in order to be thorough, we'll have to do it in every room of the house, starting here."

I laughed. "If we must, we must."

He picked me up, spun me around and laid me down on the bearskin rug. During the next three days Bodhi and I made love in every room of the house. It was sublime.

Over the following weeks my mind was preoccupied with the concept of destiny and predefined love connections. I purchased books describing the sanctity of twin flame love. It talked about the ideals of one soul forced to split into two and being reincarnated from one lifetime to the next, always in search of each other. The concept drove home the point that each soul needed to strive to become complete before they were ready and able to fully receive their twin.

At night I lay awake with imagery of the universe clouded in a web of rainbow energy, where interconnected souls roamed in search of familiarity in one another's light. The concept seemed surreal yet familiar to me. I wanted to believe Bodhi was my twin soul. He felt like home when he was in my arms and I was complete now that we had made our commitment to one another as husband and wife. There was an air of surety about our union that gave me a sense of contentment.

I had been entertaining the idea of taking Bodhi to some Tantra classes. Our connection was already profound and sexually we were so connected that I could see we would benefit from the teachings offered. The thought of enhancing what we already had would, in my mind, deepen the union. I desired to conceive a child during such an exchange.

While I was searching for classes online, I stumbled across Bodhi's Flickr account that contained all the images from his travels before he had met me. I was astounded to see the pictures he had taken were nearly identical to mine. Even the timelines were almost exact. The perspective, angles, lighting were similar. It was as though we had been following one another's path all along without knowing. It was uncanny how two people from different backgrounds could be so aligned. This provided me the confirmation that I hadn't realised I was searching for.

"What are you looking at, honey?" asked Bodhi, who had just arrived home from work.

"I found your travel blog online."

"Oh, cool. Give me a minute. I'll come and take a look too. I haven't seen it in forever."

"Okay."

I went to the bookshelf and pulled out the pictures from my travels so we could compare the images. Bodhi settled on the couch beside me as we flicked through the pages online. Every image he presented I could match from my album. I could see by the look on his face there was an air of disbelief.

"This is amazing. Our images are identical. Even the colours are the same," he said, now reaching for my album to take a closer look.

"I know. It's like we were there at the same time but couldn't see each other. Here, I have a timeline of my travels. According to the date stamp on your images, we were in the same places days apart, sometimes only hours," I said as I opened to the back of my diary.

"How's this even possible?" asked Bodhi as he ran his finger through his hair.

"I don't know. Perhaps we were always in the same space because we needed to be close to one another but were never ready to be together."

Bodhi shook his head and reached across to hold my hand. "No, I was always ready to receive you. I'd been searching for you all my life. I was ready."

"I've been reading some stuff about the concept of twin souls and how they can travel from one lifetime to another in search of their other half. In most of the cases the way the story unfolds the twins aren't even born in the same lifecycles so they're forever searching for something that may not exist in physical form for them. It's written the two appear in the same lifetime only when the lessons they were set to learn are achieved. It's only at this point they are provided the opportunity to meet and God willingly reunites their souls. It kept emphasising they only meet and recognise one another when they're ready."

"I was always ready, always aching to have you near. There wasn't a day I can recall when I didn't think about you. I may have been searching for you, but I carried you with me in my heart always."

He expressed himself in ways that made me feel so wanted, loved and special.

"You're too beautiful for words. Oh, I've been meaning to show you something," I said, raising an eyebrow and holding a wry smile.

I switched the Internet page to the site I had been looking at, which offered weekend workshop tantric classes. I gleefully watched as he read the outline of the three-day retreat package. When he was done, he cleared his throat and flashed a wicked grin my way.

"What do you think?" I asked.

"Hmm, I think you and I are going to get it on tantric-style." He made some lewd gestures that made us both laugh.

"Really?"

"Sure, it might be fun," he said, leaning in to kiss me on the lips.

"I think it could be amazing. Imagine if we could conceive a child while executing Tantra. It would be a blessed union inviting a soul to join our family."

"It sounds ideal. I'd love that."

"Me too. I'II book us in for this coming weekend. There's a retreat a couple of hours out of town. It's fully catered and offers private instruction if we want it."

"I was going to work this weekend but I'II cancel. Is there anything we need to do to prepare?"

"It recommends participants abstain from being intimate at least a week prior to attendance," I said, keeping a straight face.

Bodhi released a hearty laugh. "Hmm, I don't know about that. It seems a little extreme."

He closed the laptop and turned to me.

I stroked the side of his face. "I guess it wouldn't hurt to practice." I tilted my head to one side to invite his kiss.

He bit his bottom lip as I pushed his head towards me.

My cold breath lay on his neck as I kissed his Adam's apple. It shifted as he swallowed so I kissed it again. He reached across, bringing my fingers to his mouth. He kissed the tips and then placed them on his crotch. I stroked the outline of his erection and continued to explore the length of his neck. He raised his head so I had better access across the sides. I started to kiss him harder to intentionally leave my mark. I wanted him to feel the blood rise to the surface of his skin as I sucked and bit him.

He raised his hips so his erection was pressing against my hands. I carefully unzipped his pants to release his manhood. It stood erect, wet at the tip, awaiting my next move. Shifting to the floor, I positioned myself onto my knees and stroked the shaft of his penis while I kissed his soft lips. I pushed his chest so he was now leaning back on the couch. Maintaining eye contact, I took him in my mouth. With my tongue I licked around the edge of his perfect mushroom head. His skin was flushed red and soft. It felt like silk as I placed a blanket of saliva onto his shaft. His breath deepened as I ran my mouth up and down his penis. I gently stroked his balls as he lifted his hips to thrust more of himself into my mouth. I loved the taste of him.

Bodhi unclasped my bra to free my breasts. He leant forward and cupped them in his hands, gently squeezing them as my head bobbed up and down on his shaft. My nipples hardened to his touch. I started to squirm as he squeezed them between his fingers.

"Look at me, baby," he whispered as he settled back into a recline and placed a hand on the back of my head to guide me down.

I could feel the heat rise as he jutted in and out of my mouth. Using my hands to run up the length of his thighs under his shirt and onto his nipples, I ran across them with the tips of my fingers and then executed circular patterns around them to wake them up. I wanted to squeeze and tug at his nipples, as he had done to mine. He groaned as I did this and licked his lips. I could tell he was close.

I shifted up so I had his cock nestled snuggly between my breasts, using my arms to push them together as he drove. Bodhi was consumed by his arousal as he held my face in his hands. I could feel the friction on the sides of my breasts as he shifted into overdrive. The spurts of his cum released and settled across my breast and under my chin. I smiled as he threw his head back for one last thrust before he slumped back on the couch.

"That didn't take long," I said with a chuckle.

"A good tit-fuck never does. I love the feel of your breasts," he said, still staring at the ceiling, panting.

I got up and went to the bathroom to shower. Bodhi came in shortly after, undressed and plunged under the warm water. He took the soap and lathered me up. I did the same for him. I watched as he reached for a towel, placed it folded on the floor and got down on his knees. He parted my legs and then looked up at me, displaying a perfect smile.

"Your turn," he said as his mouth disappeared between my thighs.

I leaned my head back and squatted on his face as he used his tongue to masterfully stimulate my clitoris. My body swayed in a circular motion as I squealed with delight. He raised one hand to play with my breasts. They were still lathered with soap so his hands glided from one mound to the other and then back again. I used my hands to brace myself between the bathroom walls as I released an almighty groan. I could feel the heat rush to my burning thighs as a thundering orgasm ran through my core.

Bodhi finished his duties with a final elongated kiss on my lips. He was an incredible kisser. He placed his hands in mine and pushed his erection up against my tummy. I smiled as I shifted my leg so he could enter me. He grabbed my arse, lifting me onto his rigid erection, pushing me back against the bathroom wall so he could brace himself to strike. He rocked his body back and forth, sending shockwaves of electric pulses through my tummy and up my core. I could feel his body shudder as the crest of an orgasm loomed. I kissed him hard on his mouth and bit his bottom lip as he came inside me.

As he stilled, I stroked the back of his wet hair. He slowly placed me down on the ground and leaned his head on my shoulder.

"That was intense," I said, running my hands up and down the line of his sculptured back.

"I love you, Talia," he whispered as he kissed my neck.

"I know. I love you too, but we had better get out of here before we turn into a couple of prunes," I said, laughing.

He turned the taps off and passed me a towel. I dried him and then he did the same for me. We slipped into our dressing gowns and crawled into bed. I rested my head across his torso and lay there listening to the calming beat of his heart.

"Do you want me to organise dinner?" he asked.

"I'm not really hungry."

"I know, but you need to eat. Have you eaten anything today?"

"No," I said guiltily.

"Come on. I'll organise some take-out. All this fucking has made me starved."

Bodhi grabbed his phone on his way to the lounge

room. I remained in bed. Taking advantage of his absence, I stretched out across it diagonally and listened to him place an order for pizza.

It didn't take long for the order to arrive. Bodhi brought it into the bedroom, placing it in the centre of the bed as I shuffled across. He took out a slice of the piping hot pizza and passed it to me.

"Eat, woman. You need to get some food into you. There's nothing of you."

I looked at my legs. "Rubbish; I'm fat."

"No, you're quite the opposite, I can assure you. Lifting you in the shower was like lifting a feather. You need to eat."

"Okay, I'm eating." I took an exaggerated bite.

"What do you want to do tonight? It's still early. There're some movies being released. Do you want to catch one?"

"Sure. I haven't seen a good film in ages."

We scoffed down our pizza, got dressed and were on our way.

The movie theatre was quiet for a half-price Tuesday. We bought some popcorn, a soda to share and headed in to watch an action flick. As the lights dimmed I settled in my chair, placing my legs on the seat in front. I loved the taste of the salty butter-popcorn. I placed messy handfuls at a time in my mouth, happily munching away as the movie kicked off.

"I'm surprised there's no one here tonight."

"I know. It's cool. We almost have the place to ourselves."

Bodhi sat back to watch the film while I fidgeted. He placed his hand on my exposed knee to stop me from jiggling. I smiled and settled in to watch the movie.

There was something great about getting lost in a film. The big screen and surround sound made it easy to become a part of the scene. The only distractions were the smell of the popcorn and the welcome warmth of Bodhi's hand on my knee.

Midway through the film Bodhi shifted his hand slowly up my thigh and under my dress. He was facing forward watching the film. I turned to look at him as his fingers politely found their way under the line of my panties. He nestled his index finger between the parting of my lips and gently stroked my clitoris. I could feel myself instantly become wet. The smell of my excitement rose to greet my senses as I licked the salt off my lips.

I shifted deeper into the chair and parted my legs as he continued to stimulate my nether regions. Raising my hips to greet his pressure I found myself staring at the theatre ceiling. I placed my hand over his and assisted him in pleasuring me by applying and releasing pressure. At the point of orgasm I squeezed my thighs together, trapping his hand. My body shook all the conjoined seats in the aisle as I braced my hands on the arms of the chair and released a quiet whimper. Beads of sweat were glistening on my brow as Bodhi peeled his hand away and placed it back on my knee.

He maintained full eye contact with the screen and smiled with satisfaction. I shook my head as I attempted to regain my breath. There was something undeniably sexy about doing naughty things in public. I was so aroused that I couldn't focus on the film. In a euphoric daze I continued to eat the popcorn, allowing my mind to wander back into the space of twin flames.

As we walked back to our house I began to shiver in the crisp night air. Bodhi removed his jacket, placing it around my shoulders. The stars were out in spectacular fashion. It was unusual to see so many at this time of year.

I pointed to a falling star. "Make a wish."

"You are my wish; I already have all that I could possibly want." He squeezed my hand.

He always seemed to have the perfect response to melt my heart.

The house was still warm. Bodhi headed to bed and I jumped into the shower. I had never taken so many showers in my life. I felt like I smelt like sex all the time. I was looking forward to getting a good night's rest. All this extracurricular activity had me exhausted. Orgasms made me sleepy.

Bodhi was fast out to it by the time I crawled in beside him. His breath was steady and he always looked so peaceful when he slept. The moonlight filtered through the blinds and fell upon his olive skin. I lay awake for a while, watching him. I had never known it was possible to love someone this much. I didn't know what I would do if I lost him. Life would honestly not be worth living. He was my all of everything.

The weekend arrived.

Once Bodhi finished loading the boot with our travel bags for our tantric getaway, he ushered me into the car and we were off. Listening to the radio, I enjoyed the chance to observe the world whizzing past in a blur. There were so many lovely landscaped gardens in our new neighbourhood. I usually drove so I was never afforded an opportunity to be a passenger. It was Bodhi who insisted he wanted to drive so I could relax. I liked it when he took the lead on things. I had been in the driver's seat of my life journey, never meeting anyone I would even consider could take over the wheel for a while. I trusted Bodhi with my life. The sun beaming through the window provided me with the welcome comfort of warmth. The rays felt like a blanket. It was so cozy. I closed my eyes and drifted off to sleep.

As we arrived, Bodhi woke me. Through drowsy eyes I look at my surrounds. The lodge was amazing. It was encompassed on one side by a vast manmade lake encircled by extensive gardens. The atmosphere was alive; the sounds of wildlife penetrated the car's windows with its cacophony of diverse pitch and expression. This place felt charmed.

Bodhi opened the car door for me and held out his hand to offer gentlemanly assistance. He was so romantic.

I beamed. "Look at this place. It's so pretty."

"Yes, it's perfect."

I knew he was thinking the same thing. "It's perfect for what exactly?"

"To get you pregnant," he said, looking directly into my eyes.

"Yes, I believe it is."

"Great minds, Talia, great minds."

"Indeed."

We unloaded our luggage and went into the reception area, where a strange-looking short man with a long grey beard greeted us.

"Welcome," he said in a voice that sounded like it belonged to a cartoon chipmunk.

"Hello, we're here for the tantric weekend."

"Yes, follow me." He walked off down the hall as we followed, holding hands.

The little man had a limp and seemed to favour his

right side. I could feel sympathy pains starting to shoot down my leg watching him, the poor fellow.

"This is your room. Here is the key. You have some free time while we are waiting for the other guests to arrive. Can I suggest you settle in and then take a walk around the gardens? They are really rather beautiful. Also, it is important that you continue to refrain from doing anything sexual." He looked at our hands clasped together.

"We wouldn't dream of it," I said with a laugh.

He looked at me disapprovingly and then headed back down the hall.

"Looks like someone forgot their sense of humour," I said, a little embarrassed that he didn't see the lighter side of my jest.

Bodhi shut the door behind us. "I hope he's not the instructor. The sight of him makes my cock shrivel."

We both burst out laughing.

Once unpacked, we decided to go for a stroll around the lake. Whoever had designed the gardens had clearly been influenced by Japanese design and possessed amazing vision. Everywhere we looked the perfect postcard image could be captured. It was vast and serene. Walking the full circumference of the lake took a little over an hour. At one point Bodhi and I took pause to watch wild ducks swimming with their young. I had a good feeling about this place.

Upon our return, we went back into our room to rest. I was exhausted from the trip up. Fully clothed, we lay side-by-side on the bed, drifting off to sleep.

A knock at our door woke me. In a daze, I rose to answer.

A statuesque woman dressed in a gown adorned

with beads was there. "Hello, it's time. Everyone is congregating in the common area. Please join us when you're ready," she said in a serene melodic tone.

"Okay, we won't be long."

I closed the door. "Bodhi, we have to go."

He stretched his arms above his head and gave a little yelp. "Yep, ready," he said, stumbling to his feet.

I smiled as my tummy started to develop butterflies. This was going to be an interesting process. I was a little nervous. I hoped they didn't expect us all to be naked. The idea sent shivers down my spine. I had nothing to hide but it didn't mean I wanted to show.

Once ready, we went to the common area and sat on a mat at the back of the room. Almost everyone else was already settled. I looked at Bodhi as he positioned himself in a cross-legged position next to me.

"I'm a little nervous," I whispered.

"It'll be fine. How hard can it be?" he said in a reassuring tone.

The lady who had come to our door entered the room and stood at the front of the class.

"Thank you all for coming. *Namaste.*" She bowed.

We all responded, "*Namaste.*"

"I am Eliza. I will be your tantric instructor for this weekend. I hope that you are all ready to have a wonderful spiritual journey together. Please turn and face your partner."

Bodhi and I faced one another and held hands.

"Now I want you to stare into one another's eyes and block out the rest of the room so that all you see are their eyes."

Soothing panpipe music played in the background, filling the room. I stared into Bodhi's beautiful eyes, trying my best to silence my mind. It didn't take long for me to be completely immersed in the deep blue of his sapphire orbs. He didn't blink the whole time as he returned my gaze.

"Now without breaking eye contact gently touch one another's finger tips and explore the structure of your partner's hands."

Bodhi shifted his hands to find my tips and slowly moved them around to explore every aspect of mine. I allowed him to take the lead as I focused on maintaining eye contact.

"Take deep breaths and release them slowly. Every breath should be envisioned as white light energy invited in. Tantra is a door to opening your connectedness to your own physical and spiritual sexuality. Feel the essence of your partner's touch and observe how this electrifies your skin. We are aiming to awaken your *kundalini*."

I felt a heightened sense of awareness of my body start to emerge. I could hear my heartbeat, my blood flowing, my stomach gurgling. I never realised how internally noisy I was. All the while electric pulses from Bodhi's touch surged from my hands up my arms and to my brain, returning as tingles that made the little hairs on my body stand on end. I couldn't believe my body was falling into a sense of attunement in only a short while.

"Okay, ladies, straddle your partners in the yab-yum position. Place your arms around his neck for balance and maintain eye contact at all times. Aim to keep your breath steady. The objective is to visualise the breath as energy revitalising your body."

I looked at the couples positioned at the front that were demonstrators. I turned and smiled as I climbed onto Bodhi's lap. I could see by the twinkle in his eye he was thinking the session was finally going to get interesting. I tried to regain composure in fear that I might start to giggle. The wicked side of me felt compelled to take silent advantage of our yab-yum position. I ever so gently eased my torso down on his best friend, who was in the process of rising to greet me. An intense expression landscaped Bodhi's divine face. I listened to the rhythm of his breathing change as he inconspicuously raised his hips to press his erection, now divinely hard, against me. I continued to stare into his eyes, only partially distracted by the scent of my arousal wafting up from between our bodies. If I could detect it then he must be able to too. My mind delighted in imagining how crazy this was driving him, God knows, my knickers were saturated.

"Wonderful. Well done, everyone. You can dismount and relax."

We had been in that position for over thirty minutes. My legs had been threatening to cramp after the first five minutes. I wasn't sure I was going to make it in the end and was relieved when she called out to break. I hopped off Bodhi and sat beside him, stretching my legs. I muffled my laugh as I saw Bodhi try to ward away the pins and needles that had settled into his limbs. We all now sat in silence, awaiting further instruction. Bodhi reached across and held my hand, squeezing it hard to indicate his frustration. I smiled. I knew exactly how he felt.

After a further ten minutes Eliza broke the audible silence. "That's all we are doing for today. Dinner will be served at 7 pm sharp in the dining area. We will meet back here at 5 am tomorrow for Morning Prayer and chanting. Then we will proceed into phase two of the tantric course. Please remember to refrain from all sexual activities. It is best to be abstinent when learning the secret art of Tantra. *Namaste*."

The people stood up and bowed in return, saying, "*Namaste*."

Bodhi grabbed my hand and led me back towards our room. Once he had closed the door he pushed me up against it with his hand on the wooden frame. His was breathing heavily as he pressed his lips against mine.

"Bodhi, we're supposed to refrain," I said, feigning concern.

He ignored my words as he tore my yoga pants off and grappled at my soaked panties. Then he dropped his tracksuit pants and boxers, releasing his raging boner. I squealed as he lifted me onto him. He penetrated me hard and fast. His face was contorted and beads of sweat gathered on his brow. It took nine pumps before he was there, releasing himself inside me with a deliciously agonising gasp. I stroked his head and placed my forehead on his while he regained his composure.

"Wow," I said with a smile, kissing his wet lips.

"I thought I was going to explode. Jesus! Fuck me. That was unbelievable." He slowly let me down and placed his hands above my head against the door, still panting.

"Do you want to lie down? I'm kind of exhausted," I said, smirking.

"Yesssss," he hissed in my ear.

We climbed into bed and he held me while I drifted off to asleep.

It was almost dinnertime when we stirred from our slumber. Bodhi was looking a little dishevelled. I laughed as he covered his face and shook his head in shame.

"Don't worry. It happens to the best of us," I said jokingly.

"Seriously, I have never come so hard and fast in my life. I thought I was going to have an aneurism."

I laughed as I jumped out of bed. "I'm glad you didn't. We have two more days of this to get through and I assure you this time you are going to refrain," I said, knowing full well that was never going to happen.

I headed to the bathroom to have a quick shower.

All I heard was Bodhi's attempt at a recant. "Like hell."

The dining room was packed with people, more than had been in the class earlier in the day. We found our designated seats and sat. There were ten large circular tables with ten placings to each.

"Hi, I'm Talia and this is my husband Bodhi," I said to the people seated with us.

"Hello, I'm Marsha and this is my husband Felix."

"G'day, I'm Jules and this is Lockie."

"Hi, I'm Danny and this is my husband Sam."

"Hello, I'm Zara and this is my husband Oswald."

We all looked at the menu and poured ourselves a glass of wine.

"Who do you think breached the abstinence pact?" asked Marsha, looking around the room.

I burst out laughing and squeezed Bodhi's knee. "You don't think people would break the vow so early in the piece, do you?"

"Hells, yeah. Felix was going to pop a blood vessel. I had to for medical reasons," she said with a wink.

Everyone laughed. As I looked around the room I started to picture all these sexually frustrated people running to their rooms to have it off. I smiled at Bodhi. I knew he was still feeling a little ashamed about his quick ejaculate. I actually found it incredibly sexy. There was something totally euphoric about having him so turned on. He wanted to devour me and I wanted to let him. I was wet just thinking about it.

Dinner was delicious. They started with mushroom soup and then placed a veritable smorgasbord of food and salads on the table for people to serve themselves. I had a little bit of all the salads: Greek, potato, tabouli, coleslaw, mushroom, bean. I was seriously impressed with the catering. The food was all fresh and packed with flavour.

Bodhi and I headed back to our room feeling completely stuffed. We threw our clothes in a heap on the floor, slipped into our PJs and then both crawled into bed to flake out. The idea of a 5 am start was not something either of us was looking forward to. We weren't religious and although chanting sounded wonderful when monks did it, I wasn't sure that a bunch of wayward tantric wannabes had any business trying to chant, especially that early in the morning.

Daybreak came quicker than we wanted it to. I was toying with the idea of attending morning prayers in my pink flannel PJs. Bodhi insisted I dress.

We could hear the muffled sounds of music and voices as we headed down the hall towards the common room. Once inside, we quietly got seated.

We were late. Oops.

Everyone was sitting in the lotus position so we followed suit. The chanting didn't sound nearly as bad as I had considered it might. There was a nice echoed vibration in the room that made me feel conscious of how drowsy I was. Still feeling exhausted, without realizing I drifted off to sleep. I jolted awake when my head fell forward. Bodhi was hiding his amusement under muffled laughter. My face flushed red, embarrassed, feeling thankful that we were sitting in the last row at the back of the room. I repositioned my legs, as I was starting to get pins and needles. I didn't know how people were able to stay in the lotus position comfortably.

The chanting proved hypnotic. A tape playing in the background managed to hide the tone-deaf attempts of some of my neighbours. I once again found myself drifting off to sleep. The atmosphere was so relaxing I couldn't help but indulge. Chimes signified the end of the session, causing me to jump back to consciousness when I heard them. This time Bodhi released an almighty laugh. I shook my head and covered my mouth as I emitted a snort of laughter too. I felt ridiculous. I had never been so tired in my life.

There were two hours allocated for free time before breakfast and then the session was set to start straight after. Some people chose to gather in the garden to meditate, others stayed in the common room to do yoga. Bodhi and I headed off to our room to sleep some more. I was completely buggered.

We ended up sleeping through breakfast and were late for the start of the day session. Bodhi took the lead as we tried to sneak in. We were thwarted by the pin-drop silence in the room. Our best efforts still resonated like a stampede of elephants as we attempted to make light steps with bare feet on creaking wooden floors. Finding a spot near the exit, we sat down and mimicked the position the others were in. Bodhi was in a cross-legged position and I was to have my legs apart around his but not touching his body. Bodhi's hands were clasped together in a prayer position and settled between my legs, a whisker away from my privates but not touching. Once again we stared into one another's eyes.

I could feel warmth generating from his hands being so close to my honey hole. I steadied my breath and stared into his eyes once more. I felt a huge desire to yawn. All this sleep and still I felt exhausted. I could understand Bodhi sleeping. He was a guy and they naturally seemed to be able to spend endless hours in bed. Traditionally I was an insomniac. Lately I had recognised something had shifted within me. I hadn't felt quite right in weeks. The thought that I might be coming down with something crept into my mind. I secretly hoped it wasn't anything too serious.

"Continue to breathe in the energy and light. Feel the connection between your partner's hands to your *kundalini* power station. There should be an energy exchange occurring that warms your loins."

It was only when she said this that I started to truly feel a tingling sensation connecting me to Bodhi's hands. I wanted to shuffle closer so he was touching me. My tummy was doing flips and sweat had formed on the surface of my skin from all the heat that was being generated. I ached for him to touch me. My vaginal walls started to spasm. They tightened and released. Even my clitoris was contracting. I slowly inhaled through my nose and exhaled through my mouth as a feeling of euphoria overtook my body. Without realising, I started to make small gyrations so my panties tightened against my clitoris. My juices dripped down the side of my shorts. Bodhi's pupils dilated when he realised I was about to come. I couldn't contain myself. I shifted my hands down to touch myself and came hard, squeezing my legs together and releasing a squeal of delight for all to witness.

Much to my surprise, other women in the room were at the same point, and soon the room was filled with the echoes of their coos. Bodhi maintained his position and stared at me intensely. I smiled at him, thinking for certain, when we got back to our room, he would manage to come in under three pumps this time. The sexual energy in the room was out of this world. I wanted to inhale the sweet scent that surrounded my nasal passages forever. I had never done so little to feel so horny in my life.

Sure enough, when we had a break, Bodhi was the first to lead me back to our room. I laughed as he closed the door and started to rip off my clothes without an invitation. He bent me over the side of the bed and slammed himself inside me. In under a minute he gave an almighty grunt and heaved his body to rest on top of me. Once again I found it a complete turn-on to have him in a state of frenzy. He was out of control and I loved it.

I shifted across to lay on my back and Bodhi did the same. He was still panting from his experience. I laughed as I rolled across to lean on his torso and stare into his eyes.

"I think you broke your record."

"If this gets any more intense expect to be dazzled by my speed by the end of the weekend."

"I like it. It's a turn-on having you so out of control."

"Fuck, out of control is not the word for it. I'm so insanely horny that I feel like I have a constant raging boner and all I want to do is fuck you in as many positions as possible."

"Sounds like we're getting our money's worth from these classes."

"You can say that again. Phew," he said, wiping the sweat from his brow.

"No more sleeping. We've already slept too much. Let's go for a walk down a different path in the gardens," I said, poking at his ribs.

"Do we have to? I'm in the mood for a nap. All this fucking is exhausting."

"Yes, we have to. I'm tired too, but we need to get out of this 'eat, sleep, fuck' routine."

"Why? I rather like it," he said with the cutest sparkle in his eyes.

I stood up and put my hands out to pull him up. He closed his eyes and pretended not to notice. I waited patiently until he opened one eye; I gave him a look that made him cave. He reluctantly put out his hands so I could guide him to his feet.

Outside, the sun shone brightly. We followed the pebble-stone path around the gardens and it took us to a denser part of the park. As we walked along the winding trail I could hear the sound of running water. When we passed a bend we saw a fast-flowing little river cascading over a beautiful waterfall.

"How pretty is that?" I rushed to the water's edge.

"It's great." Bodhi sounded a little unenthused.

"Come, touch the water. It's fresh."

He knelt down and placed his hand in the water. "It's not as cold as I would have expected."

I looked at him with a wicked grin. Then stood up, kicking off my sandals, and unbuttoned my shirt. He smiled and followed suit. We folded our clothes in a neat pile at the water's edge and then stepped into the river. It wasn't deep until we reached the centre, where there was a steep drop. I could only touch the bottom on tiptoe while Bodhi was still able to stand comfortably.

I swam across to a submerged rock and perched myself on it. Bodhi came across and stood in front on me. I straddled my legs around his waist and he once again without hesitation entered me. This time he stared into my eyes, maintaining a slow thrust that made the water between our legs gush out from the sides, creating little air bubbles that tickled my legs as they travelled across my skin and up to the water's surface. I buried my hands into his back as I arched to feel him penetrate me deeper. He suckled at my breast while my nails dug into his skin.

Bodhi suddenly lifted me from the rock and held me tight as he thrust hard and shuddered with the delivery of his release. I was aroused but not close enough to come. I could see he was disappointed that he had arrived early, but I was satisfied having him inside me. I loved how he made me feel, especially when he came. I was so moved by the moment that I started to cry. Bodhi stroked my face and kissed my tears as he hugged me. The intensity of our love for one another was overwhelming. We had been through so much in order to fight for our entitlement to love. Everything that we experienced may have now been a distant memory but the bond we shared was so prominent that it would never be taken for granted.

We eventually left the river, dressed and headed down the path again. The atmosphere held an air of enchantment, a space where I imagined untold secrets were harboured, consisting of equal portions of beauty and decay. The fungi that grew on the trunks of the trees were a clear indication the ecology of the forest was in fine balance.

After lunch the next session started. This time I sat behind Bodhi, my chest close to his waist, my forehead resting between his shoulder blades. My hands were settled on his upper thighs. Bodhi sat with his legs stretched out in front of him and his hands by his sides.

This time we were expected to envisage a purple light that went from my forehead into his back, to his heart and then out his mouth to surround our bodies. We needed to use our energy breath and keep completely still. My body tingled all over as I imagined the light-force shooting from my third-eye chakra. The room seemed to spin and we were trapped in a psychedelic swirl of colours. Sweat dripped down my back as my body overheated. The room didn't have any windows nor were there any fans on the ceiling, so I started to feel overwhelmed with the lack of air circulation. The heat in the room was stifling and stagnant. My body heat was on the rise and I could feel it quickly becoming unbearable.

I woke to find I was in our room, a damp cloth across my brow. Bodhi was sitting beside me on the bed.

"What happened?" I whispered in a husky voice.

"You fainted."

"The room was really hot and my head was spinning. I remember a kaleidoscope of colours whirling around us. It made me feel ill."

"How are you feeling now?"

"Better, tired. A little hungry but better."

"I'll go fix you a plate of food. Rest. I'll be back soon."

"Okay."

I closed my eyes again and drifted off into a space of dreams where I could hear the laughter of a child behind me. Each time I turned, the direction of the voice shifted. I tried to see ahead, but the mist was too thick. I walked forward and found myself in a garden surrounded by flowers in bloom. The more I stared at them the more the colour spectrum shifted from them towards me and into my womb. I looked down and pressed my hand against my belly but all I could hear was the grumbling sounds of an empty stomach beckoning to be filled. A child's hand appeared from the left side of my torso and rested on mine. I turned to see the little girl who had always been with me.

"Where have you been? I've missed you," I whispered.

She smiled and patted my tummy. "I'm in here, Mummy."

These were the first words I had ever heard her speak. I crouched down and placed my arms around her as I cried, "Really? I'm pregnant?"

She giggled and repeated, "I'm in here, Mummy."

"Talia, are you okay? Wake up, honey. What's wrong?"

I opened my eyes and looked at Bodhi. As I reached for his arms to embrace me, I burst into tears. Between gulps of air, I tried to speak. "I just ..." gulp "had ..." gulp "the strangest ..." gulp "dream."

He reached across and wiped the tears that were falling. "Oh, honey, it's okay. Whatever it is, it's just a dream. Tell me," he whispered.

I waited until I was slightly more composed and then shifted so I was looking at him. "I think I'm pregnant and we're going to have a little girl."

He leapt onto the bed like a bouncing Tigger and placed his arms around me. "Are you serious? OMG! Really? What makes you think you're pregnant?"

"In my dream I saw this little girl that I've 'known' my whole life. Lately she's been absent. This time she appeared in my dream and told me that she was in my womb as she patted it and giggled. She called me Mummy. It's the first time I've ever heard her voice." The stream of tears continued. I was feeling overwhelmed by the experience. I couldn't stop crying.

"Wait – this little girl – is she about five years old, always wears a blue pinstripe dress, has mousy blonde hair and the cutest little smile that melts your heart?"

Shivers ran up my spine when he said that. "Yes. She's been with me, around me, for as long as I can remember. How did you know what she looks like?"

"She visits me too, Talia. Whenever I was sad or feeling lost, she would appear in my dreams and would always hold my hand or cuddle me."

I nodded my head as Bodhi's face disappeared behind the blur of my tears. "She's our unborn child, always believing and waiting for us," I said, now howling uncontrollably. "I want to name her Daniella. I've always felt that was her name," I mumbled between sobs.

"It's perfect. I love you." He touched my stomach and whispered, "Daniella."

I nodded my head as I tried to compose myself. "I love you too, honey," I said, placing my hand on his.

"Okay, let's get some food into you. I got you a selection of salads."

He shifted the plate across to my lap. I was starved. I couldn't remember the last time I had been so hungry. I guessed I was going to have to get used to the idea of eating all the time. It wasn't about me anymore. I had a little jellybean growing inside me needing constant nourishment.

"I guess I'll drink this glass of wine for the both of us then. Cheers." He raised the glass to his lips.

"Yes, I'll be missing out on a lot of things in the next few months. Not to mention getting fat," I said as I rubbed my tummy.

"Honey, you need to put on a few pounds. You're too skinny. Besides, I like the idea of you having some curves. I think you'll look sexy."

I continued to eat my salads and pulled a face at Bodhi as I chewed loudly. He grabbed his plate of food and proceeded to eat as well. Each bite made me feel better. I had felt nauseated earlier, but it had settled now that I had some food in my stomach. I didn't know much about the different stages of pregnancy. I knew I had a lot to learn over the coming months and felt exhausted just thinking about it.

"How are you feeling?" Bodhi took my empty plate and placed it on the bedside table.

"Better. I feel strong, like I could run a marathon."

"Really? Wow. You look a little peaked to me."

"It's been a long day. I still can't believe that we did it. It's a little overwhelming right now." I paused to look at Bodhi. "Honey, we're pregnant."

"I know. We'll be great parents. I can't wait to be a dad and to hold my precious princess in my arms. I'm so excited. Honestly, you have nothing to worry about. Just give birth to her and I'll do the rest. I'm going to be the best dad in the universe."

I leant across and kissed him. "I know you will."

He tucked me back into bed and we switched on the TV for the first time. There were some old Lucile Ball reruns in black and white. I snuggled into Bodhi's arms while we watched. My favourite scene was Lucile crushing grapes with her bare feet to make wine. It made me burst into fits of laughter. I don't know why I found it so amusing, but I did.

We woke just after 8 am, missing the Morning Prayer and chanting session. I couldn't say that I was disappointed but I was as hungry as a bear emerging from a winter's hibernation. Leaving Bodhi in bed to sleep some more, I jumped up, dressed and headed out the door.

"I'll meet you in the breakfast room. I have to eat something right now," I said as I closed the door behind me.

I sat at our designated table and reached for the breadbasket. I chose a slice, lathered on a thick coating of butter and started to eat.

"Where's your husband?" asked Zara.

"He's on his way. I thought I would get a head-start," I said with my mouth full.

"How are you feeling? We were all worried about you yesterday," said Jules.

"I'm okay. A little hungry and a little tired but otherwise good."

"Well, you take it easy today, young lady. You don't want that happening again," said Felix, who patted me on the back.

"I'll be fine. Can you pass me the water, please?"

Lockie grabbed the jug and filled my glass.

Bodhi arrived at the table, leant down and kissed me on the cheek. "Morning all," he said with a wave.

They responded in kind.

I ordered the big vegetarian breakfast and ate another roll while I was waiting. Bodhi poured me a cup of coffee and sat back to watch me eat.

"I could get used to this," he whispered.

I shook my head. "Seriously, I don't know how to stop. I'm starving."

"Good, eat. You need to maintain your strength." He squeezed my shoulder.

I was grateful when the food arrived. It was piping hot. Without hesitation, I hoed into my meal as though I was at the last supper with two minutes remaining. I knew the others were watching me but I didn't care. All I could focus on was the food disappearing on my plate. I even found myself eyeing off the bacon on Bodhi's plate. It smelt delicious. I salivated at the thought of having some.

The session was set to start soon after breakfast had been completed. All I could think of doing was taking a nanna nap. Outside the breakfast venue was a decking. The sun was beaming the warmth of its rays, inviting me to bask in its light. I could have curled up on the banana lounge and drifted off to sleep, but this was our last day there and I wanted to make it count. Everything I had experienced so far had been wonderful and I hated the idea of missing out or depriving Bodhi.

We all headed to the common room and found a position on the floor and awaited our instruction.

"Everyone, take your blindfolds and put them on tight so you cannot see. Focus on the music and allow yourself to feel the rhythm. Move your body in any way you feel compelled. You are free, no one is watching, so you can dance without a concern in the world."

Bodhi put mine on for me and then did his. I did as she instructed, listening to the music. Initially I swayed from side to side like the wind blowing in the trees. I then allowed my feet to sweep in a circular motion, my arms floated upward high above my head swinging from side to side. This exercise was indeed liberating. I folded myself over and swung back up again. I created a wave-like motion using my arms, and then shifted them from left to right, adding jazz hand movements into the mix for self-amusement. It was fun. The lesson lasted for five lengthy songs. By the time we were allowed to remove our blindfolds I was sweating like a maniac.

I used the blindfold to wipe off the sweat. "Are you hot?" I asked Bodhi.

"A little. Are you okay?"

"I'm feeling a little overheated again."

"I'II get you a glass of water." Bodhi rushed out the door.

When Bodhi returned, I guzzled down the liquid and passed him the empty glass. "I think I need to lie down. I don't feel that well."

"Okay." He grabbed my arm and escorted me back to our room.

I lay down on the bed and fell asleep almost instantly. Bodhi stayed to watch over me.

I didn't stir for a few hours and when I woke my eyes took a while to adjust to the bright light in the room. There was a man standing near my side of the bed, holding my wrist. I looked at him and noted he had a stethoscope around his neck.

"I'm Doctor Shlue. I'm just taking your pulse, Talia."

I cleared my throat and turned my head to look at Bodhi.

"Sorry, you left me no choice. I was worried," he said with a shrug.

"Talia, can you sit up for me? I want to listen to your heart and take your temperature."

I shuffled up the bed, placing the thermometer in my mouth. Dr Shlue positioned the cold stethoscope on my chest and listened while I breathed. I felt drained and had a slight headache. My stomach was making noises again. I was so hungry.

He removed the thermometer.

I turned to Bodhi. "Can you get me something to drink and eat, please? I'm starved again."

He laughed. "Sure," he said as he leapt off the bed and headed out the door with a bounce in his step.

"Well, my dear, it appears that you're dehydrated and running a slight temperature. Given your husband has suggested that you might be pregnant, the increase in temperature is normal. I have a test here for you to take. Can you go into the bathroom and urinate on this?"

I took the pregnancy stick and headed into the bathroom. My bladder felt like it was going to burst, as I hadn't been to the toilet yet, so the timing was perfect. I released a flood of urine onto the stick and much to my horror all over my hand. I scrubbed my hands in the washbasin, almost taking a layer of skin off in the process. By the time I returned to the bedroom the positive indicator was already appearing. I handed it to the doctor, who instantly smiled.

"Congratulations. It would appear that you are indeed pregnant."

I sat back on the bed and took the pregnancy stick back. I looked at the indicator and smiled. "Yep, I'm pregnant."

Bodhi returned with a plate piled with food. I handed him the stick in exchange for the plate so I could start eating. The expression on Bodhi's face was priceless. He clasped onto that stick and placed it against his heart, beaming with pride.

"We're pregnant," he whispered.

"Yes, we are," I responded between chews.

"Okay. Well, Talia, I think you just need to keep resting. You seem to be in good health. Your body is probably just adjusting to the changes that are taking place. When you return home you need to get yourself an obstetrician. Let them know what's been happening over the last few days. You'll need to keep your electrolytes up. Plenty of fluids, okay?"

"Sure, thanks."

"My pleasure. Okay, I'II see myself out. Congratulations again."

"Thank you," I responded.

Bodhi stood up and proudly shook his hand. "Thanks, Doc."

"No problem. Bye now." He left, closing the door behind him.

I continued to demolish my meal while Bodhi watched. When I finished I passed him the plate. "I'm sorry that we haven't been able to attend the last of the classes," I said with a pouty lip.

Bodhi kissed my pout. "Don't be silly." He waved the pregnancy stick at me. "We're pregnant."

I laughed. "Yes, we are. Hey, would you mind if we headed home?"

"Not at all. I'II pack our things. You rest."

I didn't need convincing. I released a big yawn and lay back down again. I had never realised carrying a child would be so physically taxing. Considering my current state of exhaustion I had no idea how women worked a full-time job feeling like this. It must be hell. I yawned again and closed my eyes. All I wanted to do was sleep.

Bodhi woke me when he had finished packing. He had already organised the check-out. I slowly got out of bed and followed him to the car. Within ten minutes of being on the road I was fast asleep again.

We arrived home. Once inside the door I did a beeline straight to the toilet and then curled up in bed again. I didn't bother to get changed. I had no energy. I just wanted to sleep. Bodhi unpacked the bags while I continued to rest.

I woke to Bodhi nudging me gently. "Talia, wake up, sweetie. I'm going to organise dinner. Do you feel like some dumplings?"

I did a little stretch as I turned to face him. "Yum. Yes please, and some noodles too. Oh, and if they have those small cookies we could get some of them as well."

"Anything else?"

"No, I think that's it," I said as I fluffed my pillow.

Bodhi placed the order and set the table in the lounge. I knew I would have to get up soon so I decided to jump in the shower to wash the sweat off me. By the time I came out the food had arrived. The smells wafting in the air were driving me insane. I grabbed one of the dumplings with my hand and shoved it in my mouth. Bodhi looked at me and shook his head.

"Wow, you really do have a ferocious appetite."

"I do. It's driving me insane. Imagine what I'm going to be like closer to term. God help me."

"Here, sit down. Don't stress. I'll go shopping tomorrow so we have everything here. I'll even pre-prepare some meals so all you need to do is heat and eat. Okay?"

I was chewing on another dumpling when I gave him an open-mouthed smile.

He pushed my head and laughed. "You're disgusting."

"You love me," I said with my mouth still full.

Jelly Bean

"I really don't want to tell anyone about the baby yet. I need to get my head around the concept and they say the greatest risk is during the first trimester. So I want to hold off, okay?"

"Honey, I want to scream it from the rooftops. I've already designed the pregnancy stick into a necklace," Bodhi said as a joke.

"Patience." I kissed his hand.

He sighed. "Okay, but the minute I'm allowed I'll be telling everyone. Just so you know."

"I know." I rubbed my face at the thought of all the attention. "I have an appointment with the obstetrician today."

"Oh, I never realised. Do you want me to come with?"

"No, I've got it. You go to work and I'll tell you all about it tonight."

"Okay. I'd better run. Love you." He kissed me lightly on the lips.

"I love you too."

I spent the morning researching all that I could on the topic of pregnancy. I decided the more I knew the calmer I might feel because I would understand what to expect from the whole process. I unfortunately gravitated to YouTube, where I watched some very graphic birthing clips that made my stomach churn. The bloodcurdling screams from the moms as they reacted to their contractions made the hairs on the back of my neck stand on end. Once I started I couldn't stop watching. I was officially petrified.

The obstetrician's office was three blocks from my place. I walked down and took a seat in the reception area. It wasn't long before Dr Randal was ready to see me. She had an attractive smile and a relaxed disposition. As we walked into her medical suite she had me change into a gown before assisting me into an armchair complete with stirrups. Nestled between my legs, Dr Randal gently took some internal swabs and put some cold gel on my belly to assess me with an ultra sound. She confirmed I was in my first trimester with an estimated seven or so weeks elapsed. I got to see my baby's heartbeat and it was in that moment I realised I should have encouraged Bodhi to be there. He would have loved to witness our little jellybean's heart happily thumping away.

Dr Randal patiently stepped me through what to expect during the course of the pregnancy and took some genetic tests to ensure the baby wasn't developing a predisposition for any of the known common diseases. The final part of the appointment was having me step on the scales. I watched the dial spin and then finally settle – an extra three kilos! I was going to be a heifer by the time our daughter came out.

The doc saw the expression on my face and chuckled. "It's perfectly normal and a good sign. All your indicators are in a healthy range. You should have an easy time carrying to term. You just need to keep hydrated and eat regularly but not in excess of what you require. Listen to your body. When you're hungry eat small healthy meals. We have a nutritionist available if you have any concerns. Let the receptionist know on the way out if you're interested and they can arrange a time for you. You're going to be fine, Talia. I'll see you in three weeks for another checkup. If you can bring your husband along we can talk through what you've decided about the birthing procedure."

"Thanks for your time."

"You're welcome. Take care and I'll see you soon."

I left the office and headed straight to the local bakery to buy some doughnuts. I had a hankering for pink icing and bought six, three of which I ate on the way home. I was an animal when it came to food. The idea of putting on more weight didn't sit well with me. I would have to do something to balance the increase in consumption.

When Bodhi arrived home I was lying on the couch reading a book. He had bought some Thai noodles from our favourite place. I eagerly sat up and was ready to eat again.

"How did you go today?" he asked, after fetching us some plates from the kitchen.

"I was a little freaked when she propped me up in the stirrups. It all seemed a little too real. Dr Randal was really nice. I'm seven weeks into the journey. All the signs are good. Both of us are healthy. She confirmed it was normal to be tired but has taken some blood samples to crosscheck and make sure I'm not deficient in anything. All this eating and sleeping had me concerned, but Dr Randal didn't seem the least bit worried. I've put on three kilos." I pouted.

"Aww. Honey, it's fine. You look beautiful. Eat." He handed me a fork and a bowl.

I served up the noodles and tucked in while Bodhi settled in beside me.

"I ate six doughnuts today," I confessed.

"Wow, that's a lot of dough."

"I couldn't stop eating them. I wanted to lick the pink icing. I almost went back to ask if they would sell me a tub of the icing. I'm seriously out of control."

"It's okay. You're allowed to have cravings. It's normal. Just enjoy."

"I want to join a gym," I announced mid-swallow.

"I'd prefer you didn't."

"Why?"

"Because I know what you're like. You'll overdo it, which would risk you and Jelly Bean. I think it's a really bad idea."

"Well, I have to do something. I can't just sit here and let my arse get huge."

He laughed as he patted my bum. "Let's compromise. I know a great yoga teacher. She has had three kids of her own, so I think she would be able to guide you on some yoga techniques you can do. Okay?"

I thought about it for a moment. "Okay. I'll try yoga. Can you organise for me to see her tomorrow?"

"Of course. I'll call her first thing in the morning."

I smiled. "Thank you, honey." And kissed him with my greasy lips.

"You're welcome. Now shut up and eat, fatso," he said, nudging me.

The yoga studio was ultra modern with an Asian influence. I felt comfortable the moment I stepped in the door. It had a lovely lemon grass aroma wafting from a diffuser bubbling away in the corner. Tea light candles were lined across the inbuilt shelf across the length of the wall. The music had pan flutes and soft undertones of running water. It really had a nice vibe.

"Bodhi, this place is awesome. How do you know about it?"

"Tara and I are old friends," he replied.

"Hello, you must be Talia. I'm Tara." She held out her hand.

She was lanky with perfect mid-length blonde hair and was wearing bright red lipstick on her plump lips.

"Hi," I said as I smiled and shook her hand.

She gave Bodhi a hug. "It's so good to see you. It's been too long."

"Yeah, I've been busy."

"Come in. Let's get you settled and then we can start. I thought it might be best to do a private session today so I can assess you and then nominate a suitable style and class for you to attend."

"Okay." I followed her into another room.

"Ladies, I'm going to love you and leave you. Talia, will you be right to get home?"

"Of course. I'II see you tonight."

Bodhi kissed me goodbye and gave Tara a wave. I watched him leave before placing my things on the ground to prepare for my first session.

"Have you done yoga before?" she asked.

"No, I've studied martial arts and done tai chi but never yoga."

"Okay, well we can start with the basics and then build on that."

"Sure," I said, taking off my shoes.

Tara demonstrated the moves while I watched. She was graceful and had the most perfect pear-shaped arse I had ever seen. As we went through the movements together I wondered how she knew Bodhi. There was something about her that seemed familiar.

"How long have you known Bodhi?"

"Nearly ten years now, I guess."

"Wow, that's a long time. You must have been close."

"Ha, ha. You could say that. We dated for four years. We had talked about taking the next step, you know getting engaged, married but we decided to split instead. When it came down to it Bodhi and I were always better at being friends. Didn't he tell you?"

"No. He left that bit out. He only mentioned that you were a yoga teacher with three children."

"Yes. I got married five years ago to Leon, my truest soul mate. He's a masseuse. He works in the clinic next door."

"How did you and Leon meet?"

"Bodhi and I had been talking about getting engaged a couple of weeks prior. I decided to head out to attend a weekend silence retreat on my own. I needed to collect my thoughts. My father had recently passed away. The concept of engagement then marriage only stood to remind me that my dad would not be there to give me away. It really hurt and I could feel myself becoming resentful of the idea. I also had the added pressure of trying to support my mother. She had just lost her best friend and husband after being together for forty-eight years; it was the most stressful time of my life."

I nodded my head to acknowledge I was listening. I had a feeling this story was not one that ended well for Bodhi.

"After the first day in the retreat I decided I needed to get a massage to remove all the knots on my back and shoulders. That's how I met Leon. I didn't think much when I saw him. I undressed, lay on the table and waited for him to return to the room. I'II never forget how it felt. The moment he placed his hands on my body I knew. It was like we held a current of electricity that was passing through us. He felt connected to me too."

"Ok, so you cheated on Bodhi?" I asked.

"It's not like that and then again I guess it is exactly like that. I maintained my vow of silence for the whole weekend but that didn't stop Leon and I making love over and over again. I told Bodhi when I returned. Needless to say, he was distraught and I felt like the biggest heel on the planet. He seemed to blame himself for my infidelity."

"Ouch. I guess the fact that Leon is your soul mate is in a way a justification for your inability to resist. You're married and have created a family with him so in a divine sense it happened because it was supposed to. It could have been worse. You might have met Leon after you both got married or, God forbid, after starting a family with Bodhi. That would have been so much harder."

"Yeah, it wasn't something that I expected to happen. It just happened and I as horrible as it sounds I wanted it to," she said looking at the polished floorboards.

I instantly felt bad for Bodhi. It must have been an awful experience. He thought he had met the one and she ended up with another, poor Bodhi. There was so much I didn't know about his past. The fact that he'd maintained contact with her must be an indicator that he still held her in high regard. It spoke volumes about the person that he was. I loved him so much.

"I hurt Bodhi. I'll never be able to forgive myself for that. He's such a beautiful person. He didn't deserve the way I treated him. He was really hurt but gracious throughout the process. I was hurting too because I felt as though I'd failed him. We just weren't meant to be."

"I guess that explains a few things about his inability to trust, and he has some serious jealousy issues. He goes insane at the thought of other men around me."

"I'm afraid my behaviour contributed to that. I'm ashamed. I wish I could find a way to make it up to him."

"I'm sure he's found his peace with it. He introduced us, knowing that we would talk, so maybe this was his way of reconnecting."

"I hope so. He's an amazing person. Did you know he used to talk about you all the time? I used to get jealous and quietly seethe at the thought of you, and now here you are standing before me pregnant with his child," she said, beaming and pointing to my womb.

"Terrified of being pregnant. It all seems so foreign. I know it's happening and yet at the same time I feel like I'm outside myself. Sounds strange but I need to be a little disconnected because I just feel too much emotion when I'm present to the pregnancy." I patted my stomach.

Tara took my hands in hers. "Don't be. The process takes care of itself. Just enjoy it and know that you're nurturing a bundle of love in your womb."

"Thank you. That's a nice way of seeing it. Do you think you'll have any more children?"

"If Leon had his way we would have a brood of six or more. My man is insatiable. I'm hoping to have one more. I think four is enough."

"Wow, four is huge. Three is big too. I don't know how you do it."

"It's easier than you think. I know people say this all the time but being a parent is one of the single most gratifying roles you can ever play. I wouldn't trade it for the world. You'll surprise yourself with how much love exudes from your core for your children. It's endless, and at times overwhelming, but always beautiful."

"You make it sound amazing. My reality is closer to feeling constipated and windy at the same time as never being able to sate my ravenous hunger."

Tara laughed. "Oh, that's normal. It'll subside. By the time you get to the third trimester, all this'll be a distant memory."

"I hope so."

"It will."

On the way back home I stopped in at the bakery to buy six more pink iced doughnuts. The lady behind the counter smiled as she passed me a brown bag filled with my baked delights. I did the walk of shame home while I scoffed down three before I arrived at the entrance to the driveway of our house. All I could think about was passing wind and taking another bite of the doughnut that was in my hand.

I polished off the remaining three, changed into some sweats and switched on the radio. I liked to read with background noise. I positioned myself on the couch to read for a few hours before welcoming the warm drift into a quiet slumber. It only felt like moments later that the rustle of keys woke me as Bodhi come through the front door.

"Hey, you," I said, stretching my limbs and then shuffling into an upright position.

"Hey, how did you go today?"

"It was good. I enjoyed it. I particularly enjoyed getting to know Tara and the history between you two."

His body seemed to stiffen, "Oh, what did she tell you?"

"That you were almost engaged, she cheated and is married to the man she cheated with."

"I guess that sums it up," he said, placing his hands in his pockets and pursing his lips.

"Why didn't you tell me?"

"I didn't know how. She's a good yoga teacher and I trust her with you, which is why I took you there. What happened in the past is gone. It's dead to me. I only care about making sure you're safe and happy."

"She seems really nice."

"Tara has her moments. Like I said, she's a good yoga teacher."

I took that as a sign to change the subject. "What do you want for dinner?"

"I've already organised the food. I ordered Italian from that little place you like around the corner."

I clapped my hands. "Ooo, goodie."

Once again I consumed all the food as if I had never eaten a meal before. When we had finished, I had tomato sauce stains on my T-shirt. Bodhi laughed as he wiped the corners of my lips. I sat back and patted my tummy.

"I'm stuffed," I said, feeling very satisfied.

"You should be. I've never seen you eat so much. Where on earth do you put it?"

"Please, don't start. I know I look like a heifer."

"You're perfect. Shush." He tapped me on the tip of my nose.

My stomach started making loud unattractive noises. I looked at Bodhi as he stared at my belly.

"Wow, you have an orchestra happening in there."

"Yeah, it's embarrassing when I'm out and it starts. People look at me."

"Perhaps you need to fart," he said, tickling my sides.

"No, you don't want me to do that. I promise you it'll melt your nostril hairs. There's something ungodly going on inside me."

Bodhi laughed. "We're married. Let it rip. I won't judge. I fart in front of you all the time. Go for it."

I looked at him and shook my head, but decided he needed to be taught a lesson so I released a sneaky silent one past the gates of hell. It only took a moment for it to reach his nostrils. The smile on his face contorted to a look of horror as he jumped to his feet, placing his hands in front of him as if to shield himself from the rise of death's stench.

I laughed so hard the farts escaped from my arse in bursts of bubbles, making a slapping squelchy noise that was terrifying. The more I laughed, the harder I squeezed and the more rolled out.

Bodhi ran back towards the bedroom, still with his hands in front of him. "Never do that again, okay? I retract, I retract. Oh, dear god, I think I'm going to be sick."

I continued to laugh and fart while Bodhi disappeared.

Every time he heard me pass wind he screamed out, "No, for the love of god, noooooo. I can smell it from here. Talia, seriously stop. It was a mistake. You were right. Jesus."

I was out of control in a fit of hysterics, laughing at each pass of my endless wind. I had tears rolling down my cheeks and I was struggling to breathe. There was no stopping the faucet now. My only concern was not to shit myself. At this point they were coming out so sloppy I could hardly tell the difference. I couldn't recall the last time I had laughed so heartily.

So the days melted into one another. I grew bigger and started to waddle when I walked. I developed all kinds of cravings, including the classic pickles and ice cream. All my life I had an aversion to dairy and here I was craving it. The combination of sweet and sour taste was beyond perfection to me. By the time I was about to enter the third trimester, I gave Bodhi the go-ahead to make the announcement to our families. He had been on my case for months, but I had continued to resist. I would have preferred to just send them a postcard with a picture of us saying 'surprise'. I was still very much a person who lived in a space of refrain.

Bodhi made the call to his parents, who were travelling around Africa. They were, as expected, over the moon. I watched as Bodhi told them. He was crying. I loved seeing him so happy. Then it was my turn to call Ruth and the others. As I dialled, I looked at Bodhi and took a deep breath.

"Here we go," I said.

"Hello."

"Hey, Ruth, it's Talia."

"Talia, I was just thinking about you. I was telling Shane I had the strangest dreams about you recently and last night it felt so real I was going to call you today."

"What was it about?"

"You were holding a baby. It was a little girl all wrapped up in a cloth. You were the happiest I'd ever seen you."

"That would be because I'm pregnant," I blurted out, biting my bottom lip.

"Oh, Talia, that's wonderful news. I knew it. I told Shane it was a sign. Shane, Shane, it's Talia; she's pregnant," yelled Ruth.

"I'm in my third trimester so it's not long to go. I waddle like a duck, have swollen ankles and my feet have been MIA ever since my belly grew," I said, laughing.

"The third trimester. Talia, you should have told me. I could have come over to help you. I know, I know, you don't need assistance." She released a sigh. "I'm sure you look beautiful. I'm over the moon for you. This is the best news. Talia, you're going to be a wonderful mother."

"Thank you. I'm really nervous. I still can't believe I'm pregnant."

"Honey, it'll be over before you know it, and then you'll have this bundle of joy. You'll never look back, I promise."

"I know. I just want to fast-track past the birthing."

"Take the meds. You won't feel a thing."

"I'm not sure that I will. I don't like the idea of the baby being exposed to chemicals. On the other hand there's the issue of the pain. I don't know. I still haven't decided."

"Trust me, Talia, take the pain relief. I want to come and see you. Do you want me to be there with you for the first couple of weeks to assist?"

"Thanks, Ruth. I need to just do this with Bodhi and I. It's important we have the space to work out our shift in rhythm. I think it's easier to do this on our own. I appreciate the offer, I really do. I had every intention of visiting before the baby was born, but I found the further into carrying the less likely I was to travel. I'll come or you can come here once I've found my bearings. I hope you understand."

"Talia, honestly you may need some support. The first couple of weeks with increased hormones, breast feeding, sleepless nights are really tough. You don't have to do this on your own. I'd be happy to do this for you. I'd only stay until you got settled. What do you think?"

I knew she wanted me to say yes but I really didn't want anyone around. I needed to figure this out for myself. "Thanks for the offer but I really want Bodhi and I do this. Thanks, Ruth, but I'm going to decline the offer. I love you."

"I love you too. Of course, whatever you need. If you change your mind I'll have a bag packed here ready to jump on the next available flight. Oooo, I'm so excited for you." I could hear she was attempting to mask her disappointment.

"Thanks for understanding. I have to go. Can you do the ring around and let the others know?"

"I'm sure they'd prefer to hear it from you but okay." She sounded sad and I understood her reasons.

I had always felt like an outsider even after their best efforts to have me feel like family. They were, but I was never able to let go of the feeling of being alone in the world. It was part of who I was.

"We love you. Take care of yourself. This is such wonderful news. I know the rest of the family will be over the moon. Congratulations again. Shane sends his love."

"Thanks. Pass on my love to everyone. Tell them I'll call all of them before the end of the week for a chat. I promise."

"Will do. Love you. Bye."

"Love you too. See ya."

Bodhi massaged my shoulders as I hung up the phone. "See? That wasn't so hard, was it?"

"Nope. I told you we should have told them earlier on, but no, you had to insist on keeping it a secret," I said, laughing.

"Very funny." He leant in and kissed my cheek. "I think you need to be spanked."

I turned my head to look at him with a cheeky grin. "It's about time you offered," I said, accentuating my derriere.

With this Bodhi pounced like a lion starved for a meal. There was a heightened sensuality to making love while pregnant. The intensity of the penetration was wild. All my senses were switched to overdrive and, just as my appetite was constant, I could never seem to sate myself when it came to making love to Bodhi. I was indeed the luckiest woman alive.

Nativity

I was standing in front of the mirror, buck naked, sideways, looking at the enormity of my belly. I had stretch marks that looked like bloodworms trapped under my skin. I didn't have too many but it was enough. There was nothing pleasant about what the human body had to go through in order to house a child. I was thankful at this point I hadn't acquired piles.

I called out to Bodhi.

As he arrived and stood in the doorway, he smiled. "Wow, you're huge. It's like you doubled in size overnight."

"I think the baby's turning, which is making my stomach more pronounced."

He stepped in and stood behind me and placed his hands on my belly. "Not long to go now." He rocked me gently from side to side.

I sighed. "I can't wait. This is so uncomfortable. I want it over with. Here, take this. I need you to help me." I passed him a razor and a can of shaving foam. I already laid down a towel and a small tub of warm water to rinse the blade.

"What's this for?"

I propped one leg on the side of the vanity and pointed to my nether regions. "I can't go to hospital looking like this and I don't want to get waxed because my skin's really sensitive at the moment, so you have to shave me. Take it all off. I want to be smooth as a baby's bottom. The only hair I want on my child is the hair it was born with," I said, amused at my own joke.

Bodhi's pupils dilated and his eyes widened as he immediately dropped to his knees. Without hesitation he disappeared under the shelter of my belly. I could feel the shaving cream being squirted on my skin and enjoyed the feeling of him spreading it around with his fingers.

He looked up at me and smiled. "This is so fucking hot," he said as he started to remove the hair.

I stood there while he worked his magic. It took all my energy not to pass wind the whole time he was down there. There was nothing romantic about the process for me.

"Done. There you go. All clean," he said, dropping the blade into the foam filled water and rising to his feet.

"Thank you." I kissed him on the lips.

"If you're finished in here I'm going to have a shower and masturbate like a mad man. This imagery is too hot to waste."

I laughed. "Knock yourself out," I said as I left the room.

Bodhi was suffering. I had been going through a 'distant' patch. It came over me like a cloud, leaving me feeling lost and alone. He was shocked at first then he accepted that it was phase I was going through. I hoped he was right. It was the first time since we had been together that I didn't want him to make love to me. I missed him.

I dressed while Bodhi did his thing. When he was

done, he joined me in the bedroom to help me pack my bag for the hospital.

"Jesus that was good," he said with a laugh.

I pouted my lip. "I'm glad. Sorry I haven't been more active."

"Don't be silly. I know it's a baby thing. We're good; we're more than good." He kissed me on the lips and stroked my face.

I felt better.

We had been shopping for all the nursery essentials so the house was cluttered with boxes.

I looked around and took a deep breath. "We have to unpack and sort all of this in the next couple of days so we're ready."

"I know; I'll do it," said Bodhi, looking around the room.

"Aren't you glad we bought a bigger place?"

"Yes 'we'," I said, still a little annoyed that he wouldn't let me give him some money to contribute to the purchase.

"Get over it, Talia. It's our place. The fact that I bought it means nothing. It's ours."

There was no way I was going to start up about it again. I needed to let it go, so I changed the subject. Looking at the mess, I released a big sigh. "Gosh, I hate unpacking boxes."

"Okay, I'll unpack these boxes and make the crib up. You relax."

I wasn't going to refuse the offer. I gave him a quick peck on the lips. "Thanks, honey," I said, rushing out of the room before he changed his mind.

My back was aching so I decided to lie down. I was expected to go into labour any day now and it still all seemed so surreal. I felt like I was outside of myself looking in. I was thankful that there was an air of calm and I no longer experienced any fear. All I longed for was to give birth so I could finally reclaim my body. At least that was the delusion I was currently under. I knew I was set to be a baby slave for the next twelve months with breast feeding and all the other guff that went with the process.

Later, when Bodhi had finished unpacking and assembling the crib, he joined me in the bedroom and fell instantly asleep. I lay beside him, unable to sleep, my fingers tapping the bed covers. Typically impatient by nature, I went online to look at old wives' remedies for inducing labour. I was borderline obsessed with the idea of giving birth that evening. There was set to be an eclipse, the first of its kind in five hundred years. It would be splendid to have her arrival timed with such a blessed universal occasion.

The options were surprisingly endless:
- Drink a litre of castor oil
- Eat a dozen raw eggs
- Cold shower followed by hot bath
- Eat ultra spicy food

The only one in the endless list that caught my interest was nipple stimulation and sex. I still wasn't feeling up to it but decided it was worth a try. In truth, I think my lack of desire stemmed from feeling like a bloated, beached whale. There was nothing sexy about pregnancy. I undressed and slipped under the covers.

"Bodhi, wake up." I shook him gently.

He stirred. "What's up? Is anything wrong?"

"No, I've just been reading up about how to naturally induce labour."

He turned and placed his hand on my belly. "You really want her out of there, don't you?"

"I do. It says that having sex can kick off contractions." I bit my bottom lip and smiled. "What do you say? Are you up for it?"

Bodhi sat up, placed his hand on my face and kissed me. "What do you think?"

I locked my lips with his and groaned as he pressed hard in return. He got onto his knees and dragged my body down on the bed, placing my hands above my head. I could feel my face flush red as he used his tongue to trace down towards my breasts. God, how I missed his tongue.

He paused at the peak of my mound and nuzzled my nipple until it rose for him. He used his other hand to tweak and pull at my breast while he sucked hard on the other. My breasts had almost tripled in size and were ultra sensitive. I had shivers running up my spine as he continued to devour my milk-laden boobs. His tongue skillfully darted out, licking my skin as he watched me with hungry eyes. He used his teeth to graze the surface of my tips, which made me emit a long groan as I closed my eyes.

Bodhi reached down and started to stimulate my clitoris. It was swollen and burning with desire. I shifted slightly so I could give him better access. My thighs felt like they were on fire. Bodhi moved so his face was positioned between my legs. I could feel the muscles on my thighs tighten as he swept his lips over my clitoris. Gently he kissed and then used his tongue to outline the entrance to my vagina. His slow steady strokes were driving me positively insane.

I could feel the baby kicking. It hurt enough to make me want to wince but I managed to control myself. I gripped the bed sheets on either side of me as my body tensed. Pulsations of heat surged through my core as he relentlessly tortured me with his pleasures. A blinding light flashed before me as I reefed up and roared as I came hard. Bodhi followed my movement and continued to stimulate me well beyond the point I had broken.

When he finally came up for air I could see the moist outline of my juices on his face. I kissed him and sucked on his tongue to reclaim my flavours.

"Turn over," he whispered.

I perched on my knees and bent forward.

His hands glided up the length of my back. "Fuck, you're beautiful."

He parted my legs and steadily entered me. I tightened and clamped down on his rigid penis as he thrust back and forth. Bodhi held onto the sides of my arse and released a series of groans that were synched to my muscle-clenching. I yelped as he slapped my butt and shook it. I reached down and started to stimulate myself. I wanted to come again.

Bodhi's breathing was ragged as he quickened his pace. I placed my head as low as I could on the bed so he could penetrate me deeper. Using my fingers to lightly dance around his balls, I continued to touch myself, gyrating back and forth as I massaged my clitoris in small circles.

"Fuck, Bodhi, I'm going to come."

Bodhi's body became rigid as he began a series of small deep thrusts. My body quaked as I rose to be consumed by the delights of an epic orgasm. Bodhi synchronised his climax to perfection, also shuddering the release of his ecstasy. We both were panting as we fell over and lay on our backs, staring at the ceiling.

"Oh my, I missed this," I said, reaching out to hold his hand.

"Me too," he said, still breathless.

I shuffled off the bed and headed to the bathroom. "I need to pee."

"Do you feel any different?"

"No. The baby was kicking for a while there, but that's it."

"You know, if you give me twenty, we could try again," he yelled out.

"Sounds like a plan. Pace yourself, tiger. We may have to be at it all night." I flushed the toilet.

"I am here to serve, my lady."

I hopped back into bed and lay in his arms. We switched on the TV and watched a series called *Lost*. My body still held some residual tension from the workout we had just performed. I sat up and placed my hand on my belly.

"Our little one is restless."

Bodhi placed his hand on my stomach to feel her. His face lit up as she moved. "She's feisty," he said as he leant down and kissed the side of my stomach. "Soon, little one, soon," he whispered.

Right at that moment an intense shock wave pulsed through my body. I clenched my fist and reefed forward.

"Fuck," I yelped.

"What? Are you having a contraction?"

"I think so," I said, looking down at my gut.

I stood up and placed both hands on the wall. No sooner had I done this than another contraction struck. I bent forward, accidentally banging my head against the wall.

"Oh, my god, that fucking hurts," I said.

Bodhi jumped out of bed to stand beside me. "Talia, your water's broken."

I looked down to see a seeping puddle of translucent goo.

"Is this really happening?" I asked Bodhi pleadingly, the resurgence of terror rising.

He kissed my forehead. "Hang in there, honey. I'll get your bag; we need to go."

We arrived at the hospital in record time. Bodhi took all the back roads and ignored almost every stop sign along the way. My contractions were getting closer and longer. I was sweating bullets knowing that this was just the beginning of what could take hours, perhaps days, to do. I slowly waddled into emergency, where an orderly with a wheelchair greeted me.

"Hi, I'm Jackson. Is this your first time?"

"Yes," I responded through gritted teeth.

"It's okay. We'll take good care of you. I'll set you up in your room and page your doctor."

"I feel like my insides are falling out," I said as I reefed forward in reaction to my contraction.

"I'll get you something for the pain as soon as I can page your doctor. Hang in there."

I stuck my hand down my soaked pants and squealed as I felt her head. "I'm crowning. The baby's here," I screamed.

The orderly called out for help and dropped to his knees. Shifting my pants down, he looked. "You, my dear, are indeed having your baby right now."

He turned the chair and pushed me, running towards the theatre as I screamed from the intensity of the contractions. Nothing had prepared me for the pain that surged through my body. It felt like my insides were exposed and someone was pouring hot molten metal onto my soul. I was close to blacking out when help arrived to lift me onto the theatre table. Two of the nurses stripped me bare and placed a gown on me. Everything was a blur. I was totally consumed by the pain.

Bodhi grabbed my hand and squeezed. "I'm here. You're doing great. The doctor is on her way."

"It hurts. It fucking hurts so much. I don't think I can do this, Bodhi. I feel like I'm burning alive. The pain is out of this world. I've changed my mind," I said as another contraction hit me like a sledgehammer.

Bodhi chuckled. "Breathe, keep breathing. It's meant to help. The doctor will be here soon and you can have your pain relief. Hang on, Talia."

A doctor burst into the room in a dramatic entrance.

I looked at him. "Who are you?"

"I'm sorry, your obstetrician is stuck in downtown traffic so I need to step in. I'm Dr Hallow."

Another contraction came. I reefed my head back and yelled, "Fuuuuck, fuck, fuck, fuck. This can't be real. Oh, my god, it hurts."

"Doc, can you give her something to ease the pain?" asked Bodhi.

"I'm sorry; she's too far gone. We have to proceed naturally. At the speed she seems to be contracting I expect it'll all be over soon," he said as he put on his gloves and peered underneath my gown.

"Wow, she's going to be big. You'd better brace yourself, young lady. The worst is yet to come," he said, looking at me.

My face contorted as I looked at the doctor in disbelief. "What the fuck? Seriously, are you trying to freak me out? I'm already there. You don't need to add to it. Jesus."

The doctor laughed. "Sorry, I like to tell you the truth. Now, on your next contraction, I need you to push."

I was exhausted. When the contraction came I gave it all I could. Every muscle in my body was awake and on fire. I pushed and pushed until I couldn't any longer. I lay back, panting, my eyes closed. Bodhi continued to hold my hand and spout words of encouragement, like a coach on the sidelines of a little-league game. It wafted over me like a warm blanket. I knew he would trade places with me in a heartbeat if he could. At least I wanted to believe he would.

It took three hours and twenty-seven minutes of labour before Daniella arrived in perfect form into the world. The sounds of her cries were better than any noise I had ever heard. She was tiny, contrary to what the doctor had suggested. The nurses cleaned her up, wrapping her in a swaddle, and placed her in my arms. I counted her little fingers, checked her ears, kissed her eyes and adorable little nose.

"We have a baby girl," I whispered to Bodhi, who was leaning over her, kissing her hands.

"She's the most beautiful thing I've ever seen," he said, crying.

Tears poured out of my eyes as I replied, "I know. She's perfect."

Tara was right. The love seemed to pour out of me in a gooey molten coagulated flood. I could feel my depth of love coupled with an intense desire to protect and nurture this precious life force. It was as though I had tapped into the imperial energies of Mother Nature herself. I would kill for my baby.

They took us to my private room where we were to be housed for the next couple of days. Bodhi jumped into the king-size bed as Daniella lay fast asleep between us. I couldn't stop staring at her. I was hypnotised by the rise and fall of her tiny chest. Her hands were folded near the entrance to her mouth. We had done it. The little girl who had been spiritually a part of my life for so long was now here beside me. I was mesmerised.

"I'm going to head home. I need to get the house organised in preparation for you two guys to come home. I'll call everyone to let them know."

I nodded. "Okay," I whispered, still not able to shift my gaze.

As Bodhi headed to the door I called out to him, "Hey, Daddy, congratulations."

He returned to my side, picked up my hand and kissed it with heavy lips. "Thank you. She's the greatest gift I could ever have hoped for. You've made me the happiest man alive."

"I love you."

"I love you more." He leant down and pecked my lips.

"Hey, can you put her in the bassinet? I'm really tired, I don't feel quite right and I don't want to fall asleep with her next to me."

"Sure." He picked her up ever so gently with an adorable smile on his face as he gazed upon his daughter. He gave her a gentle kiss and placed her in the crib beside the bed.

Shortly after Bodhi had left the nurse came in to do the obs. I lay there quietly while she went about her business. When she left I felt a compulsion to get out of bed. My sweet little girl was fast asleep. I felt this ache, a burning within me that I couldn't seem to settle. There didn't seem to be a position I could settle into to ease the pain. I was tired; I craved sleep.

I rose to my feet and slowly walked to the window. I felt a sharp pain run through my body as I lifted my arm to draw the blinds. It felt like my entrails were going to gush out. Hunched over, I saw a gaggle of ravens all staring at me from the tree across the way, squawking as though they were under attack, manically flapping their wings in fear. One flew towards the window, clawing at the glass. In that moment I fell to my knees as the pain resurged with intensity. I gasped and I crawled across the cold floor to activate the emergency buzzer. I managed to press it once before the room went black, my only company the distant sound of the ravens in my mind.

I was in a room filled with soft white light. There was a little child crying. Forgetting my own concerns, I went to him and knelt down.

"Hey, little one, don't cry. Shhh."

He removed his hands from his face and wrapped them around my neck as he sobbed. I instinctually picked him up and rocked him slowly. Holding him tight, I could feel this ache, a longing for his tears to subside.

In my peripheral vision something caught my eye. As I turned I saw standing before me were my mum, dad, Marlee, the old Haitian woman from the village I met when I was a child and the lady from the gypsy camp. They all looked radiant. I smiled as I ran into my daddy's arms. He picked the little boy and I up and swung us around with joy in his heart.

"I missed you so much," I said, frantically kissing him on the cheek.

I leant across to bring my mum into the embrace and kissed her as well. "I love you," I said while crying.

As Dad placed me back on my feet, I put the little boy down and held his hand. Marlee crouched and touched my face. I was so overwhelmed and filled with a feeling of love. I smiled at the little boy as I released my hand from his. He had stopped crying and was watching in silence. I turned back to Marlee, grabbing her hand, squeezing it hard. I placed my arms out in a gesture for her to pick me up. As she did, I could smell the familiarity of her skin. I smiled as I squeezed her tight.

"I love you, Marlee. Thank you for everything. Thank you," I said between muffled sobs.

"I love you too, child," she said in a familiar voice.

I gave her once last big cuddle before she put me back on the ground.

I took a couple of steps back so I could look at them all once more. If this was a dream I never wanted to wake. I couldn't believe they were all there. My family. So much love surrounded us. This place, the light; it was the purest essence of love. I felt great.

"You all look so fabulous. Mum, Dad, you're still young. I don't understand. Where am I?"

Marlee replied, "Child, you see us as you remember us."

I looked at my hands and realised I was tiny. I had become six again. "Is this a dream?" I watched as they looked at each other. "What's happened? Where are Bodhi and Daniella?"

Marlee once again was the one who spoke. "You're dying, child."

In the background I could hear the muffled cries of a child and a voice saying over and over, "I choose you. Come back to me. I choose you."

I looked up at the endless light above me. "Bodhi? Is that you?"

"Yes, he's by your body, crying." Marlee stepped forward to look straight into my eyes.

"I'm dying?"

"Yes." Marlee tilted her head to look at the little boy who had started crying again.

"Who is he?" I said, directing my gaze at the child.

"He's your unborn son. He cries because without you he cannot cross over again. You were to be his last time."

I knelt down. Wiping the tears from his eyes, I looked at him. He was the spitting image of Bodhi. I smiled at him as I felt an intense love flow between us.

"Don't cry. I'm here. I promise I'll find a way back so we can be together." I shifted the hair from his face and kissed him gently on his forehead.

With determined resolve I stood up and looked at everyone. "Send me back. I need to be there to protect my children. I'm not leaving Bodhi alone." I fell to my knees, and burst into tears at the thought of never seeing them again. "Marlee, show me the way to cross over. Please, I have to be with them. I know my cycle has not been completed. I don't want to have to do this all over again. I must go back and finish this."

The wise old Haitian woman stepped forward and placed her hand on my forehead. "You will go back, child. There's more to be done by you in that world. We united our energies to summon your soul to this place. It was the only way we could heal you and cheat death."

Through tear-soaked eyes I looked at her and felt the relief of her words wash over me. Then a new consciousness of sadness flooded my reality. I was going to have to leave them. "I don't want to leave you guys. I missed you so much. I'm torn: I need to go back but I also want to stay here with you."

"You body weakens in the absence of your soul. You cannot stay. You have received what you needed from us; all is healed. You must return, Talia. You have to will yourself to return. We love you," said Marlee.

Then they all started to chant in perfect synchronicity, "We love you, Talia. We love you, Talia. We love you, Talia."

The more they chanted the more I could feel a shift to a sense of weightlessness. The light surrounding them intensified and held a vibrational hum. I tried to focus on Bodhi and Daniella to aid my return but still felt a desire to be present. I couldn't help it. I loved them so much.

Mum stepped forward with tears in her eyes. "Talia, we never left you. We're always here. You need to go back. It's not your time. Go now," she whispered.

All of a sudden they parted to make way for a man to step towards me. He was semi-naked, adorned in a headdress with tiny shrunken skulls around it. He waved something at me and then sprayed a white powder from his mouth onto my face. The room became blurry as I started to experience the all too familiar feeling of sinking into the floor. All those I cherished melted together to become a sphere of light. I tried to touch them with my hand but fell deeper into an open cavern that was filled with the echoes of muffled voices.

"Talia, please come back to me. I don't want to live without you."

I opened my eyes to find Bodhi with his head on my chest, sobbing. I lifted my weak hand onto the back of his head.

Bodhi straightened to look at me through swollen bloodshot eyes. "Nurse, she's awake. She's awake. Help."

Medical staff came clambering in. I turned and looked at them fussing over the machines and checking my vitals. My throat was dry. I needed a drink.

"Water," was all I had the strength to say.

Bodhi placed a straw in a glass full of water and helped me sip. The staff, seemingly satisfied with my obs, left the room almost as quickly as they had entered. I turned my head to look at Bodhi. He was pale, his eyes sunken. He had lost a ton of weight. I reached out and touched his face.

"I'm fine, but you look like shit," I whispered, attempting a half-smile.

"I was terrified. You've been out for six days. They found you collapsed on the floor. Apparently you were bleeding internally. You lost a lot of blood. I was so scared I was going to lose you." He burst into inconsolable tears.

I shifted my head to look at the window. "Shh, it's okay. Everything's going to be okay."

Poor Bodhi continued to howl.

Eventually he managed to compose himself.

"Can you shift the blinds so they're fully open? I want to look outside. Please?"

Bodhi took a long look at me as if to memorise my features. As he opened the blinds, I tried to lift myself into a sitting position, but I didn't have the strength. Bodhi came to my side, leant in and lifted me. As I peered out through the window, I could see all the ravens were still in the tree. They were no longer squawking. This time they were silently watching, preening their lustrous black feathers. I smiled as I slowly took another sip of water.

Everything would be okay. I knew this now. I was loved and protected.

"Daniella?" I whispered.

"She's fine. The nurses have been expressing your milk and I've been feeding her. She's so perfect."

"I know, she is perfect," I said, resting my head on the pillow and closing my eyes to rest.